MW00579204

# Deadly Illusion

ANGUS BRODIE AND MIKAELA FORSYTHE MURDER
MYSTERY
BOOK FOUR

## CARLA SIMPSON

OLIVERHEBERBOOKS

# One

IT WAS a beautiful spring evening at the Crystal Palace in London. The sort of evening that makes one forget the past winter and those dreary rainy days.

I had been here before in the investigation of a case and had little time to admire everything that the Palace offered—exhibits of everything from exotic plants to the latest inventions in glass paneled buildings with light from a thousand lamps that reflected back into the night like so many stars, and the amphitheater with those seats that rose up over the stage where orchestras performed.

There were also musicals and theatrical plays. On the vast grounds between those enormous glass buildings London had hosted the Wild West show from the United States, with re-enactments of Indian attacks, and riding and shooting exhibitions.

However, tonight it was hosting the one-night performance of world-renowned Jean Luc Betard, expat of France before embarking on his next world tour.

My friend, actress Theodora Templeton, had been able to secure tickets to the exclusive show and had persuaded me to attend with her. I say persuaded, as I had also been commandeered to assist my great aunt, Lady Antonia Montgomery, with the final arrangements for her departure to Africa on safari, something I had been hoping to avoid.

My aunt is a remarkable woman and I adore her. More to the point, I was hoping that she would avoid pursuing that particular adventure. After all, she was eighty-five years old! Although if you asked her, she would be more likely to put her age at *'somewhere around sixty years'*.

And then there was her injury some months back in preparation for the trip when she had broken her ankle. However, a steady supply of her very fine whisky from her property in Scotland, along with standing on her head to improve circulation, had aided her recovery. I thought it might have improved the circulation to her brain. But I had my doubts.

She had been given a clean bill health three weeks earlier by her physician and it was full speed ahead for her departure, along with her reluctant travel companion, my sister, who I suspected would rather have her fingernails removed.

"Yes, we have our invitations and tickets," Templeton replied to the attendant now as our carriage arrived at the amphitheater and we proceeded to the gate.

"This is my guest, Miss Forsythe." She handed both tickets over to the young man.

"Miss Mikaela Forsythe?" he replied, giving me a curious look.

I nodded in response.

"I was here the night you ran down the spy who attempted to assassinate the Prince of Wales!" he explained. "One of the lads said that you actually shot the man! Bravo, Miss Forsythe."

The *'man'* had actually been a woman in disguise, however, I was not going to discuss that fact. I simply nodded, determined to enjoy an evening that didn't have anything to do with travel to Africa, assassination attempts, or murder.

I was hoping to enjoy a perfectly normal and pleasant evening of entertainment that also hopefully did not include spiritual interference. Templeton had promised to leave said *'interference'* at her flat, however I did wonder how one did that with a spirit who appeared and disappeared at will.

I smiled at the attendant, and we were on our way, our tickets courtesy of the theater owner where Templeton was appearing in her latest play. We found our seats very near the stage, reserved for certain guests, and it promised to be a most enjoyable evening.

Monsieur Betard had given a private performance two nights earlier for the royal family, and had performed all over the world including New York and San Francisco. He was reported to be one of the most talented of magicians with articles about him that had appeared in all the dailies.

Beside me, Templeton was as excited as a child. "He's going to present the same illusions that he performed for Bertie and the royal family, and..." her eyes sparkled, "an entirely new illusion that he's never done before."

I glanced about the audience as the performance was to begin. It did seem as if Betard had attracted a variety of persons from the most elegantly dressed, including a distinguished man in formal tails and cape, to the more average person who might not usually be able to attend one of his performances, and local workers who had somehow managed to attend.

It was not unusual to see other performers in the audience at the theater, very often a cast member of the production who then joined the other actors on the stage. It added to the entertainment for the audience. However, when I glanced back, the man I had seen was gone.

We settled back as the lights about the amphitheater dimmed leaving the center stage brightly lit, the glass panes of the amphitheater winking all about us as if they were set with stars. It was quite magical.

I had seen magicians perform before. Some were quite good. Others were barely passable, their slight-of-hand tricks resulting in a card or other object falling to the floor. Or in the case of street magicians who were always about the theater district near the Strand.

Monsieur Betard appeared and explained the next and final illusion. He was quite handsome in his coat with long tails and a swirling cape that added that bit of theater to the evening. His manner was most elegant as he began to explain, step-by-step, how his next illusion—never before performed, would take place.

"The transformation from one glass box will take several minutes," he explained in a thick French accent. "Silence is requested so not to break the spell that will transport my assistant from one glass box into the other.

The audience was silent as two large glass boxes framed with black wood and atop platforms were then wheeled to the center of the stage by two more assistants.

Monsieur Betard then led a slender young woman, who was dressed quite daringly in a skintight costume similar to a trapeze artist, to the center of the stage.

"Mademoiselle Francoise," he introduced her, then led her over to the box at the left of the stage.

She climbed the two steps at the platform and then entered the box. Betard lowered the panel of glass into place at the back of the box as the young woman reclined at the floor and smiled out at the audience.

He showed the audience that there was no trap door under the box, then asked for a cover to be lowered over it. With great ceremony, he then demonstrated that there was no trap door under the second glass box.

He entered the second box where he stood and bowed, his black cape swirling about him. On command, the back glass panel was lowered into place by an attendant. It appeared that one could see right through the box. Betard then bowed slowly as a cover was then lowered over the second glass box.

The audience waited in anticipation as the orchestra built the excitement of the moment when the illusion would be complete. We both watched as the covers were then raised from both boxes to a crescendo from the orchestra.

The first box where the girl had been closed inside now

appeared to be empty. She now waved from the second box where she stood beside Betard, to all outward appearances having magically moved from one box to the other.

"How marvelous!" Templeton exclaimed, joining the audience in thunderous applause as the curtains closed across the stage.

He had given such a brilliant performance that even someone as skeptical as myself was forced to admit that he was indeed very talented.

"How did he do it?" Templeton continued excitedly. "It would be marvelous for him to appear at the Adelphi," and in that way of hers, plunged headlong into some new scheme. "I could be his assistant!"

"It *appears*," I replied, no pun intended, "that he already has an assistant." Or one that disappears as the case might be. And there was the small detail that my friend was quite tall and might have found it difficult to magically appear in one box then move to the second one.

Due to Templeton's connection to the theater, she had also been given an invitation to meet with Betard and his entourage backstage after the performance.

"Do come along, Mikaela," she said now as we left our seats and approached the stage where she presented her invitation to one of Betard's attendants.

We were escorted backstage along with a handful of writers for the dailies, including someone I had encountered in the past, Alan Ivers of the London Times.

He much reminded me of a ferret, always poking about, dressed in his herringbone jacket with a scarf about his neck, and quite impressed with himself.

"Miss Forsythe," he greeted me. "How is your sister getting along? She did quite well with the settlement of the estate from her husband. Nasty business, divorce, and people tend to gossip."

Did I mention poking about, and how despicable the man was always digging for that next sensational story, or absent that...inventing one? I restrained the urge to punch him in the nose as I stepped past him and followed Templeton onto the stage.

I had no sooner set foot behind that red and gold curtain than there was a horrifying scream.

Betard's young assistant cried out as she stood beside that first box, hands flattened against the glass.

"*Aider*!" she screamed in French. "Someone, please! Help her!"

Betard had been speaking with others from the newspapers. He suddenly turned and ran back across the stage where his assistant was screaming hysterically.

It was difficult to tell what was the matter. Then I glanced at the box.

It should have been empty, at least according to what the audience was led to believe during Betard's performance. But I was reminded that magic is an art of illusion. The illusion here was that the girl we believed had then somehow magically made her way into the second box had never in fact left the first box.

She was lying at the floor where we had first seen her, now mostly concealed from anyone who would have been in the audience by that black wood. Lying flat as she was and admittedly quite small and slender, it had been impossible to see anything inside the box from a distance of more than a few feet.

Now, she stared up at everyone with that look I have come to recognize—a blank, lifeless stare. And then there was the blood in the bottom of the box.

She was, in fact, very dead. But there was more I realized with a jolt. The two women were identical twins!

# *Two*

I HAVE RECENTLY DISCOVERED it to be most fascinating that whenever a crime has been committed and the police summoned, everything seems to come to a standstill. At least as far as the police are concerned.

I wondered if that was part of their training—hands clasped behind their backs, like statues. Their expressions were quite stern as one among them—none other than Chief Inspector Abberline, dressed in fine coat and trousers met with Betard then his surviving assistant who was quite undone. I had the displeasure of meeting Mr. Abberline previously.

"I might have known," he greeted us when everyone present on the stage was told they were to remain. Not, *'Good Evening, Miss Forsythe'*, the simplest of good manners even under present circumstances.

I had merely nodded in response. There is a history between us.

Abberline proceeded taking the names of those present, ourselves included, questioning the various members of Betard's staff in the *'most unfortunate accident'*. He then returned to where Betard stood, the magician obviously quite upset, shaking his head in response to Abberline's questions.

More than once, I caught Betard's sad glance in our direction. Templeton and I were only a few feet away from the young woman who had discovered her unfortunate counterpart in the first box, where she sat huddled, an older woman attempting to console her. The surviving twin's name was Sophie, I heard the older woman say in French.

"How very awful," Templeton said.

The tragedy had exposed the secret of the illusion—twins with one appearing in the first box then hidden, the second twin appearing with Betard at the second box.

Now, very near midnight, Abberline had made his observations with Mr. Ivers of the London Times hovering nearby with others from the dailies.

"The chief inspector is calling it an unfortunate accident," he commented with almost morbid dissatisfaction. "Slipped, maneuvering in that small space, and fell with a severe injury to the head. What do you say, Miss Forsythe?"

As I said before, a ferret. However, I was inclined to disagree with Abberline's assessment of the situation. While I am no expert, there was something quite odd about the position of the body for something to be called an accident.

The young woman lay on her back, her head at a slight angle. There were bruises at the front of her neck and at her hands. And then there was all that blood. If, it was in fact a tragic accident, that she had simply fallen, bruises would very likely have been at the back of her head and neck.

The blood might have been from a head wound, but there was no obvious wound or bruising at her head. And I couldn't help the thought that it looked very much as if she might have fought by the bruising at her hands, something I had experienced myself in a previous case that Angus Brodie and I had undertaken. That brought me back to all that blood in the bottom of the box.

No, I was not inclined to easily dismiss her death as an accident, not that I would discuss that with Alan Ivers. It was for that reason that I had one of the constables—a young man who had assisted in a previous case, send off an urgent message.


"Mikaela."

I turned at that familiar Scots accent.

"Brodie."

"And Miss Templeton," he greeted her.

"Mr. Brodie, how good of you to join us so late of an evening," she replied.

Not precisely the most appropriate of greetings, but that was my friend; somewhat odd at times but a marvelous actress. However, Brodie was of a different opinion about her oddities. It undoubtedly had something to do with his previous encounter with her pet iguana, Ziggy, on one occasion in a previous investigation.

Ziggy was rather large—over four feet in length and quite intimidating until one got to know him. He was now a resident of the London Zoo where Templeton had declared him to be quite happy with another iguana.

"I came as soon as I received yer message," Brodie said then with obvious irritation.

He had efficiently made his way past the crowd that remained, gawking curiously, along with no less than a dozen constables. Not that it was the first time he had done so in our association. He seemed to have a great deal of respect from his former colleagues in crime.

"What have ye done now?"

What had I done? Irritating man.

"It's not what I have done, but apparently someone else," I indicated the box and the poor girl, Francoise, who lay there.

My relationship with Angus Brodie is complicated.

We first met during a previous investigation....

Well, not exactly. There was that other encounter on one of my adventures. Afterward I had only a vague memory of it, fetched back by my great aunt after I had taken myself off from my travel group. There had been a great deal of ouzo involved as well...

Sometime later, I had need of his investigative services. One thing led to another, as they say— murder that is, and I had temporarily put my adventures aside, which I often wrote about in my novels.

Brodie was once an inspector with the Metropolitan Police. He had left a handful of years earlier under circumstances that were not quite clear, and had begun his work as a private investigator.

I first sought him out on recommendation of my great aunt, and in the course of our first investigation together— I say *together*, as I am not one to idly sit by, we discovered that we worked quite well together. It was during our last investigation that things became... somewhat complicated.

I am what is considered an independent woman and of a certain age, more precisely a spinster.

There was an engagement to be married at one time which I chose to break off, something considered to be quite shocking and disgraceful.

Let me say at this point that the description of *'spinster'* does not mean that I don't appreciate a fine figure of a man. Quite the contrary. It's just that I have my travels, and my novels with my protagonist *Emma Fortestcue*. A very full life. Then, there is my great aunt who is getting on in years, as they say. Not to mention my sister who has come through some difficulties of her own, and the fact that I had decided quite honestly there was no man I wanted to share my life with.

And then there is Brodie.

We are very different in many ways. We come from completely different backgrounds—his from the streets of Glasgow and Edinburgh where he learned how to survive on the streets. While mine...? Suffice it to say we are quite different and it has caused more than one disagreement.

As he has often pointed out, I have a tendency to be stubborn, too independent, with a penchant for inserting myself in dangerous situations while he has a tendency to be overbearing, overly protective, and opinionated.

However, we had managed until now, to handle the distractions, his temper and my independence quite admirably for the sake of the cases we shared. It was the '*now*' part of it that had me waiting at the edge of the stage at the Crystal Palace and a young woman who was dead.

I had not seen or spoken with Brodie in some weeks. Part of it had to do with a fire at his office on the Strand that had reduced most everything to cinders and ash, and required him to move to other quarters while repairs were being made. *Other quarters* turned out to be the location of the Special Services in the somewhat austere offices at the Tower of London.

The Special Services, I had learned, is a somewhat secretive organization that previously handled the investigation of crimes against the Crown that were, shall we say, beyond the usual street crime that the Metropolitan Police were tasked with.

The other part of not having spoken with him had to do with that complicated matter that had come up in our partnership.

Have I also mentioned that I do appreciate a fine figure of a man? One that is tall, with dark hair that seems to constantly be in need of a trim, a dark beard, and then there is that dark gaze. It narrowed now as he walked toward the scene of the 'accident' as Abberline was calling it. Complicated.

Abberline was made aware of Brodie's appearance by one of his constables. He immediately crossed the stage toward us.

"Were you at tonight's performance?" he inquired of Brodie. "Or perhaps arrived quite expeditiously, though unnecessary," he added with an accusing glance in my direction. "However, a tragic accident nothing more, and a reminder that you have no official standing to be here."

Brodie quite handily ignored that remark. "It does seem there is a great deal of blood," he indicated the bottom of the glass box.

"It would be expected," Abberline noted. "There appears to have been a head injury that caused the death while maneuvering inside the box."

That caught my attention as I had not seen a head wound.

It was a most entertaining jousting of words with Abberline putting on his usual performance in his determination to dismiss what was, in his opinion, an accident.

"Looking for the plot of your next novel, Miss Forsythe?" Abberline added. "A crime where there is none."

I chose to ignore the pithy comment, and the chief inspector.

Brodie nodded. "And the illusionist has been questioned?" he asked.

"Monsieur Betard is quite upset as you can well imagine," Abberline continued. "A tragic end to a successful evening. I will direct one of my men escort him back to the hotel. The other young woman was quite hysterical. Quite clever as far as the illusion was concerned," he added. "But devastating now.

"As I said, a tragic accident, hardly a crime. Not your area of expertise, Brodie," he continued. "Bodies floating in the Thames, a dead ambassador, poking about in the affairs of those beyond your station? And now, your association with the Special Services?" He sniffed with disapproval.

"You will remove yourself, along with Miss Forsythe and Miss Templeton," he said in parting. He returned where Betard and Sophie stood. I caught Betard's glance once more followed by an exchange with Abberline who also glanced briefly in our direction.

"Disappointingly the same, as always," I commented about the chief inspector.

Brodie's mouth twitched at one corner.

"And ye as well," he commented.

I wasn't at all certain that was a compliment.

The three of us returned to the rail station at the Palace and caught the last train returning to London. I told Brodie about the performance, explained the illusion, and what I had observed about the young woman's body.

"And ye saw no one approach the box after the cover was lowered into place?" he asked.

"No one, other than Betard and then her sister, of course, when the poor thing was found still inside the first box. And Abberline is calling it an accident. The man is a bumbling fool, more concerned with his own advancement than any crime or the victims." I made no attempt to disguise my true opinion now that we had left the Crystal Palace.

"If I had stood by and waited for him to assist in my sister's situation, we might well have been into the next century with no answers. Not to mention several people dead, and the threat to the royal family."

"He will make his official report that it was an accident," Brodie pointed out. "We canna simply go about stirring things up when there is no one to object to his findings."

I knew that he was correct. Aggravating man.

In my sister's case I had refused to accept Abberline's complacency in what was an obvious murder and had sought Brodie's services when Abberline all but refused to investigate. While I had my own opinion in the matter, this appeared to be quite different.

I then inquired about his work with Sir Avery of the Special Services. His response was vague, a non-response to be precise. Whatever Sir Avery had him working on, he chose not to discuss. Brodie inquired as to my aunt's health and my sister's plans to eventually return to Paris.

As I said, polite inquiries that kept a distance as Templeton dozed off on the upholstered cushions at the seat beside me in the rail car, her only comment occasional snoring.

We had been fortunate to catch the last train from the Crystal Palace and returned to London in good time.

Upon our arrival, Brodie secured a cab for Templeton, then escorted me to my townhouse in Mayfair.

"Would you care for a dram?" I politely asked as anyone might, in spite of the late hour, as he walked with me to the entrance of the townhouse.

"Thank ye, no," he replied equally polite, then bid me good night. He did wait until I had entered the townhouse and then closed the door and secured it. Then left.

Irritating man!

~

I was still contemplating Brodie's polite distance the next morning as I read through the morning edition of the London Times for anything about the events of the previous evening.

That was small satisfaction that, at the very least, it appeared that Alan Ivers had not managed to get a story out of the tragedy.

I would like to say that I was indifferent to Brodie's estrangement... I was indifferent, I told myself as I poured my third cup of coffee after a restless night, or at least what remained of it after I had returned home.

Alice, my housekeeper made that observation as she had brought another pot of coffee to the front parlor where I usually worked at my next book. However, my typing machine sat undisturbed as I finished scanning the daily.

"It was quite late, last night when you returned. No difficulty, I hope," she said.

To anyone not familiar with the Irishwoman, they would consider it simply concern. But Alice had been with me for some time, through thick and thin, as they say, and I knew better.

In that way that she somehow managed to learn things, she had obviously heard about the incident at the Palace.

"Poor, poor thing," she commiserated. "And twins, I'm told. You know, twins are especially close, more so than most sisters. It's said they know each other's thoughts without even speaking. I cannot imagine what the poor thing is going through. Oh, and this was delivered just before you came downstairs this morning."

She handed me an envelope with the Hotel Metropole's crest

on the front and my name—*Miss Mikaela Forsythe*, hastily scrawled across.

Hotel Metropole?

Abberline had mentioned the night before that he was having Jean Luc Betard and his assistant escorted back to the hotel. And I knew from something I had read before that it was Betard's habit to stay at the hotel when he had an engagement for more than one evening.

A French expat, he had been living very near London the past several years on a private estate as I recalled.

It was obvious that with the performance for the royal family on one evening and then the previous night's performance that the hotel Abberline had spoken of apparently referred to the Metropole. That prestigious hotel was where my aunt had guests stay during her spring and then winter follies that she threw each year and which I tried to avoid, as they say, like the plague.

I slipped a finger under the wax seal at the back of the envelope. As I had noticed, the scrawl was most definitely a man's handwriting and one perhaps not completely comfortable with the English language. There were several places where the ink had pooled before the next word was written.

*Miss Forsythe,*

*It is most important that I meet with you as soon as possible. I wish to acquire your expertise in the dreadful circumstances of the previous evening. Jean Luc Betard.*

It was very near noon when I arrived at Brodie's office on the Strand, that note in hand.

It was good to see that the office at the second floor at number two hundred four had been quite admirably restored after the fire, the wood landing replaced along with the steps at the alcove. The office itself seemed to have been repaired as well.

"It's good to see you, Miss Forsythe," Mr. Cavendish, née the Mudger, greeted me. "The hound has been quite beside himself without Mrs. Ryan's sweet cakes that you bring him."

I had come prepared, or I should say that Alice had, with the cakes that were neatly wrapped and which I now retrieved from my carpet bag and handed to Mr. Cavendish, one of several people I had encountered in my previous associations with Brodie.

He and Rupert, the hound, lived under the entry from the Strand. When weather was most fierce he had been known to occupy the back storeroom of the Public House down the way, much to his liking. He had lost both legs below the knees in an accident years before, however that did not slow him down as he wheeled his way about the East End on a rolling platform, Rupert the hound, loping alongside.

He had proven to be an invaluable source of information in previous investigations, and I liked him very much. The hound as well, that had provided 'guard dog' services as Mr. Cavendish called it, on more than one occasion. The hound wagged his tail as I handed him a cake.

Both hound and the Mudger grinned at me, the hound from his position sprawled at the sidewalk licking his chops, while Mr. Cavendish with his gap-toothed smile. He bobbed his head.

"Me compliments to Mrs. Ryan."

"Is Mr. Brodie about?" I inquired. I had put in a call to Alex Sinclair who also worked with Special Services, quite amazing with his coding machine. He had not seen Brodie this morning and had suggested that he might be here.

"Came in quite late the night before," Mr. Cavendish replied. "Been up there ever since, in a bit of a temper, you might say."

A bit of a temper? Well, I had encountered that before. This could not wait, no matter the reason for his temper.

Forewarned is forearmed? I climbed the stairs to the second floor, determined not to be put off this time.

"It looks as if everything is in good order," I observed with a look about as I entered the office. "One can hardly tell there was a fire."

To say that the office had been remarkably transformed, much like a phoenix rising from the ashes, was an understatement.

New wood floors gleamed a rich, dark color with an area rug under a new desk that was quite an improvement over the old one. Although I missed the books holding up one end of the old desk where the leg had gone missing.

The old file cabinet had been replaced with two new ones just two drawers high each, forming a countertop with an impressive map at the wall above that showed Britain as well as Europe.

The smudged window that one could hardly see out of had been broken as we escaped the fire. It had been replaced by a window casement that looked out on the rooftops of the buildings beyond the back alleyway. The iron firebox and the mantle over it had miraculously survived.

The obvious missing part, other than my black board where I kept my notes, was the case of my aunt's very fine whisky that we had shared from time to time. It had gone up in flames along with everything else. More is the pity, I thought as I angled a glance into the adjoining room that had previously been Brodie's bedroom.

"Is there a reason yer so bloody cheerful so early in the morning?"

Cheerful? The same could not be said for himself. But I was not to be put off.

"It is hardly morning," I pointed out. "Very near midday."

He stood before the desk, much as I had seen a dozen times in the past. He was still wearing his formal shirt and trousers from the night before although he had removed his tie, the sleeves of the shirt rolled back at his arms.

He was obviously irritated by something. The lines at the corners of his eyes indicated he might not have slept well, or at all, and he appeared to be distracted by paperwork he held in his hand.

"Thank ye for yer observations," he snapped without looking up.

Yes, quite irritated. I chose to ignore it. We had far more important things to discuss.

"We have a client," I announced as I approached him and laid Betard's note at the desk, quite emphatically I might add.

That dark gaze narrowed on me as I stood beside him, not at all put off. "Monsieur Betard," I explained.

I was reminded that Brodie, even in a temper, was a most stirring figure of a man.

"He has asked us to make inquiries in the matter of last evening."

We arranged, or I should say that *I* arranged for Betard to meet with us at the Hotel Metropole that very afternoon. Brodie was still unconvinced that there was a case.

"We won't know until we investigate the circumstances," I pointed out something that he had reminded me of more than once in the past.

He glared at me as we arrived at the hotel.

"I am not in agreement of this," he reminded me.

"Of course," I replied as we entered the hotel and asked the desk clerk to notify Monsieur Betard that we had arrived.

Betard chose to meet with us in one of the hotel's small private salons reserved for guests to conduct business while in London. This was a most difficult and sad business, I thought.

Brodie stood as Betard arrived, attired in coat, trousers and shirt that might be found on any banker in the city, but no less elegant than the night before when he had arrived on the stage with that swirling cape. He nodded at Brodie, then turned to me as I also stood.

He took my hand in his. "My gratitude, Miss Forsythe. As you well know, a very difficult time, but it is so important that we learn the truth of what has happened."

"Of course," I replied as he released my hand with a sad if mysterious smile.

"How shall we begin?" he then asked.

We began by asking him questions about the previous evening —when had they arrived, was there anything different about the evening, anyone who was there not of their own people, was he called away at any time?

He was polite, most serious with a frequent glance in my direction as I also asked questions about his assistant who was found dead in the box, Francoise Dupre.

Did she seem distracted, had she mentioned anything different to him, anything she was concerned about either personally or with the illusion?

"*Non*," he replied again in French and then continued in English. "I would have noticed."

"*Bien sûr*," Of course, I replied in French, years of attending private finishing school in Paris not to be wasted. He smiled then and continued in French as well.

"We had a relationship, but it ended."

Lovers it seemed. Was there any difficulty in that, I then inquired. He gave me a puzzled look.

"*Non*," he replied, then asked, "Will you find out how this happened? Her sister, Sophie, is most distressed. They were very close. You understand?"

After translating for Brodie, I assured Betard that we would make our inquiries, that it was first important to determine how Francoise had died.

"*Oui*, I understand. I was told that her body was taken to a private facility."

He provided the name of the mortuary, one of several that had come into service over the past few years for residents in the city.

We both rose then to leave, at least with some information to begin our investigation on his behalf.

"Will you be remaining at the hotel?" Brodie inquired. "If we should have information for you."

"A few days," Betard replied. "There are arrangements to be

made, of course. Sophie wishes for Francoise to be returned to France. You understand? Then we will be returning to the country. With everything that has happened, there will need to be changes before I begin my next tour." He took my hand again in parting.

"*Merci beaucoup, mademoiselle.* I knew that you were the one to help us." He then kissed the back of my hand. I was not unfamiliar with the ways of the French, considering the interlude that I'd lived there years before.

"Monsieur Brodie, as well," he then added.

I caught the sideways look Brodie gave me as we left the hotel to begin our investigation.

"What is it?" I asked.

"Ye liked that, did ye?" he asked as the hotel attendant waved down a driver for us.

There was something in the way he said it, blunt, quite direct. Obviously, he was speaking of the fact that I had been right about my suspicions from the night before, and we now had a case.

"The man has asked for our help," I said as I climbed aboard the cab when it arrived.

"I wasna referring to his request for our help," Brodie commented.

Or obviously *not* speaking about the case. What was it I heard? Disapproval? Of what?

He climbed into the cab and gave the driver the address of the chemist's shop in Holborn. Mr. Brimley had assisted us before in the matter of determining a victim's death, and in caring for me when injured.

"The sooner we're done with this matter the better."

"Good day, miss. Mr. Brodie." We were greeted by Abby, the young woman Mr. Brimley had taken on as an assistant as we arrived at the chemist's shop. I inquired if he was about.

"In the back room as usual," Abby replied. "He has an interesting specimen that came in and he's been back there most of the mornin'," she explained.

They were two of a kind, I thought. The girl was not at all put off by the prospect of a new body part for Mr. Brimley's collection—a hand, a foot, or some other appendage. I didn't go further with the thought.

Mr. Brimley had studied to be a physician at King's College, but circumstances took him in another direction—that of pharmacist dispensing treatments and pills in the East End, along with being quite a hand, no pun intended, in stitching up wounds. I could personally attest to his skill in that regard.

He was slightly shorter than myself with thinning grey hair at his head, curious eyes, and somewhat distracted with some thought as now when we made our way back into his workshop, a separate area with countertops and microscopes, and camera.

"A pleasant surprise, Miss Forsythe," he greeted us. "And Mr. Brodie, as always." He looked from me to himself. "Is there something I may help you with?"

As Brodie was still in somewhat of a disagreeable temper, I explained the events of the night before and our new client's wishes for us to make inquiries on his behalf.

"Yes, yes, quite sad. There was a bit about it in the afternoon paper."

Alan Ivers, I thought. So, he had managed to make a story out of it after all.

"Nasty business, a young woman's death," he commiserated. "Let me put this hand away, and I'll be able to join you. Abby can handle anyone who comes in until I return."

In addition to being a chemist and well-schooled in medicine, he was also most curious about the human body. The last time we had met, he had been studying a hand that he had come by, suspended in a glass jar with a preservative so that he could make notes about the inner workings that included tendons, muscles, and bones.

However the hand had suffered a fate similar to the rest of his collection during our previous investigation when his shop was broken into and left in a shambles.

The workshop had been well-cleaned with everything in order once more. Much like a collector of fine art, he beamed as he presented the jar with the latest specimen, and what appeared to be an eyeball!

"The one in the first jar is from a cow, courtesy of the stock-yards," he explained. "This second one..." He cleared his throat. "I was able to acquire it after an altercation between two men at the Old Bell."

I knew it well. The Old Bell was a local tavern with a reputation... well, let's just say that the reputation included sailors from vessels that put into port from places across the empire, local ladies, and the occasional grifter.

"Most interesting." It was all I could think to say.

"An aspiring young artist has agreed to illustrate it once I've dissected it," he continued to explain far more than I needed.

An artist. I thought of my sister. This was not precisely her area of preference. "Fascinating," I commented, and I had to admit that, distasteful as it might be, it was fascinating.

"That will allow me to study the inner workings of the eye," he told us.

Mr. Brimley was quite well studied on the human anatomy; the better to treat wounds that might come his way, and something I did appreciate.

He was ready in quick time, quite excited about this latest diversion from hands and eyeballs.

"Come along then," he said, reaching for his coat. "Let's see what this young woman's body has to say for itself."

# Three

WE ARRIVED at the Bedford Mortuary where Francoise's body had been taken just before three o'clock in the afternoon.

Betard had made arrangements for us to view the young woman's body. Brodie gave his name, and an attendant escorted us to what was referred to as 'the viewing room' which seemed so very tasteless; bodies put on display like the latest specimen collected for public exhibition to then be sent off in a box like so much rotted fruit.

I much preferred other means; the Vikings had it quite right I thought. I preferred to be sent off in flames much like the Vikings.

No moldy, slow rotting in a box with some ridiculous headstone overhead etched with host of angels. Although the likelihood of angels was remote given my chosen course in life—my novels, my travels, and solving crimes.

There would be only my sister to mourn my passing, assuming that I went first, and she had specific instructions to see to the final process. Ashes to ashes, dust to dust as it were.

"That is so barbaric!" she had once declared at the end of that somewhat morbid conversation.

"But most efficient," I had added. "Don't you dare lay me out in the front parlor for gawkers to parade by with their comments, or I swear, I will haunt you."

That had effectively ended the conversation.

It wasn't that she necessarily believed in ghosts and such, but her acquaintance with my friend Templeton and her spiritual companion, William Shakespeare, who had a habit of popping in from time to time, had her leaving that particular door open.

Now, I turned my thoughts to my observations of the previous evening.

I was no expert by any means when it came to dead bodies, however I know what I had seen and what previous experience had proven out. As Mr. Brimley said, bodies gave up their secrets. It was simply business to be seen to. This from a man who collected the odd hand or foot, kept in jars for him to study. Along with the occasional eyeball.

Brodie was also always quite circumspect. Again, having seen his share of bodies, he made his observations with the experience of the police inspector he had once been.

On the other hand, there was always that first jolt of shock for myself as I couldn't help but notice the similarity of the attendant drawing back the sheet to Jean Luc Betard whipping the cover back from his latest illusion, and *voila*!

Once I had my initial reaction under control, there was surprise that it looked very much like the young woman was merely resting, surely to waken at any moment and call us all fools. Except for the slight bump at her forehead just at the hairline and the bruising about her throat.

*It's quite all right*, I wanted to assure her, thinking of my sister and our first case. *Don't be frightened. We're here to help.*

Mr. Brimley began his own observations. He was quite methodical, glasses in place, talking to himself as he leaned over the table inspecting the body while Brodie made his own observations, and I made notes in my notebook.

The victim had an approximate two-inch laceration at the forehead, quite superficial, bruising about the neck, and something I had not noticed previously—additional bruising at the left cheek.

"There was considerable blood in the box," Brodie commented.

"Could be from the head wound," Mr. Brimley explained but sounded doubtful. "Head wounds bleed quite a lot."

Brodie and Mr. Brimley were like two schoolboys circling about some item of curiosity, each lost in their own thoughts, morbid as they were.

I watched with curiosity as Mr. Brimley then proceeded to turn Francoise's body onto one side.

"Ah, another wound," he commented. "That would most probably account for the amount of blood ye saw, and it appears to have been made with a sharp instrument, probably a knife," he added. He looked over at me then.

"What color was the blood?"

What color? It was blood, thick, dark, almost black as I remembered my initial observation before Brodie had arrived. Mr. Brimley nodded. I described it as best I remembered it.

He nodded. "The knife pierced the liver as well." He gently eased Francoise back onto the table. And to make the process perfect, she groaned, that momentary escape of air from the lungs, almost as if in protest. I took a step back.

"It would seem that you may be correct, Miss Forsythe. The young woman's death was not an accident."

Mr. Brimley accompanied us back to the Strand where he explained what he had found and what it told him.

"None of the other bruises would appear to have caused the girl's death," he explained.

"She was obviously assaulted, and fought back as there were scrape marks at her fingers. However, it would all have been done quickly."

"What else were you able to determine?" Brodie asked.

Mr. Brimley drank from a coffee mug, his gaze thoughtful.

"The wound at her back was the one that killed her, and accounted for the loss of blood.

Brodie turned to me then. "Can you make a guess how much time passed when she first appeared to when the discovery of the body was made?"

I thought about the performance the evening before, Betard's charismatic presentation, his explanation of what the eye sees as opposed to what was actually happening, then the illusion itself from the moment the young woman entered the box, the way Betard built the anticipation in the audience with his theatrical performance, then stepped into the second box with Sophie.

The orchestra had then built on the drama of the illusion as the covers were slowly lowered over both boxes. Then the conclusion as the covers were removed to reveal the young woman had supposedly been transported from the first box as she and Monsieur Betard both stepped from the second box.

"Possibly twenty minutes from when she entered the box to the end of the illusion and her body was found."

"That could have been enough time... But the question remains how was it done? She was alive when she entered the box. So the question then is what happened after she entered the box, and the cover was lowered?"

"Ye may use the desk to make yer notes," Brodie commented after Mr. Brimley had left. It was now a certainty that she had been murdered. But who was the murderer, and how was it done?

"I didn't want to inconvenience you," I replied, "if you have some other business that needs attending to."

"Not at the moment. Though it's getting on in the evening and I understand if ye wish to leave before dark," he replied.

It seemed that we were dancing around each other with an awkwardness I hadn't experienced since that first case. And the truth was, that I didn't want to leave just yet. I wanted his opinion in the situation and his suggestions as to the course we should follow.

I sat at the desk as I had a dozen times in the past as I made notes in my notebook. When I had finished I set my pen down.

"How should we proceed next?"

"Ye no doubt have a thought in the matter," he replied.

"We should contact Betard. He needs to know what we've learned."

"Have ye considered that the magician..."

"Illusionist," I corrected him.

"Have ye considered that the *magician* might be involved?" he continued pointedly.

"A relationship that ended?" I repeated what Betard had told us. "He decided to retaliate in front of an audience of four thousand persons?"

There it was again, that look, as if there was a question but he chose not to ask it.

Brodie sat across from me as he had so many times before when we discussed a case. His mug contained his second dram of whisky.

"Aye, he will need to be told. Ye seemed to get along quite well," he added in a way that had me looking up. "Perhaps ye want to be the one to speak with him regarding the matter, and the sister as well."

He took my hand—the one that had been injured during our last case in what I had to admit was a reckless escape from a hot air balloon. However it wasn't as if there was a place to land the thing.

"Yer hand seems to have healed well enough." He gently stroked my fingers.

"Yes, there's hardly a mark."

I should have pulled my hand away given his surly attitude but didn't, even though I sensed we might not be talking about the injury at my hand.

"Be careful, lass," he said, completely surprising me. The only time he called me that was when something had happened that upset him.

Where did that come from, I wondered? We were talking about a conversation at the Hotel Metropole with Betard and Sophie to let them know what we knew.

"Yes, of course." I pulled my hand from his.

"And I will want to speak with his handlers and other assistants before they return to the countryside," he added. "They may have seen something. I will return to the Palace tomorrow morning and see what I can determine without Abberline, and several thousand people gathered about.

"I will let him know," I replied. "We should plan to meet in the afternoon afterward," I said then. "And determine how to proceed next."

I left then, my thoughts turning to the conversation I needed to have with Betard and Sophie. Not at all a pleasant conversation, but one that was necessary. And then there was that conversation with Brodie. There was something different, something had changed.

I told myself I had no idea what that was. However, there was that little voice that whispered that I *did* know. I thought of Wills and the conversations Templeton supposedly had with him, and chose to ignore it.

I was not into things that went bump in the night, as they say, or some sort of other spiritual presence that my aunt insisted existed; most particularly after getting together with her 'ladies' and a substantial amount of her very fine whisky.

When I returned to the townhouse, I placed a call to Jean Luc at the hotel and set the time of nine o'clock the following morning to meet and discuss what Brodie and I had determined.

The Hotel Metropole had opened five years earlier with much excitement, one of four towering hotels built to accommodate the vast numbers of international travelers who arrived daily in London.

It was seven stories high built in a triangular wedge due to carriageway restrictions at the corner of Northumberland Avenue and Whitehall Place, with easy access to Charing Cross Station that brought travelers from Dover or Folkstone.

It boasted accommodations for officers of the military attending the levees at St. James, and ladies attending state balls and concerts at Buckingham Palace. Not to mention, American visitors and those from the British Colonies along with foreign ambassadors. That also included the renowned Jean Luc Betard who had performed in the salons of royalty and presidents.

I stopped at the front desk. An attendant accompanied me to Betard's rooms. There were two of them, adjoining rooms on the fourth floor.

The attendant's knock at the door was answered by one of the young men who had assisted with the performance the previous evening. He was quite young with a rough way about him, his tone anything but welcoming as he greeted us in French with a dismissive attitude.

I explained that Betard was expecting me. The young man who answered the door was dismissed. He pushed past then disappeared down the hallway.

"You must forgive him," Betard said as he stood aside for us to enter the suite. "The last several hours have been... difficult. The newspapers, even the hotel staff; most curious... Details to be taken care of," he added with a dismissive gesture.

"I appreciate your attention to this, Miss Forsythe." He was most engaging, with a faint smile. He was also quite handsome with dark hair and piercing blue eyes.

I put him of an age with Brodie, very slender of build but with an appealing manner typical of the French that I had discovered some years before during my years in Paris at private school.

"*Avec une habileté incroyable,*" he told me then. "*Vous avez peut-être passé du temps en France?*"

"Yes," I replied of my familiarity with his language. "I spent several years in France, in private school."

"Ah, a lady of some station, it seems." He indicated the chair beside the table, then took the one opposite.

I thought how best to inform him on what we had determined, never a pleasant task. I decided it was best to simply tell him, then proceed.

"With the help of someone very familiar with these situations, we have determined that Francoise's death was not an accident." That seemed somehow better than simply blurting out that we were convinced she had been murdered. He was visibly shaken.

"Please continue."

I explained as delicately as possible what Mr. Brimley had discovered and his certainty that the knife wound had been the direct cause of death while the bruising had very likely occurred as she was initially attacked and fought to save herself.

"Mon Dieu," he replied. "Who would have done such a thing?"

"That is precisely what we need to determine next," I explained. "She was the sister of your assistant, correct?"

"Yes, " Betard replied. "Poor Sophie. This has been very difficult for her as you must understand, and now..." He shook his head. "For her to learn that it was murder?"

He appeared quite grief stricken. I understood with what he had told us previously of their relationship.

"The illusion was a new one, was it not? Performed before the audience for the first time?" I then asked.

Betard composed himself. "Yes, however, not new as far as my experience with it. I had perfected it over many months with both Francoise and Sophie, and it was always perfectly executed. There was nothing new, no difficulties. It should have been perfect, and now..."

"Would it be possible to speak with Sophie about happened?" I then asked.

"I don't know what she can tell you. All of this has been most devastating for her."

"Of course, I understand. Still, it might be helpful to ask her a few questions."

He rose from his chair then crossed the suite to the adjoining room.

I have encountered people, both men and women, in the most tragic of circumstances—the loss of a loved one, the cruelty of murder that leaves so many unanswered questions.

I glimpsed the adjacent room through the doorway as Betard knocked on the door then opened it. The adjacent suite included a sitting room and what appeared to be another room beyond. He spoke quietly in French announcing that I was there to speak with her.

Having seen Sophie Dupre the previous evening in her stage costume with stage make-up, much the same as my friend Templeton wore for a performance, the contrast now as she stepped from the adjoining room was quite startling.

She wore a dark blue dress with a high neck that framed a pale, heart-shaped face with delicate features and swollen dark blue eyes with smudges below.

She was much smaller than I had previously noticed and looked more like a sad, fragile child. But the startling resemblance to her sister was there. I would not have been able to tell which was Francoise or Sophie.

The smallness and fragility of her made me want to wrap my arms around her shoulders and comfort her, although I knew as well as any that there was no amount of comfort that was enough when a loved one died. I couldn't imagine what it was like for a surviving twin.

Betard gently took Sophie's hand and led her into the sitting room, then introduced us. I felt a hollow ache inside as he spoke to her in French. By her reaction, no translation was needed as he explained the reason I was there, the sudden widening of her eyes, the way her face became even more pale. She took a step back and for a moment I thought that she might faint.

He held on to her, gently supporting her as he led her to the settee across from the table.

I sat beside her and took her hand in mine, and felt the fragility in the slender fingers that clung to mine.

I explained in French that I knew what it was to lose someone that I loved very much. Then, difficult as it was, I told her that it was important to find the person who had done this and that we would need her help. This, I also knew, might be a way of helping her at this most difficult time.

I then made a decision that I was certain Brodie would have objected to had he been present. I explained that I would like to return and speak with her later. What she had learned today, was enough for now.

She slowly nodded, and simply murmured, "Oui." Yes.

Betard then escorted her back to her suite.

I then explained that Brodie had returned to the Crystal Palace to inspect the stage area, and that we would also want to see the boxes that were used for the illusion.

He nodded. "Everything is at the warehouse at the rail station to be returned to my estate. However, I will make certain that they are available to you and Mr. Brodie. I will send word to one of my people there."

He sadly shook his head. "Tragic. When I think of Francoise, so full of life, so beautiful, and now..." He shook his head. "Who could have done such a thing?"

That was precisely what I wanted to find out, and that brought us to the next part of our conversation.

"We will need to question all of your people," I added. "Those who travel with you—attendants, stage people, anyone who would have had access to the stage and the boxes."

He nodded. "I will make my people available to you, of course. I will provide a list."

"What about any threats you might have received?" Was it possible someone was angry over his affair with Francoise? Or had there been professional threats?

"There are many who imagine themselves to be masters of the illusion," He replied. "There were some in the audience last night, but very few are capable of such things as I have created."

Nothing like confidence in oneself, I thought. Or possibly some small amount of conceit as I had noted in some actors of the stage?

"We will need the names of those you recognized as well," I told him.

"Yes, of course."

"I will need to return to speak with Sophie."

"Tomorrow would be better," he suggested. "When she has had a little time to understand what has happened."

From my own early experience, I wasn't at all certain such tragedy could ever be understood. It was simply something that was always there.

He then explained how the illusion that night was fabricated with mirrors set at specific angles that created a narrow space at the back of the box where Francoise was meant to hide herself once the cover was lowered into place. Then when the cover was removed all that was supposed to be seen was an empty box, the mirrors inside reflecting off one another.

Then Sophie was to step out of the narrow space in the second box where she had been all along to suddenly appear alongside Betard. The fact that they were identical twins made the illusion of the transference, as he called it, possible.

He smiled sadly. "Francoise was most excited to perform the illusion after rehearsing it so many times." He shook his head. "Tragic, so very tragic... She was so very beautiful."

And then dead.

I thanked him then rose to leave. He took my hand once more.

"I am most grateful for your assistance, Miss Forsythe. And your kindness with Sophie most certainly." He bent over my hand again.

Whitehall Place, one of the streets that bordered the Metropole Hotel, was filled with the usual congestion found in central London, carriages and cabs lined up in the carriageway waiting to deliver guests to other destinations in the city, the walkway crowded with those arriving.

As I stepped up into the cab, I glimpsed a man who had made his way through the crowd of hotel guests, then quickly disappeared. There was something odd about him, about the way he seemed to be looking directly at me. But there was something else about him... something at a glance that might have been familiar.

I gave the driver the address of the office on the Strand. As he drove off, I looked back through the opening of the cab. However, the man I had seen was gone. Most strange.

Brodie and I had agreed to meet back at the Strand after I had spoken with Betard, and he had returned to the Crystal Palace to make his own investigations. It might provide some insight into precisely how someone had accessed the one box before an audience, and then committed the murder.

We were to meet later in the day and visit the warehouse at Victoria Station so that we might examine the boxes that were used in the illusion.

That was several hours away, and I had my own thoughts on something that might be useful.

I contacted Templeton at the Adelphi, with her vast experience on the stage, and asked if she knew of someone who might be able to explain how someone might have gotten into that glass box and murdered Francoise.

She agreed to meet me for luncheon after rehearsal had ended.

"Julius Stroud, do you know him?" Templeton commented as she read the names of the other illusionists that Betard had provided, who were also at the Crystal Palace the night of the murder.

"He's positively ancient. He hasn't performed in some time. I thought he was dead... But then, that often doesn't mean anything," she casually added. Conversations with Templeton could be most entertaining.

"And then there is Albert Smyth, not his real name of course. He has performed at the Adelphi, rabbits in hats, that sort of thing, and Reginald Toomy, also known as the Great Waldo. He works the street."

Most interesting I thought, although none of them seemed on a level with Betard. I would pass the information on to Brodie. She handed the list back to me.

"Now, do tell me everything," Templeton insisted as I joined her in her dressing room after the completion of her rehearsal. In spite of the fact that the night's performance was the closing of the play, she was in high spirits.

A lunch awaited us in her dressing room. There was caviar with hard cooked eggs and small pancakes called 'blinis'.

I have become quite accustomed to different foods from my travels, and I've never been hesitant to try something new. Hence, my recently acquired appreciation for meat pies, an amusing dish called 'bubble and squeak', and then there were 'neeps and tatties', served on any given day at the public house near the office on the Strand. When one is hungry, one might eat just about anything. However, I drew the line at fish eggs.

"You know," Templeton explained. "It is rumored that caviar increases... certain urges." Her eyes gleamed. "I will have to see if I can persuade Mr. Munro to try some."

It was possible, considering the Scots were inclined to haggis —a sheep's belly filled with oats and vegetables then roasted.

I didn't care what you called it or what you put on it, caviar was still fish eggs and one of Templeton's favorite meals. I felt the same way about 'animelles', French for bull testicles that were considered quite the delicacy. Thank heavens, Templeton wasn't into French cuisine.

I chose to keep with the blinis and hard cooked eggs, along with a nice white wine. It wasn't my aunt's very fine whisky, but it was most pleasant.

Over our shared luncheon, I explained what I could about our investigation into Francoise Dupre's death at the Crystal Palace.

"Do you know how the illusion was created?" she asked, eyes closed as she took a bite of blini stuffed with caviar and made a rapturous sound.

She is my very good friend and in spite of her eccentricities about certain things, she was someone I trusted and much enjoyed spending time with. Hence, our evening at the Crystal Palace to see Monsieur Betard's performance the night of the murder.

"He did explain it since he won't be performing it again due to the circumstances," I explained.

"Do you think he has a mistress?"

Oh dear. I didn't bother to explain that he had been having an affair with Francoise. That was far too much information.

"I wouldn't know," I replied.

"It might be most interesting to find out," she announced. "What about Mr. Brodie?"

"What about him?" I had the distinct impression that we were beginning to wander in a direction I might not want this to go.

"Have you... You know, yet?" she asked, savoring another bite of the blini with caviar. At this rate she was going to need several cups of very strong coffee to rouse her up from her euphoria.

I tried ignorance on the subject. "I don't know what you're talking about."

"Oh, do come along," she exclaimed. "Have you slept with him? That forceful, very masculine, glowering, dark-eyed Scot. Personally, I find Scottish men to have great endurance, and they can be most creative." She took another swallow of wine.

It had to be the caviar.

"That is none of your business," I replied.

I did not consider the few times I had needed to stay over at the office on the Strand as the same thing. That had been strictly for medicinal purposes after I was injured. There was, of course, the time that Brodie stayed at the townhouse in Mayfair. But that was strictly for my protection.

The question was, what was I supposed to do about Brodie? That was for another time, and another conversation.

"What I do want to know," I moved the conversation back to the topic at hand, "is how the murderer might have been able to kill Francoise without anyone seeing anything," I explained.

"Yes, of course," Templeton commented somewhat vaguely.

I had the distinct feeling that she had gone off somewhere, even though she was still sitting across from me. It wasn't the first time. There was another possibility, of course. It happened from time to time, and I had become quite used to her wanderings of the mind, as Brodie called them. Or as he put it less delicately, 'mad as a hatter'.

"He might be able to help," Templeton mentioned.

She was back, or at least appeared to be back in the moment.

"Who might that be?" I inquired. These sorts of conversations with Templeton were always a little like falling down the rabbit hole when she came up with her ideas.

"Mr. Alamy. Wills thinks that he could be very helpful."

I emptied my wine glass and poured another. Before the evening at the Crystal Palace I hadn't shared company with Templeton in some time due to her schedule at the theater and my work on my most recent book. And therefore, we hadn't shared company with 'Wills'—Mr. William Shakespeare, the somewhat dubious spiritual connection she claimed to have.

I will admit though that on previous occasions Wills had proven himself to be a reliable source of information. Most intriguing.

I definitely needed more wine. "Who is Mr. Alamy?" I inquired as I poured.

"He is quite talented and has a shop in Holborn. You really must speak with him. Wills is most insistent that it might provide valuable information for your case."

I had nothing to lose, and it was some time before I was to meet with Brodie at the office on the Strand.

"Do you need to send round a note or ring him up?" I asked.

"Heavens no," Templeton replied. "He's always there. His shop is just off the High Street. It used to be a brothel. Wills will set everything up for us," she continued.

Perhaps it was the wine, although I'd only had three glasses, but I felt as if I had already gone down that rabbit hole and was looking up at the opening that was rapidly disappearing.

"I do need to return by five o'clock to prepare for tonight's performance," Templeton reminded me as our cab arrived in front of Mr. Alamy's establishment, formerly, of all places, a brothel. The sign across the bow windows at the street read, *The Magicks Shoppe*.

"I've been thinking of another endeavor," she announced as we entered through the front door of the shop, quite surprising me. Leaving the theater?

"Something a little more exciting," she continued. "Although there are so few opportunities for women as we both know, beyond seamstress or lady's maid. So very boring."

I had visions of her as a lady's maid in black gown with white apron, providing advice on make-up, style of gown, possibly a costume. As for seamstress? My thoughts didn't even continue in that direction. Either one would not be a good choice. It was probably simply a phase she was going through with the closing of her latest play.

# *Four*

THE MAGICKS SHOPPE was on the side street set among the usual taverns, and public houses with Reeves Bookseller and Publisher to one side and an eyeglass maker to the other.

The buildings were over two hundred years old in this part of Holborn, black and white half-timbered affairs in the Elizabethan style. At least the walls used to be black and white, but were now black and sooty grey from coal smoke and time, with high chimneys, jettied upper floors and dormer windows.

I could just imagine a lady of the evening leaning out of one of those dormers plying her trade to those on the street below. I did wonder what the going rate might have been.

The shop was set back with an array of colorful characters in the windows—ventriloquist dummies in various poses much like human beings; a charwoman with a broom, a street monger, a grubby faced boy with a toothless grin, and a washer woman with her cap and apron, along with a character who might have been a magician. There was also lettering that advertised decks of cards, a crystal ball for conjuring up spirits, disappearing powder whatever that might be, and everything for practicing the art of magic.

I looked about for the proverbial top hat with a rabbit poking up out of it among assorted stuffed birds, including a fierce looking falcon at a perch near the door. The rabbit appeared in the form of the proprietor.

"Mr. Alamy!" Templeton greeted the small man who stepped from behind the counter to greet us, his cherubic face framed by a wreath of white whiskers and oversized ears—. Rabbit indeed, I thought.

"Miss Templeton!" he greeted her. "It has been some time since you visited my shop," he replied. "I had word that you would be calling. And you've brought a companion."

"My friend, Miss Mikaela Forsythe," she made the introductions.

Oh, my, I thought. Mr. Alamy as well, communicating with the spirit world? But then this was a magic shop, I supposed that it was good for business.

"What brings you here?" Mr. Alamy asked, eyes bright as that rabbit I had imagined.

"Your expertise, of course," Templeton explained. "In the matter of conjuring an illusion."

Like most artists, he beamed, a mixture of delight and shyness at the prospect of discussing his craft. "Secrets, perhaps?"

"How something might be done without being seen," my friend explained.

Mr. Alamy's eyes sharpened. "Miss Forsythe... That name is familiar. From the dailies I believe." He came around the corner of the counter and approached me.

He took my hand, turned it over, then lightly brushed his fingers across my palm very much the same as Brodie had.

"I sense a curious nature, intelligent, but obstinate at times, and quite passionate." He looked up at me then.

"And there is a man, one that you are often at odds with, and... Oh, my dear, the answer must be 'yes' of course," he announced, and with a flourish produced a beautiful red rose seemingly plucked out of the air and presented to me.

"Yes, well that is all most entertaining," I replied avoiding Templeton's amused expression.

Mr. Alamy grinned. "Just a bit of palm reading. It can be most insightful. Now, tell me what may I show you? Disappearing powder perhaps?"

He picked up the jar, opened it and sprinkled the powdery contents all about himself.

The dust from the powder filled the air... and he was gone!

Good heavens!

"Oh, bravo," Templeton exclaimed and clapped her hands together as I looked about the shop for some sign of Mr. Alamy. He had truly and completely disappeared. At least he seemed to have disappeared.

"What brings you to my shop, Miss Forsythe?"

I turned about and discovered the shopkeeper behind his counter once more.

Was it an illusion? Or had he truly disappeared, then reappeared?

Templeton was most amused while I was extremely curious.

"Poppy seeds, myrrh, wormwood and mistletoe with a bit of mica added," he explained. "It works quite well, although I rarely share the recipe with anyone. Only those who come seeking my skills, young men eager to expand their skills."

Whether it was merely an illusion that took advantage of my inexperience or truly some feat of magic, still I was impressed.

"How may I assist?" he asked with a courtly bow.

"It's in the matter of an incident that happened two nights ago at the Crystal Palace," I explained.

"Ah, the murder of Monsieur Betard's young assistant. Most tragic and perhaps the end of his career And you have come to learn how it was done."

Murder he called it. How very interesting.

"The police are calling it an accident," I replied.

"But you have determined otherwise, with intuition, skill, a touch of magic..." he cocked his head as if someone had just whispered in his ear. "A new case perhaps."

I had seen that same pose before with my friend, Templeton.

As if someone were whispering in his ear. I was not given to believing in that sort of thing. Most strange.

"And the man I spoke of earlier is quite accomplished in these matters." I commented of Mr. Brimley's observations.

This was a very odd conversation. There had been nothing in the dailies yet. The situation had been called a tragic accident. And most certainly nothing had been written about Brodie's taking the case.

Mr. Alamy picked up a deck of cards and laid it at the counter. "Please, if you will, Miss Forsythe."

"I am here for information, Mr. Alamy," I attempted to explain.

"Precisely," he replied with that cherubic smile. "Please cut the cards and we will begin."

I wasn't certain what that was supposed to mean. I cut the cards as he was most insistent.

He gathered them once more, then spread them at the counter as I had seen when my aunt had her ladies gathered for such entertainment.

"Select three cards, Miss Forsythe."

I thought again of that rabbit hole as I selected the cards at random, indulging him if it would move everything along as to the reason I was there.

"Oh my...!" Then, "Yes, most certainly," he commented as he looked at each of the cards I had selected.

"The sword means intellect, this card means transformation— things that will change..."

Quite a performance, I thought. "And the last card?"

"Oh, that is part of the arcane that means passion. Most exciting wouldn't you say, Miss Forsythe?"

Oh dear. I wondered if he was perhaps channeling Wills?

"Monsieur Betard was gracious enough to explain how the illusion that was presented at the Crystal Palace worked," I explained. "I was hoping that you might be able to tell me how one might have gotten inside the box without anyone seeing it done."

"Of course, the sword—intellect," he repeated. "Most interesting. So, tell me, Miss Forsythe, how did Monsieur Betard create the illusion?"

Since it was very likely that Betard would not be performing that illusion in the future and had not hesitated to tell me how it was done, it didn't seem that I was divulging any great secret.

Taking out my notebook where I had made a sketch of the box with the angled mirrors that created the illusion, I showed the drawing to Mr. Alamy. I explained that it was empty when the cover was raised with that narrow compartment at one corner where Francoise Dupre was supposed to hide herself. The audience then saw what appeared to be an empty box with the help of those mirrors.

"Yes, of course. Most ingenious," Mr. Alamy replied quite fascinated. "One set of mirrors would have reflected off the other creating the illusion that the box was empty."

"My question is, how might someone have entered the box and attacked the young woman?" My thought was, if we knew how it was done, it might help determine *who* would have done such a thing.

Motive, means, and opportunity.

"I quite see what you wish to know," he replied. "The art of illusion is the art of deception, Miss Forsythe. What you are led to believe that you see, as opposed to what is actually seen—someone who disappears in a puff of powder," he smiled. "Someone who was concealed inside a box. What happened inside the box? How did the person disappear? Or not." He came out from behind the counter.

"Come with me."

I exchanged a look with Templeton. She was quite amused by all of this.

"Do come along, Mikaela," she said, slipping her arm through mine. "You did want to know how it can be done."

"Shouldn't you set the lock at the door?" I inquired as we followed Mr. Alamy behind the counter—potential customers or perhaps others considering where we were.

He smiled again. "Everything is quite safe. It is well known that anything that someone might steal would only bring them harm." He indicated the stuffed falcon on that perch and smiled again. I could have sworn the bird turned its head, sharp eyes looking straight at me.

Behind the counter was a door, very likely a closet or store-room I presumed. However, the presumption of a closet was deceiving at what appeared before us as we followed Mr. Alamy through that doorway into the gaping darkness of a huge room.

He pressed a button at the wall and the electric came on, several lights glowing at the ceiling down the length of an enormous room. It must have filled most of the entire ground floor of the building.

It was filled with a hodge-podge of what reminded me of theatrical props—swords mounted in stands, screens, a barrel filled with wood balls, clothes that included men's cloaks. Ornate tables stood about, one holding a crystal ball or two, no doubt for conjuring of images, while an array of puppets mounted along one wall stared back at us as if we were intruders.

As we followed Mr. Alamy deeper into the storeroom, I felt something brush against my leg. A black cat no doubt, I thought sarcastically.

A shadow moved into the deeper shadows amid the props and costumes, and I thought of Ziggy, Templeton's pet iguana. However, whatever had brushed against my leg was a bit smaller than Ziggy's five-foot length. There was a cackling sound —laughter?

"No bother," Mr. Alamy assured us. "It's just Mr. Stumpf, there." He gestured toward that wall of puppets.

There seemed to be a stirring among those odd fellows, and I fully expected one of them to start talking as we passed by.

44

However, rather than a puppet, a lanky man emerged from the shadows.

He was dressed in a somewhat threadbare frock coat and trousers with a hat atop his head which he swept off in a grand gesture as he bowed to us. He was quite thin, his features gaunt with sunken cheeks, but there was a gleam at his eyes.

"Good afternoon," Mr. Stumpf greeted us most eloquently. "A grand, fine day it is when two lovely young women appear. Perhaps an apple," he suggested and promptly produced one as if plucked from the air.

"Or possibly a comb for your lovely hair?"

As he spoke, I realized it was his laughter that I had heard from the front of the shop.

"Or a sweetmeat provided by my assistant." He made a gesture to one of those dangling puppets, what appeared to be a combination of a boy's body with a clown's head. It was quite startling.

"He is quite harmless," he assured us.

"There, there now, Mr. Stumpf," Mr. Alamy spoke up. "You've found what you were looking for, then?"

"Yes," Mr. Stumpf replied most eloquently. "The boy will do." He chuckled then. "Unless one of these young ladies would care to become my assistant." His gaze fixed on me.

I decided it was best to simply go along with the charade. "Thank you, no, Mr. Stumpf. I have a previous engagement."

"Ah, yes." He bowed again, and then gathered up the '*boy*' with the clown's head.

"I have an idea for a trick that I believe the children will be most excited to see. You will add this to my account, Mr. Alamy?"

"As usual," the shopkeeper replied, and Mr. Stumpf swept from the cavernous room like a performer exiting the stage.

Mr. Alamy continued to lead us deeper into the warehouse of magic paraphernalia. "He's been perfecting the trick with the sweetmeat for several years. He's not well, and I may never see coin for the 'young chap'."

By '*young chap*' it appeared that he referred to the puppet. It was somehow quite sad, but it seemed that Mr. Alamy had a good heart and had previously assisted Mr. Stumpf.

We continued to follow him into the depths of the warehouse, stepping around props, elaborate fabric screens, various items including a skeleton clothed in formal long tails and top hat —most startling when come upon amidst shadows. We rounded a cart much like a food vendor's wagon with a head wearing a turban.

Was it my imagination or were the eyes in the head following us as we passed by?

Nonsense, I thought! I did, however, glance back at the head. Nothing more than an illusion, I told myself. But by far the most intriguing was the full-sized statue of Admiral Nelson in uniform as we continued deeper into the storeroom.

"Things are not always what they seem, Miss Forsythe," Mr. Alamy commented with what could only be described as a mysterious smile.

The statue was remarkably lifelike from portraits I had seen of the hero of Trafalgar. I had just stepped near when he moved! He bowed to me, sweeping his bicorn hat before him.

"Good heavens!" I commented and looked closer, or as close as the meager light in the warehouse allowed.

"He seems to be admiring you," Mr. Alamy commented. "I do have to keep an eye on him." He chuckled then at the joke he made, considering that Admiral Nelson, when he was alive, was known to be blind in one eye.

"He was created by the artists at Madame Tussaud's museum for Trafalgar Day celebrations. It is most entertaining to see reactions when he salutes bystanders."

Most entertaining, I thought.

"How does it work?" I asked.

"There is a clockwork device inside Lord Nelson with a spring that creates the movement," he explained. "He's never bowed like that before. There must be a malfunction. I will need to have him looked at before the next celebration come October next."

Looked at, indeed, I thought with amusement as I imagined people's reactions when the Admiral actually moved. I nodded in the direction of the figure of Lord Nelson. He then slowly stood to his full height, and nodded in return. I kept my eye on him as we continued to the location the shopkeeper indicated.

Things not quite what they seemed?

"Here we are," Mr. Alamy announced as we approached a half-high cabinet, much like a sideboard for storing China pieces and linens. He opened both doors to indicate that it was empty.

"To simulate the box you have described, Miss Forsythe," he explained. "Miss Templeton, if you please."

She stepped around me with smile at her face. It appeared she was familiar with what was about to happen next, dropped to her knees, then crawled inside the cabinet.

"Are you quite comfortable, Miss Templeton?" he asked like a master magician performing before an enthralled audience.

"Yes, most comfortable," she assured him and waved to me. "You may proceed."

Mr. Alamy then closed both doors.

"This has been used for private performances by several esteemed magicians. One in particular, I believe, may have performed for Lady Montgomery," he suggested with a look over at me.

I nodded. Why was I not surprised.

"Please feel free to inspect the cabinet, Miss Forsythe."

The sideboard was made of mahogany wood, approximately five feet long and three feet high and deep, perched on carved legs. There were designs carved into the doors. On the whole, it was an elegant piece that I might have found in my aunt's formal parlor.

I made my inspection, circling about the front and both sides of the sideboard, then down on my knees and passed my hand underneath.

"Are you quite all right?" I asked my friend.

There was a vaguely muffled response. "Of course."

I stood then and inspected the exterior of the cabinet once more.

"Are you going to wave a wand or announce some magic words?" I asked the shopkeeper with more than a little amusement.

He smiled indulgently. "You may now open the cabinet, Miss Forsythe."

I opened both doors, fully aware that there was an obvious illusion he wished to show me. However, having inspected the cabinet with that illusion in mind, I was still surprised to find it empty. My next thought, of course, was how it was done? And where was Templeton?

Before I could ask that particular question I heard Templeton's amused laughter as she approached from the front of the storage area, making a bow to Admiral Nelson, and then rejoining us.

"Mr. Alamy is really quite talented, wouldn't you say?" she commented.

Talented indeed, I thought, turning to our host. He chuckled.

"All of the props and devices you see I have used myself at one time or another. I discovered, however, there was more profit to be made in providing them to other magicians, particularly the young ones hoping to make a reputation for themselves. The more successful ones will not show you how an illusion is done."

I was aware that artists rarely gave up their secrets, and Mr. Alamy was clearly as much an artist of the craft as Betard, but we had come there to learn how Betard's illusion worked and had somehow gone wrong.

I thought of the man I had seen at the amphitheater just as Betard was beginning the illusion, quite overdressed— there, and then gone.

An illusion? I then asked the obvious question.

"How does it work?"

He stepped to cabinet and began to explain much like an instructor.

"Each illusion is known only to the master who creates it, and as you saw, there are no mirrors in this cabinet as you described of Betard's illusion. However, my cabinet might provide you with some idea how similar illusions are created.

"How much time would you say passed between when the young lady stepped into the box and when the body was discovered?" he asked.

I told him what I had told Brodie, that it could have been as long as twenty minutes as Betard continued with the performance. He had explained how Francoise would disappear and he would then make her reappear inside the second box.

"Would you be so kind?" He then told me and held out his hand.

He obviously intended for me to enter the cabinet. Intrigued, I went to my knees, took his hand, and then crawled inside the cabinet.

My initial thought was that it was a very good thing that I was not bothered by tight spaces as the cabinet didn't allow for a great deal of movement.

"Are you comfortable, Miss Forsythe?" he then asked.

"Yes, quite," I replied and prepared myself for the total darkness of the cabinet once those doors were closed.

"Excellent," he announced and then did close them. "Still quite all right, Miss Forsythe?"

I acknowledged that I was and waited.

"Do you have a hairpin in your hair?"

I replied that I did.

"Remove the pin if you please, then feel along the inside of the cabinet, top left corner until you find a small hole in the wood and insert one end of the hairpin into the hole."

I did as he instructed and heard a faint click. The back of the cabinet opened. However it didn't open into the warehouse but into a small room that was obviously behind the wall at the back of the cabinet.

I crawled out, took a moment to orient myself, then

approached a door at the back of the room. It opened into a passageway. I followed the overhead lights until I emerged into the shop once more.

That certainly explained how Templeton had escaped the cabinet and then come up behind us in the warehouse.

Mr. Alamy was most amused as they rejoined me in the front of the shop. I now realized how the illusion of the young woman's disappearance might have been intended. No doubt after hiding behind one of those mirrored panels inside the box. But it didn't explain how someone else had gotten inside the box and killed her.

"That is the question you must find the answer for," Mr. Alamy agreed. "The back panel of the box would have to have been removed..." he paused, "if it had been lowered into place. Remember, this is the art of illusion, what is expected by the audience as opposed to what actually happens."

I saw his point.

"Was it possible she left the box, and then her body was placed back inside the box?" Templeton asked.

"Again," Mr. Alamy reminded us both. "It would have required the back of the box to be opened or the back panel removed entirely, the body placed inside, and then the box closed once more."

Secret compartments, back panels that opened, mirrors that created the illusion of an empty box. That explained how a person inside seemed to disappear, but what if the person never left the box? How would someone else have gotten inside and then killed Francoise? And who would have wanted her dead?

I had come to the Magicks Shoppe hoping to find answers, or at least some indication how Francoise had been murdered without anyone seeing it done. However, I had to admit that I now had more questions. The next order of business was to inspect the box that was used that night at the Crystal Palace.

Still, the shop was most fascinating, with automatons of

Admiral Nelson and the falcon in the front of the shop—lifelike recreations that moved. Amazing!

Templeton needed to return to the theater to prepare for her evening performance, while I needed very much to return to the Strand, make my notes and have a conversation with Brodie about what I had learned.

I thanked Mr. Alamy for showing us his creations and props, along with revealing the inner workings of the cabinet that had indeed provided a valuable clue. If there was such a mechanism inside the box in Betard's illusion, then it appeared that Francoise could easily have stepped out of the box before she was killed.

And then?

I called the office on the Strand, eager to meet with Brodie. However there was no answer, as he had obviously not yet returned.

I then decided to call on someone whom I knew had a great deal of experience with fortune tellers and magicians in her various charitable endeavors, and knew everyone who was anyone about London the past sixty years or so.

My aunt's head butler, Mr. Symons, met me at the entrance at the foyer of her house at Sussex Square.

I had called in advance, however that was always a problematic situation. Our great aunt, Antonia Montgomery, had raised my sister and me after the deaths of both our parents. Linnie—my sister Lenore, had lived with our aunt for some time after her recent difficulty.

Either Linnie or one of the servants would have usually answered the telephone. However, she had recently moved to her own residence to establish her independence and the servants were reluctant to answer a 'contraption' that my aunt considered rude and undoubtedly the portent of disaster for polite society. She would only speak on it in the case of a dire emergency.

I had no idea what she considered 'dire', and simply accepted the fact that she would not respond. Hence my decision to call on her without announcement which she did *not* consider rude, or a portent of disaster for polite society.

As she once told both of us, Sussex Square was still our home and we were welcome whenever we chose to *'drop over'* as she put it; one of those phrases that young men, and now women, at university were said to use.

"I do believe in taking on these modern things," she was fond of saying, excluding the telephone of course. "I have no intention of becoming a boring, stuffy, old dowager. However I suppose that I cannot be a dowager, as I have never been wed."

"Is she about?" I asked Mr. Symons, almost afraid of the answer I would receive. My aunt also had a penchant for unusual habits, such as planning an African safari in her advanced years.

"I believe that she is in the arboretum this afternoon." His faint smile was more a grimace. "The creature escaped again and caused a great deal of havoc with the kitchen staff."

The creature, I knew, referred to the monkey she had acquired on loan from the zoo in preparation for her safari with the thought that it would prepare her for wildlife she would encounter there. My sister and I were still attempting to dissuade her from taking the grueling trip. I'd had great hope for Linnie's success, before she moved to her own residence. I braced myself and went to join our aunt.

There is something to be said for being raised by an independent, forward-thinking woman at the end of the nineteenth century. I kept that in mind as I stepped into the jungle née the formal parlor and was suddenly set upon by a creature that leapt from a tree branch toward me and wrapped its arms around my neck.

"Bloody hell!" Not how I usually greeted my aunt, but under the circumstances...

"Mikaela? Is that you dear?" my aunt called out from somewhere inside the jungle.

I attempted to wrest the creature from about my neck. I finally succeeded. It squirmed out of my arms, dropped to the floor, and skittered off down the long hallway. There was a some-what startled shout—presumably from one of the staff, and the monkey appeared once more and headed in the direction of the kitchens.

"Where has Hercule gone now?" my aunt demanded as she emerged from the jungle in what could only be described as a very colorful presentation.

Said presentation being the formal gown in a brilliant shade of purple that she was wearing.

"Mikaela, so good to see you," she greeted me. "Did he pass this way?"

Presumably she meant the monkey which I had just learned that she had named. Then, with a captive if stunned audience, she asked, "What do you think?"

She proceeded to do a pirouette, or as close to one as a 'sixty-year-old going on eighty-six years' woman with a recovering ankle might manage. However, the *pièce de résistance* was the equally brilliant purple wig piled atop her head. At least, I hoped it was a wig. And there was something a bit odd at her face.

"I..." I searched for the words to best describe what I thought without hurting her feelings. I settled for, "Brilliant!"

"I quite think so as well. It's for my annual May ball that I'm holding next week at the Park."

St. James Park, which was closed down each year to anyone not invited to her spring extravaganza. She was the only person other than the queen who could pull off closing down one of the most exclusive parks in all of London.

"Juliette designed it for me," she went on to explain. "I wanted something that would make a statement."

Juliette, her seamstress, designed for an exclusive clientele, including the Queen. I could think of several comments, none that I would have said in front of my aunt.

"I wanted to get the feel of it, as the skirt is quite heavy," she explained. "Juliette recommended that I practice walking about in it as my soiree goes on for several hours and there will be a great many people there... however the damned corset is giving me a bit of a pinch. I haven't worn one since acquiring my hunting costume for my safari and this is a bit constricting."

There was a word—constricting. It seemed it was more than a 'bit' as she looked to be about to pop out of the bodice. Oh, dear.

I'd read about certain maladies of the elderly, one of them being a sort of mental impairment, prone to odd behavior, even the mention of an elderly fellow who went about stark naked while giving a violin concert on the street.

However, that seemed to be something that set in with advanced years. My aunt had been described as being somewhat eccentric her entire life. I wondered if that sort of thing passed on to others in the family.

Considering my travels and the heroine of my novels, Emma Fortescue, I had been called somewhat 'eccentric' myself. I'd even been judged thus in a review of one of my books:

*The latest tome from the mysterious author who hides behind the name of Emma Fortescue exemplifies a somewhat pithy sense of humor, abandonment of social mores, and quite befuddles this reviewer as to her enormous success. It cannot bode well for proper English society.*

I did love that review and had clipped it from the daily when it came out and had it framed. It was on the wall in my own front parlor where I worked on my latest novel.

"And I did have a bit of a go this morning with my fake eyelashes," my aunt continued as she batted her lashes at me to demonstrate. Or rather one eyelash as the other eyelid was quite naked. That explained what had seemed... different in her appearance other than the purple gown and wig.

"However, I will have Juliette resolve the issue when she comes to make her final alterations."

There was suddenly a loud crash that sounded very much like China breaking, presumably Hercule encountering one of the other servants.

My aunt squirmed a bit. It had to be the corset. She looked at me, then batted her one eyelash as if returning to the present.

"It is so good to see you, dear. It has been a while. Did your sister send you? She has been most difficult and declared that she would not go on safari next winter. I may have to cancel, most disappointing. She has become quite independent since moving into her townhouse."

Said the queen of independence. Hurrah for my sister. It was about time, I thought, after the disaster of her marriage.

"Actually I came after a visit to the Magick's Shoppe in Holborn."

"Mr. Alamy? Such a devilish man, but so very entertaining. I may have him for my May soiree. Excellent idea, my dear."

"And to ask what you might know about the artist Jean Luc Betard?" I quickly redirected her before she went off in another direction so to speak.

"Betard? Ah, yes, unfortunate business the other evening at the Palace. Such a handsome man. I might invite him. It would be quite a coup, don't you think, with all the publicity around that illusion and... there are rumors of course, as there always are." She blinked one eyelash again. "Were you there? Another case for you and Mr. Brodie? Do come along into the encampment." She gestured to the jungle. "You must tell me everything."

Mr. Symons had reappeared, attempting his most dignified expression amid the chaos of Hercule apparently still causing havoc, my aunt in purple, and a very distinct scream from the direction of the kitchens.

"Whisky, if you please, Mr. Symons. For myself and Miss Mikaela."

"We are making inquiries," I explained as I later sat with my aunt at the 'encampment' that she had constructed in the middle of the jungle in her front parlor.

I had to admit, everything—including her gown, the wig, and lack of eyelash not to mention the chaos of Monsieur Hercule as she called him— all seemed to fade in importance with a second dram of her very fine whisky.

"Jean Luc Betard," she commented over her own glass with a somewhat dreamlike expression. "One of the expats from France. I believe that he's been staying in the old estate at Hampton Manor at the edge of the city when he's not abroad, under some arrangement with the owner's family. Cecil Northridge lived there until he passed."

That was some distance, and the fact that he was to have departed on tour explained the reason that all the stage props, including those glass boxes had been brought to the Crystal Palace by rail.

"And of course there are all those rumors about the reasons he left France all those years before," she continued. "Supposedly it was because of all the political turmoil the past several years— assassinations, bombs, that sort of thing."

There was only one person I knew who would have brushed off assassinations, and bombs as 'that sort of thing', with a casual wave her hand. Of course, I supposed when one had lived as long as my aunt and undoubtedly seen her share of things, one could be excused for waving them off.

"What about rumors of any affairs?" I asked.

"Well, the usual, of course. And he has always had quite fetching young assistants. I heard that his final illusion of the evening was spectacular.

"That is if one considered a murder to be spectacular," I commented.

"Murder?" my aunt then asked with a look at me. "How exciting!"

As I was saying about having lived that long...

"What about any threats against him in the past? Any scandals that made the dailies?" I asked, even though I had asked the same question of Betard.

My aunt had a tendency to know everything about everyone.

While I didn't consider her to be a gossip, she was often a source of information that had been quite useful in the past.

She was fiddling with the fake eyelash that wouldn't stay put.

"Gossip, you say? Well, there was some talk going round when he first arrived. Of course one never knows if that is a bit of self-promotion as he was trying to establish himself here." She was thoughtful.

"And more recently it's said that his last tour was quite abysmal, and he's been working to re-establish himself. That may be the reason it's been rumored that he was working on several new illusions."

Most interesting, I thought. His career was waning. I tucked that away for later.

"And I believe there was something about a situation over one of his illusions," she continued thoughtfully, a font of knowledge. Or rumor, as it were.

"His sort is always so protective of their work. Have I mentioned how very handsome he is? Oh, but of course, you would know as you attended his performance. Was Mr. Brodie there as well?"

Speaking of handsome, mysterious, men. Or possibly brooding was a better description.

"He arrived some time later. He is assisting with our inquiries." I chose to leave it at that.

I was well aware that there was a certain 'interest' in Brodie on my aunt's behalf. She had been the one to recommend his investigative services to me most satisfactorily. However, there was that other part of our partnership that I didn't care to discuss.

"Have you? You know... shared your bed. I dare say that could be most exciting—and quite effective for insomnia which I know you have from time to time."

Bloody hell! That was the second reference to my sleeping arrangements in the same day.

I did wonder if she had been discussing my personal affairs with Templeton. And the truth was, though, I was not about to respond. Brodie and I had shared the same bed. Only not in the way either she or Templeton suggested. I took the easy way out of that particular aspect of the conversation.

"Our relationship is strictly professional."

She poured us both another dram. "Of course, dear."

Once she had settled back into her camp chair with her glass, she added quite thoughtfully, "You know, Juliette might be the one to inquire about Betard. They arrived in London about the same time. It's quite possible she would know more about him. And you will be needing a new gown for my May celebration."

# Five

IT WAS late afternoon when I arrived back at the Strand, and the Mudger informed me that Brodie had returned.

Considering that I'd had no food since breakfast, having avoided fish eggs followed by three drams of my aunt's very fine whisky, it was a wonder that I wasn't quite well foxed. The fact that I wasn't, or not quite, had to be what my aunt referred to as proper conditioning. I did enjoy her whisky very much.

I thanked Mr. Cavendish and climbed the stairs.

Brodie was at the desk. He had just hung up the earpiece at the telephone that was now installed. He looked up from a note he'd been scribbling at a paper in front of him.

Imagine that, I thought. Brodie making notes! I smiled to myself. There were times the man surprised me. When I had more or less given up on the male of the species. And there were other times...

As I contemplated Brodie with furrowed brow, the frown at his mouth wreathed with that dark beard, I had a moment to contemplate what I knew about him.

He preferred the dress of the working class, the sleeves of his shirt rolled back to the elbows. No doubt in deference to the warmer days we were having lately, his collar was open at the neck, revealing the strong column of his throat and the light dusting of dark hair that teased just at the neck opening.

He had been 'released'—a polite word for terminated—from the Metropolitan Police over some matter he chose not to discuss. Not that he owed me any explanation.

The man came with other qualities—well-respected by those he had served with, trustworthy, honorable, and most dependable.

All on recommendation from my great aunt and which I had discovered as well for myself. Add to that, I had also discovered there was a dark side as well. Something that didn't quite fit with the image of the polished, uniformed police constable.

I had seen that firsthand when I was physically threatened and in a situation that I thought I might not survive. Brodie had been there, that dark side no doubt acquired on the streets.

It was all over in a matter of minutes and a murderer was dead. The expression at his eyes when he had looked at me, however, was something I had not seen before—something darker, and quite dangerous.

Wherever he had gone in those few moments, he returned and the expression I saw then was one almost of sadness and regret.

Afterwards, there were no lectures as he was wont to do when I had gone off on my own when he had warned me against it. No reminders that I was too stubborn for my own good. He had simply gathered me up and escorted me away from the carnage.

Quite shaken by the events that night, babbling nonsense, trying to make some sense of it all—yes, I will admit now that I had babbled a bit—seeing someone dispatched as they say; Brodie had simply tucked me into his bed, then held me until I finally fell asleep.

He did not fit the image of the police constable in his perfect uniform or inspector, far different from Abberline. Brodie had chosen his own path, left the MP on his own terms —that much I did know, and had once again made something of himself.

He had been called a misfit by Abberline. The word seemed to suit him, and I would take it over any other man I had made the acquaintance of. Not that I would have admitted that to anyone.

He looked up now, that dark gaze narrowed in thought. I was quite familiar with it when it was narrowed in disapproval. This was different. This was his look when we were on a case.

"Ye met with the young woman this morning?" he asked. "Was she able to tell ye anything about the night of the murder?"

I shook my head. "Very little. She's quite undone by all of it. I don't think she will be able to tell us anything more." I added, thinking of other things.

"But there was something that bothered ye? About Betard?"

There it was again, something vague when Brodie spoke of him.

"It was afterward, something I saw as I left the hotel. Or someone..."

"Someone ye recognized?"

I shook my head. "It was more of an impression."

"An impression?" he asked with a trace of amusement. "Is that anything like yer woman's intuition."

"Something else," I replied. I was thoughtful, then asked, "Were you able to learn anything from your return to the Crystal Palace?"

"Aye, the stage where he gave the performance hadn't been swept or cleaned yet. There was quite a bit of debris about, as to be expected with so many people around—the usual trash one would expect and something peculiar."

Something peculiar about trash?

Brodie then handed me an envelope of the sort that he kept at the office, and I had dashed off notes to others in the past. But it was what was inside the envelope that had apparently drawn his attention. I frowned.

"A cigarette?" Not unusual at all, I thought. Most particularly at an evening event with a great many people in attendance.

Brodie was given to smoking as well, although he preferred the pipe. And I had been known to smoke a cigarette occasionally with a preference for the Turkish variety I discovered on one of my travels. The tobacconist who occupied the ground floor below had begun carrying it.

"Not your average variety," he replied. "Cannabis is often prescribed for pain. It's found on the streets from time to time."

"Something you're familiar with?" I asked.

"Mr. Brimley has had some experience with those he provides services for."

What did that tell us? Cannabis had been used in China for centuries as a medicine.

"Possibly from someone in the audience or one of the constables?" I made a guess. Or someone else?

"Most likely not from the audience considering where I found it, directly in the proximity of the box where the young woman was killed. Nor one of the constables. It would have meant their job."

A special cigarette smoked for pain.

"Perhaps Betard?"

"It is possible."

There it was again. "You believe that he could be the murderer?"

"For now, it could be anyone."

"He murdered the woman he was having an affair with?" I shook my head. "In front of an audience? When it could be done at his estate, or on tour? And for what reason? It makes no sense."

He watched me with that dark gaze, with something else behind it.

"I have found that murderers possess certain qualities much the same. No matter the motive, they feel invincible, powerful, in control. We've both seen it."

I thought of the previous cases we'd been on together. I had to admit that in those particular instances he might be correct. But I refused to believe it of Betard.

I had seen other things in him—grief, his concerns for Sophie. And he had been most cooperative, and that included providing us access to his props and the boxes that Brodie wanted to inspect.

I shook my head. "He hasn't attempted to hide anything."

"That we know of," he added.

"Impossible," I said then.

"Impossible because you're enamored with the man? A kiss of the hand? I thought better of ye."

Enamored? Thought better of me?

Was this was I had seen in that dark gaze?

"You're wrong. And a kiss on the hand has nothing to do with this. I've experienced far more..." I caught myself before I let my anger overrule common sense. I had learned that arguing a point with Brodie was often quite... pointless.

I had to admit, discovering the cigarette might be useful.

"Were you able to learn anything else?" It was a moment or two before he replied.

"There was a powder all about the stage."

"It could have been from an earlier illusion. He turned a bear into a rabbit. The bear was restrained by a collar and chain in a case. He made it disappear in a cloud of smoke. When the smoke cleared, the rabbit was where the bear had been."

"Rabbits and bears," he muttered. "It's a wonder the creature didn't escape."

"You noticed something there as well?"

"Footprints, specifically a man's boot print."

"There were undoubtedly several, as others gathered about the stage," I pointed out.

"These were most interesting, or in the very least one of them was, as one seemed to have been dragged about. There were several long scrapes at the stage amid the powder just where that glass box stood."

"A limp? Someone who was impaired?"

"Perhaps."

Most interesting.

"What of the constables who were on duty that night?"

"Unfortunately most were kept some distance apart from the stage at Betard's instructions. And Betard hires his own people along with a man by the name of Jerem Fitzsimmons for security purposes when he travels on his tours."

He'd have taken such precautions in his effort to keep his illusions secret.

I could tell by the sound of Brodie's voice that he did not approve of Fitzsimmons.

"Still, it might be important to speak with the man," I replied. "He might be able to provide information about anything unusual that night, or if someone other than Betard's people had access to the stage."

I was aware of a certain ill-feeling between certain peoples in the East End, most certainly the Irish and Scots among the working classes. It was a dislike that had more to do with old hostilities than anything else, and most certainly there were exceptions. Most particularly my aunt.

She had several Irish among her household staff, and there was Mr. Munro, a Scot if ever there was one. And then there was Brodie's friendship with Tommy O'Rourke and countless others in the East End. It seemed that he perhaps had a particular dislike for Jerem Fitzsimmons.

"Do you know the man?"

Brodie made that sound. Definitely dislike there, I thought.

"He's as bad as any of those he supposedly guards against," he replied, then with a look at me, "He steals with one hand the same time he's shaking a man's hand with the other. He been known to quote a fee for his services, then attempt to extort his client for more. Those who don't want their activities known gladly pay."

"That sounds very much like blackmail," I commented, something well known in the Scottish borders in the past where *'rents'* or other payments were demanded in exchange for not turning individuals over to the Crown. He eyed me thoughtfully.

"Aye, blackmail. There are not enough constables to provide

security for those like Betard. I investigated the security around the stage and discovered it was being handled by Fitzsimmons."

"In other words, the MP looks the other when it suits them," I replied.

"Ye might say that."

"And what of your relationship with Jerem Fitzsimmons?" I asked.

It was obvious that he was thinking how best to answer that.

"We crossed paths in the past."

Was it possible that someone like Fitzsimmons might be responsible for Francoise's murder? But what reason? Spurned by her? Or retaliation for something else?

"I see."

"No ye don't, and ye won't take yerself off to speak with the man. I'll take care of it. As I said, he's the worst sort. I wouldn't want ye in the same room with him."

"After I met with Sophie and Betard I met with an acquaintance of Templeton's. He's quite proficient in the magical arts. We met with him at his shop in Holborn. I wanted to know more about how illusions work. It was most interesting."

"Did the man disappear in a puff of smoke as well?" Brodie asked.

Not quite, I thought, but Templeton might. She had purchased some of his disappearing powder and was quite excited to give it a go.

"He's familiar with Betard's work, a most interesting little man. He demonstrated how the disappearing illusion works with a person inside a cabinet able to escape.

"Aye. We're assuming that the girl was trapped inside when she was murdered, but perhaps not," Brodie speculated. "That could be useful."

He then told me that he'd made contact with the man at the rail station where the props and those boxes were stored for now.

It was only quarter past four in the afternoon. "How soon can we go?" I asked. After my visit with Mr. Alamy I was most anxious to see the boxes Betard had used in his illusion once more.

~

We made Victoria Station in good time where the boxes were being held until they were returned to Betard's estate. Brodie directed the driver to the rail warehouse where other passengers who traveled abroad stored shipping containers, trunks, even a private coach or two which I found most interesting. What no horses?

The attendant was most cooperative. "The items you mentioned are this way." The man led them into the cavernous warehouse.

As someone who preferred to travel light with only one case, the idea of traveling with an enormous trunk or shipping container was astounding. Although when my aunt traveled to her property in the north of Scotland she was known to take her own bed with her.

Betard's props, much like those in a theatrical production, had all been carefully stored in large wood containers with his name and destination affixed to the side. Among those were the two large glass boxes he had used for his final illusion the Crystal Palace. They were covered with the same thick canvas he had used that night.

"The owner said as how you was to be given access to these." He shook his head. "A right awful tragedy about that young woman."

I hadn't had time to read the dailies yet, but it seemed that everyone in London was now aware of Francoise Dupre's death. Alan Ivers had been busy.

"Has anyone else asked to see the boxes?" Brodie inquired.

"No, sir."

Brodie nodded. "Nothing is to be removed without my

knowledge," he informed him and handed him a card. "Is that understood?"

The attendant nodded.

"Can ye give a hand with the covers then?" Brodie asked.

"Yes, sir. Mr. Brodie, sir."

Together they untied the ropes that bound the covers then removed them.

"I'll be at the office if you need anything else," the man told us then left.

The attendant had dropped the card in the process of unwrapping those boxes. I picked it up, then frowned as I read the front of the card.

"Angus Brodie, Special Services?" I read the print on the face of the card.

"It's something Sir Avery insisted on," he replied. "He thought it might be useful from time to time."

Useful. As in? Other matters that Brodie was investigating on behalf of the service?

Most interesting, I thought. It seemed that Brodie was doing some work for Sir Avery Stanton, whatever that might include, but there'd been no explanation from Brodie what that was. Not that it was any of my business.

He began a slow, careful inspection of one box then moved to the other with the dried blood, in that methodical way I'd come to know that came from experience.

"It appears that all four glass panels are capable of being removed, not just the one at the back of the box," he commented and lifted each side of the one box with gloved hands, then lowered each back into place into that black frame of the box.

"So, it would be possible that someone could access the box from any of the sides as well as the back or front," I concluded.

"Aye, and it contains the mirror panels that create the illusion of an empty box with that narrow compartment concealed at one corner," he continued.

"Then it would be possible to conceal someone in the

compartment," I concluded the obvious. "But then, how would that person be able to leave the compartment?"

"It appears that the mirrors collapse one onto the other." He proceeded to carefully fold one mirror back onto the next one beside it, until all were collapsed against the opposite side of the box."

I set my notebook and pen on top of a nearby crate and approached the other box.

"Can you make me disappear?" I asked somewhat cheekily.

"Verra tempting," he admitted. "However, this requires a very small, slender woman. Yer a bit tall."

Disturbing as the memory of that night was, I forced my way past it to the task at hand. I stepped closer as Brodie continued his inspection of the other box. It appeared to be an exact duplicate of the one he had just inspected.

While Brodie took dimensions of the other box and compared it to the one he'd already inspected, I circled round and made my own inspection of what I had seen that night.

Supposedly the boxes were sealed with that back panel lowered into place as the audience had seen, Francoise then entered this box and was concealed by the cover that was lowered into place. Betard had entered the other box, the panel slipped into place, and then that box was covered.

Based on what was discovered afterward, it seemed obvious that the murder had taken place during the approximately twenty-minute interval between when the first box was covered, the second box was covered, and the attendant removed the cover from the first box. The intention—that it was to be seen as empty with Betard to emerge with Sophie from the second box.

I thought of what Mr. Alamy had shown Templeton and me in the storeroom behind his shop.

Was it possible there was a hidden mechanism in each box, that allowed those inside to leave...? Or perhaps someone else, the murderer, to open the box that Francoise was in?

I ran my hands down each panel of glass, and then across

where one panel joined the other in the frame of the box to create the glass square. As with the other box, the mirrors on the inside of the box were set at precise angles that created a hidden compartment just large enough for a very slender, small woman to conceal herself. Then when the cover was removed, it appeared to be empty.

The mirrors moved freely, reflecting the blood-splattered interior of the box in multiple macabre images that then reflected back at each one. It was really quite bizarre.

I continued my own inspection, running my hands down the next panel at the back, then across the top where the back panel that was lowered into place met the top of the glass box. I pulled back suddenly at something sharp.

"Bloody hell!" I exclaimed, most appropriate it seemed as I drew back my bloody hand.

"What have ye done to yerself, now?" Brodie exclaimed as he came round the box and took his handkerchief from his coat pocket. He inspected the cut then bound my hand.

"It's a deep cut. We should have Mr. Brimley see to it when we return to the Strand."

"Nonsense," I protested. "It's only a cut, but it certainly made a mess."

He proceeded to tie off his handkerchief, then went to the box to inspect the scene of my injury.

"Ye should have worn gloves."

Yes, that was all well and good after the fact, I thought, and looked up at a faint clicking sound.

Brodie stood at the back of the box where he had been inspecting the panel that now stood open. I looked over at him quite surprised.

"It seems that you discovered something," he commented as he then opened the panel all the way, revealing that compartment where Francoise had hidden herself.

I joined him and stared at the small button that blended perfectly with the wood frame of the box. It was now covered with blood from the cut at the glass panel where a small piece had broken away, possibly when the box was moved from the Crystal Palace? Or perhaps when the murderer had hastily closed the box once more afterward?

Motive, means, and opportunity.

We had the same thought. Betard had not bothered to mention the button or the mechanism at the back of the box.

We discussed what we had found as we left the warehouse and found a cab. In that way that I had discovered in the past, a development—in this case the additional way someone might have entered the box, raised several more questions, particularly about Betard.

"We need to speak with him again," I pointed out.

"Aye," Brodie replied thoughtfully. "And Sophie as well. It is obvious that she would know about the mechanism in the box."

What were they hiding? And what might it have to do with Francoise's death?

It had grown quite warm inside the cab, the weather most welcome, but this was almost overwhelming. I fanned myself with my other hand as everything about us suddenly blurred.

"Brodie?"

I was certain I called his name, then everything went dark.


There were voices, quite distant at first as though through a fog, vaguely familiar. Then, there was an image that appeared, then disappeared. I thought of the White Rabbit as if I had truly fallen down a hole. But when I tried to reach for it, it was gone.

"You know these things as well as meself, Brodie."

Was that Mr. Brimley? His voice seemed to fade.

"You've seen it enough on the street. She'll be all right, she just needs to sleep it off."

"How could it have happened?."

Brodie. I was almost certain it was him. I did so like the sound of his voice.

"My guess would be..." Mr. Brimley again as I slipped back into that fog and drifted.


"Mikaela?"

It was Brodie, I would know that voice anywhere, deeper than usual and with something else that wrapped around the sound of my name. He sounded worried about something. Me? Silly man, as I attempted to clear my head of the fog that seemed to have wrapped itself around my senses.

"Aye, there ye are," he said as his face slowly came into view.

*There I was.* But where was I? And why was I in bed with Brodie sitting in the chair beside the bed?

Then as things slowly focused I realized I was not in *my* bedroom at all, but his bedroom next to the office on the Strand. I tried to sit up and immediately regretted it. My mouth was dry as parchment, and I had a raging headache.

"Take it easy, lass."

I wasn't at all certain how I would manage even that. My arms and legs seemed to have detached.

"Drink this," he told me and pressed a cup to my mouth. I prayed for whisky. It was water. I would take what I could get and would have swallowed all of it except he pulled the cup away. I groaned.

"Just a bit now, ye can have more later. Yer stomach may be a bit unsettled."

Unsettled? I was ravenous, but I hadn't the strength to argue the point.

"What happened?" I asked, my voice barely more above a whisper.

"Apparently it was morphine," he replied.

Morphine? That was ridiculous. I would have pointed that out, but there seemed to be some sort of breakdown between my brain and what I was trying to say.

"How?" I winced at the dry sound as I lay back at the bed.

"Apparently the cut at yer hand," he replied. "It appears there was morphine residue at the glass at that box."

I noticed the expression at Brodie's face for the first time—the frown, the faint lines at the corners of those dark eyes. Concern?

"Ye gave me quite a turn, lass, when ye went out."

"How long?" Two words. I must be improving.

Brodie held the cup for me once more and I took another swallow.

"How long have ye been out, or how long until it goes away?" he replied.

"Both."

"Ye've been out for a couple of hours. Mr. Brimley said you should be fine by morning. Yer hand will take a little more time to heal."

I saw the neat bandage at my hand. So inconvenient.

"Betard...?" I started to ask a question. It was there, but once again the words slipped away.

"Don't think about that now," Brodie replied. "Go back to sleep. I'll be right here."

That seemed odd in my befuddled state, but I didn't question it. I was aware that my boots had been removed, and that wasn't all. That didn't seem to matter either.

Brodie pulled the blanket up over me, and there was that wonderful scent about him—orange and cinnamon as he leaned close.

I felt his hand against my cheek. Then, I was drifting off once more.

I wakened some hours later. There was only a faint glow from a lamp at the side table as I came out of an old dream, the feeling the same as it was that day as a child when I found my father dead by his own hand, the tightness in my chest.

Brodie was still there, his head resting against the back of the upholstered chair beside the bed as he had dozed off, his hand over mine at the bedcovers.

It wasn't even a thought, merely something natural as my

fingers slipped through his and I felt that strength, the warmth—holding on to me. I closed my eyes and drifted off once more and there were no more dreams.

When next I opened my eyes, it was morning, slivers of light slipping around the edge of the shade at the window. The chair was still there beside the bed, empty now as I heard Brodie moving about in the office just beyond.

The headache was not as severe as before as I slowly swung my legs over the edge of the bed and carefully sat up.

Morphine? How the devil...?

It came back to me now. Mr. Brimley had been there, his presence slipping in and out of things that I remembered. And Brodie had been there, apparently all night.

My fingers curled over my palm as another memory returned, of his hand over mine. I hadn't imagined that either.

What sort of man did that? Holding my hand through the night? Watching over me?

My steps were slow and careful.

I found him standing at the coal stove. He had just poured himself a cup of coffee. It smelled wonderful, and I was suddenly starving. The after-effects of my accidental encounter with morphine, I wondered? I had no previous experience with such things.

"Oh, yes please," I said. He looked up, then poured a second cup.

"Ye should eat something as well." He gestured to the plate with the cloth over at the desk.

"Courtesy of the Mudger," he explained.

Dear man, I thought, as I descended on the desk and uncovered the plate of sausage and potatoes.

"He was worrit about ye, and proceeded to point out that I should take better care of ye."

I caught something in his voice and looked up. "I'm quite well recovered, except for the headache." And my hand, of course.

Take care of me, indeed. I started to say that I didn't need anyone to take care of me.

Instead, I admitted, "I am hungry."

"Ye're always hungry. I've never seen a woman put away food like ye do. Ye'll probably be as big as a horse when ye're older."

"My mother was quite slender," I replied, remembering her. "And Linnie as well. So, not to concern yourself, Mr. Brodie."

"Aye."

There it was again, the way the conversation had wandered into other things. And there was something else.

"I brought you here last night as I thought it might be better than your townhouse in Mayfair... gossip and such from others who live nearby," Brodie then explained.

Gossip. There'd been enough, mostly when Linnie and I were much younger. I'd learned to ignore it.

"I've never been concerned with such things," I replied and wondered where his concern came from.

"Aye, still, I wouldna want others to be thinking badly of ye."

"And what of your reputation?" I asked in return.

"Aye, well, not much to be concerned about there."

I didn't agree. He was very well thought of by those who mattered. He had proven himself to be more honorable than any man I had ever known, even when he was grumbling at me or contradicting me over something, which was often.

Then, there were other times when I felt that he actually valued me, a most unusual experience. I felt awkward and off balance. I blamed it on my encounter with that box and the cut at my hand.

"Have you eaten?" I asked.

"Aye." He nodded and gestured to the plate. "And a good thing. It seems there won't be anything left."

I needed to focus on the case as I munched, my thoughts going back to the day before and my encounter with what apparently was morphine at the glass panel at the back of that box where Francoise had died.

"What do you think it means?" I asked as I proceeded to down most of the breakfast the Mudger had brought with a second cup of coffee.

Brodie sat back at his chair at the desk, wearing that expression I was most familiar with, his own cup of coffee in hand.

"The morphine?"

I nodded. "It would seem that someone brushed against the glass box after using the drug."

Someone, who just happened to brush against the box, as it was being moved about before the performance? Or the murderer?

Neither of us believed in coincidences.

"The question is, who?"

Brodie nodded. "Who would have access to the box?"

That obviously fell under *'opportunity'*. That raised the next obvious question... What was the *motive*?

"After yer encounter with the morphine, I asked Alex Sinclair to examine the box as well. He took one of their people with him along with a new machine that he's been working on and was able to confirm that there was a substantial residue just where ye cut yer hand."

By *'people'*, I presumed he referred to one of those who worked for the Special Services. He still had not explained his participation with them. Not that he owed me any explanation.

"It must have been very recent to still have been present on the glass," I commented.

Betard came to mind, as well as Francoise and Sophie. And others among those who traveled with him for his performances?

"Apparently, the residue was quite clear along with a man's larger fingerprints," he added. "I've seen cases of others effected by coming into contact with opiates."

What did that tell us, other than they were neither Francoise nor Sophie's prints?

As we had learned in an earlier case, the only prints that were maintained by the police were those of known criminals who were arrested and taken into custody. It was a fairly new aspect of police work.

As for prints made by others? That sort of identification system did not yet exist and most certainly not of foreign individuals. Although Brodie had spoken of a time when everyone would undoubtedly be finger-printed and registered with the authorities.

"We might attempt to obtain Betard's prints," I suggested. "However, I suppose it would be natural for them to be all over both boxes."

"I want to speak with Mr. Brimley about the possibility of being able to obtain those prints," he said then. "With his old-fashioned way."

Old fashioned? I thought with some amusement. His old-fashioned way had proven to be most effective in the past.

"I'll go with you," I announced.

"Mr. Brimley did say that ye should rest until the effects of the morphine are gone," he reminded me.

There was no arguing with him. Still, I gave it a good try. He was quite adamant, and I had to admit that I was still a bit off although the headache was less severe now.

In the end I conceded. There were other ways to win an argument, and I did have someone whom I wanted to speak with.

BRODIE HAD DEPARTED SHORTLY after our conversation. I poured myself another cup of coffee and decided my course of action. It most certainly did not include staying in bed for the day, or in the office as it were, waiting for his return to hear what he might have learned.

A young woman was dead, and I was determined to find out who had killed her.

Brodie would have called me obstinate, lacking all common sense, but I was not about to sit idly by while the murderer was still out there somewhere and might strike again.

I made use of the water closet and dressed, with only a few waves of lightheadedness from the after-effects of my encounter with that residue that had been left at the glass at the box. I downed the cup of coffee and was on my way.

I could see the reasons that some used morphine from my ventures onto the streets of the East End—the need some felt to numb themselves against the endless poverty and pain I had seen on the streets.

Opium, that morphine was made from, had been outlawed, but obviously, like anything, there were ways to obtain it.

"I suppose that he told you to keep watch over me," I

commented as I reached the entrance to the alcove where Mr. Cavendish could usually be found. He rubbed his chin in that thoughtful way I had seen when he was contemplating what to say.

"He might have mentioned that you needed to rest, and not go out and about on account of your injury." He looked at me suspiciously. I sensed a conspiracy between the two. Brodie could be quite devious.

"Somethin' I might get fer you, miss?" he then asked.

"Not at all... A short walk is all, for some fresh air." Not precisely a lie as far as it went. I did want some fresh air that might clear my head.

"I suppose that would be acceptable," he replied. "And ye'll be takin' the hound along so there's no difficulty, of course."

Which raised the question just what the hound might be able to do if I had a difficulty either with my hand or the effects of my encounter with the morphine. The obvious was that Mr. Cavendish didn't believe me for a moment.

I met that narrowed gaze. I had no wish to bring Brodie's wrath down on the man, although I was confident Mr. Cavendish had seen it all before.

One didn't live on the streets and not acquire a certain expertise in defending oneself. And I had seen Mr. Cavendish hold his own against cabmen, carters, and the occasional pickpocket who thought to take advantage of his situation. Handicap indeed!

"Just down the way," I explained. "The publisher's office."

Mr. Cavendish was well aware of my publishing endeavors. However, I didn't specify *which* publisher.

"Not out to purchase some *'lady things'*?" he inquired with the wink of an eye, an excuse I used previously. "That might make it difficult to take the hound along."

It seemed that he wouldn't fall for that excuse again.

"Not this time," I replied.

"Well, I suppose there's no harm if it's just down the way," he decided and whistled for Rupert. "This one could do with some fresh air as well," he commented.

Most amusing since the hound lived on the street, which of course meant that he had fresh air—or as fresh as possible on the streets of London, most of the time.

"He'll just go along, to make certain you don't encounter any difficulty."

Clever man.

It was quite obvious to us both that I couldn't take the hound just anywhere, as a great many places wouldn't let him through the door.

I looked down at Rupert who sat at my feet, tongue hanging out the side of his mouth, ears perked up at the prospect of an adventure. And that smile.

I had to admit the hound was an admirable companion and he had saved my life on a previous occasion.

I supposed that I should be grateful that he hadn't appeared with something recently alive, or possibly still alive, clutched in his teeth.

"Come along, then," I told him and set off afoot, Rupert trotting along beside me.

The publisher I had in mind was not the publisher of my books, but another publisher not far at all—the Times newspaper and someone in particular who worked there.

I had met Lucy Penworth in the course of a previous investigation. At the time, she worked as secretary to the reporters who wrote articles for the newspaper, ran errands for things they needed that included making coffee and bring in lunch from one of the local taverns.

In short she was relegated to the position of hired 'caretaker' to a group of obnoxious, egotistical men who were perfectly happy to keep her in her place if they even noticed her at all, other than to bark out orders at her.

All of that had changed with the story she had secured regarding that previous case, an exclusive as it was called. That had elevated her to the position of reporter and the only female reporter in the city. I needed her assistance.

I would have left Rupert at the main entrance of the Times building. However, he was most insistent on carrying out his orders. There were times that I wondered if one of Templeton's spirits inhabited the animal as it seemed that he understood what people said quite well.

I signed in at the main desk.

"I don't believe the owners would approve," the young clerk commented with a glance down at the hound who sat most congenially at my feet.

"Please feel free to explain that to him," I commented and headed for the lift.

"Miss...?"

I heard footsteps behind us and ignored them. When the lift arrived, I opened the gate and stepped inside. The hound followed as if he did that sort of thing every day, the clerk mumbling something at his desk.

"Good boy," I praised the hound, closed the gate, and we were off.

"Miss Forsythe!" Lucy called out from across the 'pen', the area where the reporters congregated. Each sat at a desk, either madly writing, typing away which was most interesting to see, or talking on the telephone.

"How very good to see you again," she greeted me with an infectious smile.

She was not quite as tall as myself, but a bundle of energy with enormous blue eyes and a splash of freckles across her cheeks which I noted were now hidden under an application of powder. No doubt, to make herself appear more mature.

She chose to downplay her feminine status lest she was forced to threaten one of the other reporters with bodily harm when they became too 'friendly.'

I had provided her the name of the owner of the local gymnasium where she might polish her self-defense skills on a previous occasion. I had also provided her with a small but very sharp knife, the sort that folded in on itself.

"And you've brought a companion!" she continued enthusiastically. "Not Mr. Brodie by the looks of him, but a fine fellow indeed!"

Lucy reached down and scratched the hound behind the ears, and he immediately flattened himself at her feet, head across the toe of her boot in a bid for more. Typical male!

"I see you've recovered from your last case," Lucy observed. "Horrifying. You might have been badly injured, or worse." Then she noticed my bandaged hand. "Or perhaps not?"

"Merely a scratch," I replied. "I've come regarding some information you might be able to assist with."

"A new case?" she responded, eyes sparkling as she kept her voice low. "A story for the newspaper perhaps?"

"Perhaps, but you must keep our conversation in strictest confidence for now."

"You have my word, however, it might be best if we discussed it in private," she suggested and led the way down the hall past the pen.

"You don't have a private office of your own yet?" I remarked.

"I'm hoping for one. Perhaps a story about the case you're working on might assist in that," she suggested with a smile.

I explained what Brodie and I were inquiring about over the next hour and a pot of tea her replacement brought—a dour older woman with one eyebrow at her forehead.

"Thank you, Elvira," Lucy commented.

We waited for her to leave. Lucy closed the door behind her.

"The walls have ears," she commented, then when she was sure the woman had gone, she returned to sit across from me at the small table.

"The original story about the young woman's murder was given to Alan Ivers, of course, as he was there that night," Lucy said as she poured tea.

"Yes, I did see him there."

"There was nothing mentioned about your investigation into her death, nor has he spoken with Monsieur Betard as far as I know."

"I have no desire to further the career of Alan Ivers," I announced. I had encountered him and his poor choice of clothes previously and considered him to be quite deficient as a writer, creating stories for the newspaper for sensationalism rather than substance.

He was easily distinguishable by that herringbone checkered coat that he usually wore. It was a garish affair that he announced always let people know he was about so they wouldn't have to look far to provide some bit of gossip or a story to him. Now there was a man very full of himself.

"It would go far for my career if I were able to provide the full story once the murderer is discovered," Lucy pointed out.

We were not there yet, but I had every intention of helping her along if we could.

"Have you decided to make a career of it then?" I asked.

"Oh, yes! Absolutely! However..."

I heard a great deal in that one word. "However?" I asked.

"Alex is not in favor of it."

Ah, I thought. That had to be Alex Sinclair of the Special Services. It seemed that their original acquaintance had progressed. I did remember that he was quite taken with her.

"He considers it too dangerous, the long hours... we've had to put off several occasions. I've tried to explain to him that this is as important to me as his work with the Service is for him. He's been quite stubborn about it!"

Oh dear, I was familiar with that.

"How were you able to convince Mr. Brodie to allow your involvement in his investigations?" she then asked.

"In the first place, they have not been *his* cases." That was splitting hairs a bit since I had hired him to assist in my sister's disappearance.

"And in the second place, he doesn't *allow* my participation. I don't need his permission."

"Does Mr. Brodie disapprove? I don't believe for a minute that you would stand for being set aside," Lucy replied.

Disapprove? That was putting it mildly. Although lately, it seemed we had progressed to his grumbling and grousing only on occasion about my involvement.

"We have reached a mutual understanding," I explained, which was the best way to put it, although I was not at all certain that was how Brodie would have described it.

She sighed. "It seems that Alex and I will need to reach a mutual understanding in the matter."

"If the man is worthy of you, you'll find a way. Not that it won't be challenging," I replied, the voice of experience.

"I'm up to a good challenge." She angled her head in the general direction of the *'pen.'* "I've had a great deal of practice with that of late. And I will admit that he does quite take my breath away."

Similar to curling one's toes?

"So," she continued, "what you're saying is that I need to simply go on about my career."

"If he truly cares about you, he will understand."

"I hope so, however you didn't come here to discuss my prospects," she concluded.

"I need your assistance," I told her then. "I've searched library archives for information in the past, but I need information that is more current. I'm hoping it might be in the Times' archive." I then explained specifically what I was looking for.

"About Betard," she said, sitting back. "That is if we carried any articles about him in the first place. However, I will check. I've done research for some of my other articles, about society, prominent families, all of it most boring. We do have a substantial archive on microfilm that goes back at least ten years—that is, if the articles have been catalogued correctly. It can sometimes be a nightmare to find anything."

She was thoughtful. "It might help if I knew specifically what you are looking for."

"Anything that might have to do with his past performances, tours, encounters with any rivals. I've been told that the art of an illusionist can be competitive, guarding of secrets and that sort of thing. And he has been most successful over the past several years with performances across Europe."

"Threats perhaps from others in the profession?" she speculated. "I'll search the crime archives as well. I should be able to find something if it's there as he has been here for some time."

There was a growl from Rupert where he lay at my feet. Speak of the devil? The door opened and Alan Ivers poked his head in the office.

"Mr. Roberts is looking for you," he told Lucy.

That would be Hiram Roberts, the editor in chief of the newspaper. The summons seemed a little odd since no word had been sent for her, most particularly from Elvira whose position it seemed was that of assistant, procurer of tea, watchful over all things.

Rupert stood, the matted fur at his back standing up, always a good indicator of his dislike of certain people and not a good sign for Mr. Ivers.

Was the man perhaps curious as to my meeting with Lucy? Nosing about? The man was such a ferret.

Rupert appeared to share my opinion of him. There was another rumble from him, attention fastened on the doorway.

"What the devil is that?" Ivers demanded.

"He's with me." I explained no further as I rose and bid Lucy good-bye.

"I'll send word," she assured me. "At the Strand, of course?"

I nodded, then called to Rupert as we left the private office. He padded along beside me and Lucy, quite docile now. However, he did swing that large head about as Alan would have followed. The reporter then apparently thought better of it and ducked back into the *'pen.'*

"Good boy," Lucy told him with a scratch behind the ears. He grinned.

It was very near noon time as I left the Times newspaper building. I thought a reward was in order for Rupert as he had behaved most admirably.

"We don't allow his sort in here," I was informed at the entrance to a tavern. I thanked the proprietor and headed for one of the many vendors who had returned to the streets with the fair weather. I would simply take my business elsewhere.

"What will it be, miss?" a rosy cheeked woman selling meat rolled in a pastry asked as I approached.

I purchased one of the pastries for myself and two for the hound, and sat at a small bench with the Rupert beside me while I contemplated what the next order of business should be.

It would take a while for Lucy to find information on Betard in the archives, *if* there was anything to be found. The Times and other tabloids were far more concerned with local crime, the latest news about the royal family, and political events across the Empire.

I had finished my meat pastry and placed the brown paper it had been wrapped with in the nearby receptacle. For his part, the hound had practically swallowed the two I gave him, paper and all, in one gulp.

It was undoubtedly an improvement over his usual fare—the odd bones and dead rodents found at the street, or the occasional handout from Miss Effie at the public house that often included fish heads and entrails from the day's fare that was served up. There was a telltale belch of appreciation.

"I thought so," I replied. I was also feeling quite restored from the previous day's encounter with morphine and most curious how it had gotten on the box.

"Mr. Brimley might be able to answer my questions," I commented.

The hound looked at me as if he understood and I shook my head. I was beginning to remind myself of my friend

Templeton and her conversations with Wills, not that I expected an answer from the hound. Still, it reminded me as well of dotty old women with their small fluffy dogs that lived better than some people. Not that the hound was small or fluffy.

There was a low rumble from him. Not the conversational sort but the warning sort I had heard before. I glanced the direction he stared down the sidewalk.

There were the usual sort of people at the sidewalk—vendors, customers, others who had business in this part of London near the warehouses and shops. But I had learned to trust the hound's reaction to things. Something obviously bothered him.

"What is it?" I asked, as if he might answer.

For his part, the hound remained by my side but was obviously displeased as he kept glancing down the way.

"Do come along," I told him, seeing nothing to be concerned about as I stepped to the curb and waved down a cab.

There had been no opportunity to question Mr. Brimley the previous evening after my encounter with what had been identified as morphine, an experience I had stayed away from in the past although I knew others who partook of the drug from time to time.

Brodie had explained that it was made from opium, a narcotic that was now banned. However, as with anything, there were those who still managed to acquire it.

That included my sister after the loss of the child she had hoped for, a dreadful experience for her. Her physician had prescribed morphine for the pain.

While it seemed to relieve the physical pain afterward, it had made it difficult for her to remember anything. To her credit, she had refused to take any more of it after a few days. There was no narcotic that could dull the pain of the heartache in the months that followed.

The hound continued to stare down the sidewalk as the cabman arrived.

"If you don't come along, I will leave you," I told him to the curiosity of the driver.

The hound gave one last look down the sidewalk, and then jumped into the cab.

"That will be extra fair for the animal, miss," the driver informed me.

"And if the other passenger had two legs?" I argued.

"Extra fare," the driver repeated. "I'll have to return to the yard afterward and wash me rig down to clean the smell of the beast before I can take another fare."

"Oh, very well," I conceded and climbed into the cab, the hound jumping in beside me.

"You could use a bath," I commented. The hound looked at me with those big dark eyes. I could swear he grinned.

I paid the extra fare when we arrived at Mr. Brimley's shop in Holborn. "I will take it out of the cost of your next meal," I informed the hound with a scratch behind his ears. He followed me into the shop where we were greeted by Mr. Brimley's assistant, Sara.

"Afternoon, miss," she greeted me with a look down at the hound. "Is that a horse you have with you, or a dog?"

"This is Rupert."

"Out for a bit? Feelin' better are you?" She gestured to my bandaged hand. "Mr. Brimley said as how you were injured."

"I thought to have him check the bandage," I replied with a glance about. It appeared that Brodie had already been there and left as there was no sign of him.

"Is Mr. Brimley about?" I asked.

"Just there in the back room," Sara replied. "He's been there all morning, dissecting that hand. Said as how he wanted to see how it worked."

Oh, dear. I had a fairly good idea what that meant. I liked Mr. Brimley very much. It could be said that I owed him my life on at least one occasion, but I was not of a mind to observe one of his examinations as to the anatomy of the human body.

"I wouldn't want to disturb him," I told her.

"Is there a customer?" Mr. Brimley called out.

"Miss Forsythe," Sara announced.

"I don't want to bother," I explained as he emerged from the back of the shop and looked at me through his glasses with a smile in greeting.

"No bother. And how is the hand today?"

"On the way to recovery it seems, thanks to your care," I replied. "I understand that Mr. Brodie was going to inquire about possibly assisting us."

"That he did, and then went off on some other business." He motioned in the direction of the back of his shop.

"Come along. I'll check your hand and make certain he is taking good care of you."

I had become accustomed to Mr. Brimley's somewhat odd nature, such as a preference for severed hands in jars, not to mention the many times I had seen him refuse payment for his assistance or a medicine with one of the people of the East End who could barely afford food, the care he took with others who were injured.

It was a strange path that had brought such a learned and compassionate man to one of the poorest parts of London where he barely earned a living and would not have been able to continue offering his services without the help of others who provided coin in passing or paid the monthly rent for him. Brodie came to mind.

And then there were the women who earned their living on the streets and found themselves in a *'difficulty'* as it was called. He provided the means to deliver their child and then turn it over to one of the charities. It was a grim fact of the East End that I was forced to confront in my work with Brodie.

I rested my hand at the small table, spread with a clean cloth. Mr. Brimley cut away the bandage as efficient as any surgeon, and then proceeded to inspect his handiwork.

"No additional bleeding," he commented. "And no putrification of the wound. By what I've been studying over there, there doesn't seem to be any residual damage." He smiled.

I assumed he referred to his dissecting of the hand I had seen at the counter. I was grateful for his observations but not of a mind to inspect the specimen that he had been working on. He then instructed me to slowly flex my hand then make a loose fist.

"Excellent, everything seems to be in working order," he declared. "No tendon or muscle damage." He then spread some of the salve he had applied the night before to the cut and proceeded to apply a new bandage.

"No other symptoms?" he asked.

"Only a slight headache," I replied.

"That's to be expected," he replied as he expertly tied off the bandage. "The effects of morphine."

"I do have questions about that."

Mr. Brimley looked up at me then. He smiled. "I thought you might."

# *Seven*

I SAT with Mr. Brimley after assuring him that Rupert wouldn't go after any of his specimens, most particularly that hand he had staked out on a board. At least I hoped that he wouldn't.

One could never tell. At present, he had remained at the front of the shop quite taken with Sara.

"Tell me about morphine," I asked. "How do people come by it?"

Mr. Brimley sat back at his chair much like a school master about to begin a lecture.

"It's a product of opium, used for centuries by different cultures for medicinal and other purposes. It's said that the Egyptians first cultivated opium from poppy plants, then discovered the process for making morphine, almost two thousand years ago.

"They were far advanced in many medical procedures and medications," he continued. "They were the first to perfect brain surgery for injuries and ailments of the brain. A fascinating culture." He sat back at his chair much like a storyteller with a captive audience.

"The cultivation and use of opium spread throughout the Byzantine Empire. It was banned by the Holy Inquisition. Like many things, the use of opium and morphine had become a

commodity for profit and often abused with devastating conse-
quences—smugglers, thieves and such.

"The import of it into Britain was banned a several years ago,
the widespread use in the poor areas devastating for many people.
There are still those who are able to come by it," he added. "Physi-
cians, and those in the upper classes for *recreational* pleasure."

"You've seen the effects of it here in the East End?" I asked.

He nodded. "The import of it may be illegal, but people find a
way around such things. It's either the drink or some other means
to dull the pain of their existence."

"What form might morphine be in?"

Mr. Brimley rose from his chair and went to a locked cabinet
across from his desk. He opened it and retrieved a bottle of clear
liquid.

"Most usually it will be in liquid form so that it can be
injected."

"You told Brodie that I had very probably come in contact
with it when I cut my hand," I recalled.

He nodded. "Most likely since you are not one to indulge in
the drug," he pointed out.

I had my reasons.

"I do remember that my sister was given morphine after the
loss of her child by her physician."

"It is usually give for pain," he replied. "Judiciously of
course. However, there are those who come to rely on it." He
went on to explain, "It is an opiate and can be very addictive.
However, you don't have anything to be concerned about with
one encounter."

"How might it have gotten on the glass where I cut my hand?"
I then asked.

"It could have been from residue on the hands of someone
who had recently used it. Or, possibly given to the girl before she
was killed."

I looked over at him in surprise.

I had not thought of that possibility. To ease her pain and

make her more docile? A merciful killing? The thought was horrifying.

"I did not see any indication of an injection when I examined the body," he continued. "Nor was there any other indication that would be obvious if the poor thing was known to use the drug."

Left then by the murderer?

"How long might it have remained on the glass?" I was trying to determine a time frame regarding the performance and who might have had access to the glass box.

"It is possible that residue from morphine syrup might remain on the glass for some time," he replied.

And that same substance that I had encountered had also revealed a man's fingerprints, according to Alex Sinclair who had assisted Brodie.

Betard? One of his attendants? Or someone else?

"You've had some experience with morphine and opium?" I then asked.

"Too much experience I think at times," he replied. "As I said, opium might be illegal, but there are those who acquire it from the ships that come in before the cargoes are unloaded to avoid confiscation. It's then sold to others on the streets."

He was speaking of the crews on those ships. There was no way to determine who might have brought it to the Crystal Palace that night, unless it was someone who might use it.

"Brodie has seen a great deal of the troubles it causes, the way it takes a man's soul," he continued.

I nodded and thanked him for his time and his care.

He walked with me to the front of the shop. "Be sure to change the bandage daily and keep the wound dry. And be careful."

The hound had found a friend in Sara. One who would scratch his ears and apparently had parted with whatever was left of her midday meal.

"He was hungry," she explained.

"He's always hungry," I replied.

"I did notice that he showed a particular interest in Mr. Brimley's specimens," Sara added. "I thought it might be best to distract him."

Crafty beast, I thought. Distract him, indeed.

I thanked Mr. Brimley again and then managed to get Rupert back out onto the street. He'd undoubtedly made another food connection and with his streetwise habits would no doubt be back. He really was such a scoundrel.

I hailed a cab, once more paid the extra fare for the *beast,* and gave the driver the address on the Strand.

On the ride back to the office, I thought about what Mr. Brimley had shared with me about the uses of morphine.

Although I had never met Francoise Dupre, I couldn't help but think about what had brought her to her sad fate.

Motive, means, opportunity.

What could possibly have been the motive to kill a pretty young girl whose life had just begun?

Anger? There was no mention of it from Betard, or Sophie who was obviously very close to her sister.

Jealousy? There was no indication of any jealousy, certainly not from Sophie. However, that didn't mean there wasn't any from someone else.

Rivalry? A possibility.

Greed? Sophie had been well dressed and had stayed at the Hotel Metropole with her sister. It appeared they traveled well and lived well, certainly not impoverished. Or someone else?

Lust? An unknown admirer perhaps?

Certainly Betard was a very handsome man. He could be most charming, and charismatic.

I had learned in my travels, and more particularly the past year working with Brodie, there was often far more hidden beneath the surface when a crime had been committed.

The task was to find out what that was. Then, we would know who had killed Francoise and why.

The hound and I arrived back at the strand. He bounded out

of the cab in a manner that startled the horse. I noted the disgruntled look from the driver as he brought the horse back under control. I paid him the extra coin and made a mental note to leave Rupert with the Mudger next time.

"Has Mister Brodie returned?" I asked Mr. Cavendish as he greeted me.

"That he has, miss, and has a man with him—foreign sort, French would be my guess," he said with a disapproving frown.

I thanked the Mudger and climbed the stairs to the office at the second floor.

Jean Luc Betard sat across the desk from Brodie as I entered the office.

I caught the look Brodie gave me. It was a casual nod. However, there was far more in that dark gaze that I had learned to read. Something had happened, something quite serious it appeared, at least serious enough to bring Betard to the office on the Strand.

I also caught Betard's glance in my direction, the slight frown. Gone was the smile from the day before that was almost seductive which I had also noticed in his performance at the Crystal Palace. It had been replaced by an expression that seemed most uneasy.

"I thought you must know about it as soon as possible," he said. "I received it today."

Brodie nodded. "Miss Forsythe is an associate," he explained. "I value her participation as well as her experience in certain things, and she has already had an encounter in the matter."

Betard frowned, however, Brodie chose not to explain the incident of the cut at my hand or my encounter with the residue of morphine left at the glass box we had inspected.

"Whatever you have to say may be said in front of her," Brodie continued. "Or you may consider our business concluded, sir, and take your concerns to the local constabulary."

I smiled to myself, then took one of the other chairs that sat before the desk. I was not prepared for what Betard shared next with us.

"Very well," he began, then handed a folded piece of paper to Brodie. "This was delivered to the hotel this morning."

I caught Betard's frown as Brodie read the note. He then handed it to me.

It had been written on good quality paper that might be found in any stationer's shop, and there was a single line of the message.

*Life is a torch to be extinguished.*

I exchanged a look with Brodie. A threat? And from whom?

"Do ye have any thought who might have sent this?" Brodie asked.

Betard shook his head. "The clerk at the hotel said that it was delivered by one of the courier services."

"Do you know the meaning?" I asked.

"No!" he replied. "I have no idea."

"When did you receive it?" I then asked.

Betard made a dismissive gesture. "What does it matter when it was delivered? I've already said that it was today. I left the hotel then, I didn't want Sophie to know."

"The delivery services in the city keep records," I explained. "If we know the approximate time it was dispatched, we might be able to learn who sent it."

He looked at me with an expression of something very near desperation, then at Brodie. "First Francoise... Now this!"

"It would seem, by the note, that someone has sent a warning," Brodie commented. "Is there anyone who might hold a grudge? Over an insult? Another performer, perhaps?"

"No!" Betard replied.

I wondered if there was something else as I noticed something in his manner. Had there been a threat of some sort, as Mr. Alamy indicated was not uncommon among those who also performed illusions? I said nothing of it for now.

"Very well," Brodie replied. "In the very least, whoever sent the note obviously knows where ye can be found," he continued. "We must consider this to be serious." He gestured to the note.

"It would be best if both of ye left the hotel and remained someplace safe where ye can be protected until we know who has done this."

"I must return to my residence," he insisted. "There are things that must be taken care of now... arrangements for Francoise and I was to depart on my next tour to the continent... I have performances that I must honor," Betard replied.

"It is impossible for us to continue without your participation," Brodie replied. "You must cancel your arrangements to leave until we know who is responsible for this. If ye will not, our arrangement is ended."

I saw Betard's hesitation. "Of course, I understand." Again that hesitation and I thought of what my aunt had shared, that he was attempting to rebuild his career after a disastrous previous tour.

"I will do as you ask," he finally replied, then added, "There is Sophie to consider."

The note Betard had received seemed to indicate a threat against him, not her. Yet, it was best to take precautions and she had been through a great deal.

"I know a place she can stay until this is resolved, with a friend of mine," I told him. "She was at the performance at the Crystal Palace and can be trusted. She will be quite safe with her." I ignored Brodie's expression, and those raised brows.

"No one will think to look for her there," I assured him.

"I will have someone I know provide additional protection," Brodie commented. "We will then be able to proceed with finding the person responsible for this."

"I must speak with my manager. He is still at the hotel."

"You will tell him as little as possible, only that you will be returning to your residence."

Betard nodded, not at all pleased but at least resigned to the situation. "I will explain to Sophie."


It was late afternoon and I needed to make arrangements for Sophie. I rose and went to the door. I might just be able to catch Templeton after her late rehearsal. Brodie accompanied me to the landing at the street.

"Templeton?" he commented as he followed me down the stairs after making a phone call and leaving a message for Mr. Conner.

"She will be happy to assist us," I replied. "She's in between as she calls it, with her next play not to begin for a few weeks."

"The woman is not right in the head..." It was a frequent topic of conversation. I chose to ignore the comment.

"Actually, they have a great deal in common with their work in the theater," I explained. "And Templeton can be most entertaining. I would have Sophie stay with me in Mayfair..." I thought again of that feeling that I might have been followed. "But it might be too obvious to anyone looking for her, and I wouldn't want to put Alice in jeopardy."

"Templeton—entertaining, with her card reading?" Brodie commented. "Not to mention her communication with the spirit world..."

"You must admit that Wills has been quite helpful with information in the past." I pointed out and had another thought. "I wonder if she might have Ziggy back from the zoo. She had mentioned it."

There was a muttered curse. "Ye're as strange in the head as she is. Next ye'll be communicating with ghosts."

"I doubt that," I replied. "Wills seems quite taken with Templeton, and according to her, this sort of thing only works for a few. And they do have the theater in common interest." I waved down a cab, with another thought.

"I do think it might be a good idea to have someone watching over Templeton's flat. Mr. Munro perhaps," I suggested. "I'll contact my aunt and have her speak with him."

That seemed the logical choice. He was a friend of long-standing to Brodie, a fellow Scot he had known since arriving in London as a boy. Granted he had a somewhat mysterious background, but he had proven himself to be absolutely trustworthy in my aunt's service, and could be quite intimidating. He could handle himself as they say, most often by displaying considerable skill with a knife.

Munro had provided me with one when I was about to set off on my first travel adventure, along with lessons in the use of it. He had been most complimentary of my skill, or as complimentary as one might expect with a mumbled compliment, something along the line of, *"Ye'll do."* I always carried it with me. It had come in quite handy more than once.

I had discovered that most people, men in particular, were not prepared for a woman to carry a blade, much less be quite proficient with it and willing to use it. Most often it was secured in the pocket of my dress or skirt, or down the inside of my boot.

I set off for the Adelphi theater. I had called before leaving the office and was informed that Templeton had finished rehearsals.

"This is so exciting! I will be part of your investigation!" Templeton exclaimed when she joined me at her dressing room and I had explained what had happened, and that Sophie needed a place to stay for a while. At least until we had determined who had sent that note and what was behind it.

I could only imagine what Brodie's reaction might have been to that, something that included several curses.

"You're certain it's no imposition, with your performance schedule and all?" I asked.

"Absolutely not. I would be put off if you hadn't asked."

"She is most congenial. You should get on quite well." That seemed the best way to describe her with the limited conversations we'd had. I could only imagine how devastating all of this has been for her.

"Poor thing," Templeton replied. "I cannot imagine how difficult it must be to lose one's sister, having never had one." She looked at me then. "I didn't mean to bring up unpleasant memories. But they were twins for heaven's sake!"

And she was off in that way of hers, rattling on about this and that.

"I've heard that twins are unusually close," she continued. "Some even know each other's thoughts. Do you think that she knew when her sister was...? Well you know what I mean."

"I have no idea," I replied. "I haven't asked, and you should not either. I imagine the whole thing is quite painful for her."

"Of course," she replied. "But if she should want to talk about it..."

I was beginning to think Brodie's objections might be well-founded.

"She's much too fragile right now," I insisted. "If you have any reservations about this at all, you must tell me now."

"Absolutely not. Wills and I will be happy to have Sophie with us, and," she pressed a finger against her lips, "not say a word to anyone."

I then mentioned that it would be best to have Mr. Munro keep a watchful eye on her flat. She became quiet at the suggestion, a novelty for her.

"You should probably be the one to make the request," she suggested. "He's quite put out with me of late."

Oh, dear. A lover's quarrel? Although there was some speculation about that part of it.

However, there was that mural Brodie and I had seen at her country home, most erotic and quite revealing.

"Of course," I replied, not wanting to pursue that. However, it wasn't Templeton's nature to be shy about anything.

"He seems to think that I've been in the company of another man," she explained. "Now, why would he think that?"

I really didn't want to discuss that, but there was no stopping her. I suppose this is what friends were for.

"It was all a misunderstanding, an admirer who became quite bold after one of my performances...Wills did warn me about the man."

"I really must be going, matters to be settled, and all that." I stood abruptly, hoping to escape. "I will let Sophie know and make arrangements for her to meet with you as soon as possible."

"What was I to do?" Templeton continued. "I found the man here in my dressing room quite naked and fully..." She looked at me. "You know what I mean..."

I did, however I wasn't going to discuss that either. It was quite a while ago and best left on a Greek Isle during one of my adventures. However, moving on.

"I did the only thing I could do..." she said with a wave of her hand.

That was certainly open to several possibilities.

I left the Adelphi and my visit with Templeton, everything in place for Sophie to stay with her until we could resolve the case. I would arrange for her to meet with Templeton before her last performance, then return with them to her flat.

Templeton had shared far more details than I needed to know about her relationship with Mr. Munro. It went beyond toe curling, and I was still fanning myself as I stepped aboard a cab.

After what she shared, I could well understand that Munro might have taken offense. However, all that aside, he was the best man for the job and Brodie trusted him implicitly. I made a mental note to put in a call to my aunt's residence at Sussex Square to enlist his assistance.

Before leaving the Strand earlier, Brodie and I had agreed that I might be the better one to return to the Hotel Metropole to inquire with management when that note had been delivered and by whom. My aunt and her circle of friends were much favored guests, and they might be more cooperative with me rather than Brodie.

However...

"You must understand our position, Miss Forsythe," the day manager of the hotel explained. "Our guests' privacy is most important and paramount to their association with the hotel. What might happen if they were to learn that we provided the information you are asking for?"

When my polite request failed, it was time to use influence.

"My aunt, Lady Antonia Montgomery, has spoken highly of the Metropole for her guests when they visit. I believe there were very near one hundred people who had accommodations at the Christmas holiday event that included the use of your ballroom."

I swore that I saw the wheels turning behind that beady gaze, and the moment when influence won over hotel policy.

"Monsieur Betard, you say," he replied, and not politely. "Yes, his party has been staying here." He commented with more than a little displeasure. "We don't usually see actors or actresses for guests," he added with obvious disdain.

Yes, of course, I thought, ignoring his attitude in the matter. I simply replied that I would be very appreciative of information and would make Lady Montgomery aware that he had been most helpful, and...

Once again, name dropping did have its advantages.

I was able to learn that the note for Betard had arrived just after nine o'clock that morning, delivered by courier service as he had told us.

"According to our log, it was the Remington Courier Services that delivered it," he provided.

I was familiar with the company and had used them myself in

the past when it was necessary to send a note across the city or to send off a package to my publisher.

Quite pleased with the information, I thanked him and decided to pay a visit next to the Remington Courier Service.

There were times when I think my friendship with Templeton was beginning to have an effect on me—messages from the spirit world, perhaps? Or, simply that little voice that seemed to whisper every once in a while.

Now, it was like a tap on the shoulder and had me turning around as the concierge at the hotel entrance waived down a cab for me. My gaze swept those who came and went at the sidewalk and the street beyond.

"Miss?" the hotel attendant reminded me as the cabman waited.

I saw nothing out of the ordinary now as I climbed into the cab and gave the driver my destination, but that feeling as if there had been someone watching me persisted and had me looking back through the opening of the cab. It was the same feeling I had experienced earlier.

Remington Courier Services worked with merchants, businessmen, even members of Parliament when it came to providing courier services across the whole of London or beyond.

There were at least a half dozen offices throughout the city, however it made sense that the person who had sent that note to Betard might very likely have chosen one nearest the Hotel Metropole.

Remington couriers also provided service to the clubs where gaming and entertainment of a private nature were held through all hours of the night. It was rumored that late night service had been at the suggestion of the Prince of Wales who apparently relied on Remington rather than palace couriers. I could only speculate the reasons for that.

I arrived at the office very near Whitehall Place and explained to the assistant manager that I had been waiting for a message at the Metropole that had not yet arrived and was most concerned that it might have been lost along the way.

He sniffed indignantly. "We do not lose messages, miss," I was informed. To prove his point, he checked his logbook.

"There was a message that went out this morning very early, and was delivered."

"It's very important that I know if it was the message I've been waiting for," I continued my ruse. "Do you have the name of the person who sent it?" I asked.

"The name is not shown."

"How is that possible?" I knew from my own experience that information for both the sender and the person receiving a message or package was requested when using their service.

"We have a drop box at the entrance for those wishing to leave messages after closing hours to be delivered afterward," he indicated a box beside the door.

"As long as payment is included, or a well-known client with an account, we send out the message according to the sender's instructions when we return the next day," he explained.

"In this particular case," he continued. "The request was made for the same day that the envelope was found in the drop box upon opening our office."

"Do you perhaps still have the envelope it arrived in with those instructions?" I asked. "So that I might know if it is the message I have been waiting for."

"I will see what might be found, miss," he replied.

"I do appreciate your assistance as the hotel suggested that it might be the fault of your company that the note hadn't yet arrived." A slight stretch of the truth.

That seemed to put a fire under him, along with the possibility that once he provided me the information he would soon be rid of me. He signaled for a clerk.

"Mr. Hanby, would you please search through the rubbish for the day. You will be looking for an envelope that would have been received in the drop box quite early with instructions for the contents to be delivered to the Metropole."

The clerk was a slender lad with hair that spilled onto his forehead. He ducked his head slightly in acknowledgement. I smiled at him as he disappeared into the back of the office.

I was prepared for the possibility that nothing might be found when Mr. Hanby finally emerged with an oversized brown envelope in hand.

"I found this, sir."

The manager of the office nodded. "Thank you," he curtly replied and took the envelope from him.

I caught a glimpse of the writing at the front of the envelope. It appeared to be the same as on the smaller envelope and note Betard had received.

"It is noted here that it was retrieved from the drop box at half past eight this morning, the contents then dispersed per instructions on the outside of the envelope to the Metropole Hotel, exactly as indicated in our ledger with payment included. There is no name on the outside of the envelope," he continued. "Not unusual."

"Yes, that is it. I recognize the handwriting." I grabbed it from his hand before he could return it to the trash.

"You've been most helpful. I do appreciate your assistance." I smiled and quickly left. It was doubtful that he would summon a constable over an envelope that had been retrieved from the rubbish bin.

I returned to the Strand to inform Brodie what I had learned. Sophie was there. Betard and one of his men had escorted her to the office and left her in Brodie's care earlier.

Brodie indicated the door to the adjacent bedroom that was slightly ajar. I glimpsed her at the bed, a blanket pulled up over her street clothes.

She hadn't slept the night according to what Betard told him.

"I gave her some of her ladyship's whisky," Brodie quietly explained.

Elixir of the Gods as my aunt called it. Whatever name, it seemed to have worked.

While Sophie slept, I explained what I had learned. I also told him what my aunt had shared about things she'd heard about Jean Luc Betard, including the importance of his next tour in reestablishing himself as a premier illusionist.

The bell at the landing sounded and he rose from the desk. He went to the stairs, then returned with a small wood box of the sort used by green grocers at market. He set it at the desk.

"I sent Mr. Cavendish to the public house," Brodie commented as I removed the cloth that covered the food.

The public house provided the usual fare preferred by workmen and those who lived in the East End, most which I found quite acceptable. *Most of the time*, I thought, as I stared at the fish at one of the plates, complete with head and scales still attached, and beady dead eyes.

"The Mudger mentioned that Miss Effie wasn't about," Brodie explained with a gesture toward the two fish at that plate. I detected a note of disgust at his voice, and this from a man whose people ate haggis!

I had encountered a most interesting variety of foods on my travels and in my partnership with Brodie. However, I drew the line at what stared back at me from that plate. I pulled the cloth back over, then seized the plate and set it out at the landing.

When I returned, Brodie had opened the office window near the desk. While the air that moved through the opening was the usual mix of remnants of coal fires and the river, it was an improvement.

The fish dispensed with, there remained assorted vegetables, a loaf of bread, and a bowl with a baked crust over—a fruit cobbler!

Brodie wasn't hungry. Instead, he inspected the brown envelope I'd retrieved from the courier service.

"Whoever sent that note went to great lengths to make certain not to be discovered." He turned the envelope that had contained that smaller envelope and note, over in his fingers as he examined it.

However, what did that tell us? We had no name. It was disappointing.

He was quiet in that way that I knew he was turning things over in his head. Then, he held the envelope up and passed just below his nose.

"Just here, at the edge of the flap," he said, then handed it to me.

# Eight

"IT SMELLS LIKE LICORICE!" I exclaimed. There was no mistaking it.

"Or more precisely, absinthe," Brodie replied. "I would say that yer time this afternoon was not wasted."

Beyond a glimpse at the writing on the outside, I'd had no opportunity to examine the envelope until now. Nor had I noticed that faint, pale green smudge just at the edge of the envelope flap.

Left by the hand that had tucked that note inside?

Absinthe was a liquor favored by those on the continent, that had an unusually high alcoholic content. That dark gaze met mine.

"It's quite strong," I commented. I knew of it from my travels, not unlike ouzo.

Brodie nodded. "Not usually carried by merchants here, but used by some in the medical profession."

"For what purpose?"

"Much the same as laudanum for sleep or to relieve pain," Brodie replied.

"Morphine and absinthe," I commented.

There was a sound at the landing. Mr. Munro had arrived. He stood as tall as Brodie with dark hair and piercing eyes.

"Have I interrupted yer supper?" he asked with that Scot accent slightly different, from the streets of Edinburgh.

He had received the message I left with my aunt.

"It seems ye left part of it at the landing," he commented. "At least an empty plate."

It seemed that the hound had his share of the supper.

"Her ladyship gave me yer message," he acknowledged, taking the chair across from Brodie.

To see them together, in spite of Brodie's white shirt and trousers, and Mr. Munro's 'uniform' as he referred to it; there was that shared look about them.

Neither had spoken of anything specific, however Brodie had shared that they did what they had to in order to survive. Considering his experience in certain matters it seemed that had included a fair share of things that the authorities at the time would have frowned upon if they'd been caught.

That had been the end of the discussion. However, those early experiences, as I knew only too well of myself, had made them who they were. Quite ironically, Brodie had become a police constable then inspector. Mr. Munro had acquired other experiences after they arrived in London, and equally ironic or perhaps not, had eventually found employ in my aunt's household as manager of her properties.

Might that have been like the fox guarding the henhouse?

Not according to my aunt who shared that there was a scoundrel or several in the family, including some nefarious highwayman according to her own father. Welcome company as far as she was considered. And he had proven himself to be most capable as both manager and protector over the household.

His relationship with Templeton was destined to hear her tell it, brought together during one of our previous cases. It did seem a perfect match. Scoundrels and highwaymen, indeed.

Who was I to question?

I chose not too then, not now whatever might have passed between them that brought on that estrangement. However, I did trust Munro completely to see to Sophie's safety.

Brodie explained our new case.

"A magician, ye say," Mr. Munro commented.

"It will be the girl, his assistant, that ye will be looking after until this is resolved. Most recently we received this note." He passed it to Munro.

Somehow, much like Brodie, he had learned to read, not usually something found on the streets. The skill proved most useful in managing my aunt's accounts for her properties.

Brodie then handed him that envelope from the courier's office.

"Along the edge," he told him. "Faint, but it's there. Absinthe would be my guess," Brodie told him, then explained my encounter with the glass box and the cut at my hand. "Mr. Brimley is most certain it was morphine."

Munro nodded. "A person with habits."

"Just so ye know what we might encounter," Brodie added. "And the reason for protection of the girl. It was her sister, found dead at the end of the performance."

Munro studied the message at that note. "Most people who intend murder simply get on with it, they don't tell ye about it before hand."

Brodie agreed. "Someone who wants to make certain Betard knows what will happen."

It had become quite late of the evening as Brodie told him the rest of what we knew, and that Sophie would be staying with Templeton. I saw the change at Munro's expression.

"Aye," he said simply and emptied his glass of my aunt's very fine whisky, a case sent to the office to replace the one lost in the fire.

With arrangements made, it was very near time for us to meet Templeton after her performance of the evening. Munro was to accompany us.

I knocked lightly at the bedroom door, then entered the room. Sophie had already wakened. At the sound of voices— Brodie and Munro as they quietly spoke— I saw the fear in the expression at her face.

While Betard spoke English quite well, Sophie whispered in French, terrified.

*"What has happened? Who is there?"*

I gently assured her that all was well in French, and told her that it was time to meet Templeton, and that Brodie and I would accompany her along with someone we trusted to keep her safe.

In spite of the few hours sleep, there were still dark patches at her eyes much like bruises. It would take some time for those to go away.

I helped her smooth the wrinkles from her gown and straightened her hair, her appearance far different from that night at the Crystal Palace.

We introduced her to Munro, and I saw some of the fear ease from her pretty features. He did make quite an impression. For his part, Munro was courteous and assured her that he would make certain no one harmed her. I translated into French for her.

Brodie then retrieved his coat and tucked his pistol into the waist of his pants, and we departed.

In spite of the recent warmer weather, the night air was sharp as we rode along the Strand to the Adelphi. Shadows seemed to reach out from the darkness, and I found myself searching them for someone who wasn't there.

I looked over at Sophie. I had come very close to losing my own sister and sensed her feelings of helplessness and fear. No wonder she was so shaken, considering everything that had happened. She was so far from any family with someone very dangerous out there.

I could only hope that we would be able to find the person responsible for Francoise's murder and perhaps provide Sophie some sort of closure for that horrible loss.

We didn't have much to go on. Only that note and the envelope—*Life is a torch to be extinguished.*

A threat as Brodie had commented? But for what?

From what I'd learned from Mr. Alamy, those like Betard guarded the secrets of their illusions, sharing them with no one outside the circle of those who performed with them. And it did appear that he was desperate to resurrect his career with new illusions, including the box illusion.

Or was it something personal against Francoise that had caused this tragedy?

I looked over at Sophie where she sat across from me in the coach. She seemed much smaller and even more fragile in the passing light from a streetlamp that spilled through the window of the coach.

Brodie had been hesitant about leaving Sophie with Templeton in consideration of Wills' penchant for popping in from time to time, as it were. He thought that it might upset the young woman. Not that he believed that such visitations were possible, mind you.

I pointed out that it might be entertaining for Sophie, not unlike the illusions she was part of.

Templeton and Sophie had a great deal in common. Both were familiar with the theater. They had performed in some of the same cities across Europe. Birds of a feather as they say. And I was confident Sophie would be quite safe with Munro nearby.

In a conversation earlier that day with Templeton regarding the arrangement for Sophie to meet her, she had mentioned that it would be good to have someone about as Ziggy as still in residence at the London Zoo.

We met up with her and introductions were made. For his part, Munro chose to remain apart but watchful. Not a good sign, I thought as we then continued to Templeton's flat very near the Adelphi.

In true Templeton style, she showed Sophie the room she was to occupy, then the rest of the flat that included Templeton's bedroom—the door discreetly closed, a small parlor, and the convenience of a water closet. And it appeared they would not be alone, as a creature swept past my head.

Its wings were at least four feet in width, somewhat smaller than Ziggy, and brightly colored. However, what it lacked in size it more than made up for in the string of obscenities that filled the air as it flew past.

"Isn't he marvelous?" Templeton announced, making the introductions. "His name is Eduardo. He's a Brazilian macaw and speaks three languages."

I wondered if that included curses in three languages.

Most other people I knew were in the habit of collecting small dogs with bows around their necks, docile creatures until they left teeth marks on one's hand or a puddle on the carpet.

My aunt was the exception, having acquired Hercule, the monkey she had installed at Sussex Square in preparation for her departure to Africa. And then, of course, there was Rupert. However the hound didn't actually *belong* to anyone, although the Mudger insisted that the animal was quite taken with me. I wasn't at all certain that was a compliment.

"A damned bird?" Brodie exclaimed.

"Be careful what you say," I warned him. "According to Templeton he's fluent in three languages. He might take offense." Although I was fairly certain that did not include curses in Scots Gaelic.

It was after that brief introduction that Eduardo perched himself on the back of Templeton's settee, head bobbing back and forth as he seemed to be listening to our conversation. Then he made a sweep of the front parlor once more, screeching profanities first in English, then in what was very likely Portuguese.

Munro preferred to remain outside the flat and I wondered about the estrangement between them. Although, there was also Wills. In the past, Munro had made his opinion known about Templeton's claims about being able to communicate with the man.

Brodie made another comment under his breath and immediately joined Munro as they set off to investigate the rest of the building. However, I was not fooled.

When they returned from their inspection and after seeing that Sophie was quite comfortable in the arrangement with Templeton, Brodie escorted me home to Mayfair.

We shared some of my aunt's very fine whisky until my housekeeper, Alice, pointedly informed me that it was quite late, and she was retiring for the evening.

'And was there anything else she could get for us?' A hint if ever there was one.

After Brodie's leave-taking, I spent the next few hours in the front parlor at my writing desk, putting pen to paper in my notebook about what we had learned so far.

When I looked up next from my notes it was well after one o'clock of the morning. However I was not tired. I was restless, pacing back and forth across the front parlor, going back over what we now knew.

Brodie had pointed out that my determination to solve the case might have something to do with my own experience at very nearly losing my own sister. I saw his point but argued that it had absolutely nothing to do with that.

He had also pointed out that with so little to go on, Francoise's murder might never be solved. He reminded me of the Whitechapel murders, now a few years old and still unsolved.

I was not of the same opinion. There was more to this, and I was determined to find out what it was.

Brodie had questioned those at the rail storage about the props and equipment Betard used, most particularly the glass boxes used in his performance.

According to what he had learned, no one had seen anyone unusual about the storage area when the boxes were shipped to the Crystal Palace in advance of his performance there, nor afterward when they were returned to await transport back to the next location as he embarked on his new tour.

He wanted next to question others in Betard's employ, the handful of assistants who were still at the Metropole before they departed for Hampton Manor. He thought that I might be useful in that regard, particularly with Marie Genesse who traveled with Francoise and Sophie and saw to their costumes for their performances.

*Useful.* Never let it be said that the Scots were effusive with their compliments. Irritating man.

Betard had earlier provided a list of those who had accompanied him to the Palace the evening Francoise was killed. It was amazing how many were required for him to put on one of his performances.

~

Brodie returned the following morning and we proceeded to the Metropole where I might be *useful.*

There were several people who usually accompanied Betard when he was on tour, and they were still at the Metropole.

Brodie met with the others while I met with Marie Genesse who was less than accommodating.

"*Je ne comprends pas,*" she snapped and refused to say anything more.

I politely asked another question regarding how long she had been with Monsieur Betard, and received the same response. Perhaps, she preferred to speak in French.

"*Peut-être êtes-vous plus à l'aise en français.*" I then told her. She gave me a withering glance. However, the conversation proceeded from there, surprisingly in English.

She explained that she had been in charge of the costumes and make-up for both Francoise and Sophie. The costumes had to meet Monsieur Betard's exact requirements for the success of his illusions.

After further questions, she shared that she had been with Betard for several years, and had in fact once worked with him on the stage—an illusion that required her to be 'sawn in half' inside a box. Not what I would have chosen for a career, however it was, after all, an illusion.

I asked if she was angry that she had been replaced in Betard's performances.

*"Non,"* she snapped with a shrug of the shoulders in that way of the French when responding to a comment. "It would not have worked for the new illusion. There is only one of me. *Comprenez vous?"*

I did understand quite well. She had been replaced as Betard's illusions changed, including Francoise and Sophie, twins who were perfect for the new illusion, and younger.

She was complimentary of Sophie—referring to her as *petit ange triste*—a small sad angel. However, she was less fond of Francoise, even critical of her, lapsing into French once more.

*"Elle était... une pute,"* she spat out, calling her a whore. Quite uncomplimentary.

"She was always out for herself, her affair with Monsieur, calculating. It was she who demanded to be in the first box with her smile for the audience. She was not like *mon cher*, Sophie," she continued. "Not a care for her sister by that one. Only Francoise was important to Francoise! Cruel and demanding. Nothing was ever right for that one.

"That night, Sophie was in tears and did not want to go on with the performance. However, Betard persuaded her. She would have done anything for him."

Most interesting, I thought. She then insisted that she hadn't seen anything or anyone suspicious the night of the performance. But then, as she explained, she was in the dressing room that had been provided for them, and knew nothing of what had happened until she heard the police called for.

*"Il n'y a rien de plus."* There was nothing more she could tell me.

I joined Brodie afterward in the hotel salon, provided for

those meeting others at the hotel, and told him about my conversation with Marie.

"There is something troubling ye," he commented.

"I couldn't help the feeling that there was something more, something she refused to tell me."

"Protecting Sophie, perhaps?" he suggested. "It's understandable."

His conversation with others in Betard's entourage had fared little better. Two of the men, a father and son by the name of Lescole, were responsible for seeing that all equipment, props, and those glass boxes were maintained and properly installed for a performance, and carefully covered afterward. Neither of them had seen anyone near the boxes prior to the performance.

A third man by the name of Fouquet was Betard's manager. He angrily repeated what Betard had said, that upcoming performances in Berlin and then Madrid before traveling on to Budapest, would have to be rescheduled because of the delay.

The *accident*, as Fouquet had called it, was most unfortunate. However, as Templeton had once said of the theater—the show must go on. No matter that a young woman had been killed and the murderer was still unknown.

Two others he spoke with were 'handlers', as he described them. They were responsible for arranging for Betard's transportation to and from the Palace.

Brodie had the hotel concierge summon a cab. When the driver arrived, we boarded the hansom, and he gave the driver the location of the rail storage at Victoria Station.

"I've asked Mr. Brimley to meet us there to see if those fingerprints can be obtained from the glass at the box. If so, they might tell us something."

It was a fairly recent method the MP used to identify criminals in the fledgling fingerprint bureau Alex Sinclair had been instrumental in creating. However, as Brodie had explained at the time, that depended on a criminal's print previously entered into the records.

The person we were searching for might not have been entered into the records, or had only just arrived in London. I was thoughtful as we rode to Victoria Station.

"Sophie is in love with Betard," I commented, something I was quite certain about.

Those dark brows angled sharply as Brodie looked over at me. "Is that yer woman's intuition?"

"It is quite obvious, and apparently her feelings were not returned. It seems that Betard and Francoise were lovers."

"Unrequited love?" He commented. "Ye think that Sophie could have murdered her sister?"

Jealousy certainly could have been a motive, but I shook my head.

"It would have required her to enter the box unseen, strike the fatal blow, then enter the second box at the end of the performance still unseen, and," I continued, "most certainly Betard would have been aware. Considering his relationship with Francoise, he would undoubtedly have attempted to protect her. And I hardly think that Sophie is strong enough to have done it."

They were sisters, I argued with myself. Twins, supposedly more closely bonded than other sisters. I couldn't imagine that one would want to harm the other, no matter the issue between them.

It was just another aspect of the tragedy. Then, there was Marie Genesse. Clearly, she had not liked Francoise. However, what did that mean?

We arrived back at Victoria Station and found Mr. Brimley waiting for us with a black case in hand. We then went to the storage area where those boxes with the glass panels were stored. They had not been moved and were covered as before when Brodie and I had first examined them.

Brodie removed the cover from the box where Francoise had died and showed Mr. Brimley where we had seen the fingerprints. He immediately set to work. I watched, fascinated once more with the process as he set out items he would use—

a candle on a stand, matches, and iodine crystals in a vial.

He heated the crystals in a small brass salver over the flame at the candle. As the crystals heated, a vapor appeared. He then held the salver next to the glass. The prints gradually appeared.

Brodie looked closer, his brow furrowed as he studied the image that the vapor revealed. He exchanged a look with Mr. Brimley.

"What is it?" I stepped closer for a look, and I saw...nothing.

Three prints were in fact there and as before, apparently made by a man's hand by the size and the spread between the fingers. The outline of each was quite clear, but there was no other detail revealed by the vapor, just a muddled smudge at each one.

Mr. Brimley produced a magnifying glass from his kit and proceeded to examine them thoroughly. He stepped back and handed the glass to Brodie.

He looked at the prints once more, his reaction the same as before. He looked over at Mr. Brimley.

"I've not seen it before, however, my experience is limited in these things," the chemist explained.

"The outline of the prints is clear. What would be the reason that there are no other marks?" Brodie asked.

I took the glass from Brodie, and I had another look to see what he was speaking of. There were only those smudges inside the outline of those prints, not the usual loops, arches, and whorls I had seen in other prints.

"One appears to be most irregular, distorted. It could simply be a deformity of some kind," Mr. Brimley explained. "And it's not unusual for a man to lose a finger at the docks or in the workhouses. It happens quite frequently."

However, that didn't explain the other prints lacking any of the usual marks on them.

"How is that possible?" I asked.

"The prints might have been smudged," Mr. Brimley replied, however, he didn't seem convinced.

"Or there are no marks."

I looked at my own thumb with its lines, whorls, and arches.

"How might that happen?"

"I would need to examine them more closely," he said and retrieved two items from his kit. "A little trick young Mr. Sinclair showed me. This might work," he said with a wink of the eye.

He dusted the prints with a fine black powder, then covered them with what he called a lifter that appeared to be a piece of thin, white rubber. He then placed the rubber back in his kit.

"I can then photograph these. The image may show us more once the photograph is created." He smiled, much like a cat with a mouse.

Ingenious. Hopefully that might tell us something, or in the very least we might be able to have them compared to those collected by the Metropolitan Police.

Mr. Brimley left to return to his shop, while Brodie wanted to check on Mr. Munro to make certain there had been no unusual encounters through the night. Every precaution had been taken, however he was still uneasy.

Lucy Penworth had sent a message round to the office that she had information for me.

Our driver let Brodie out very near Templeton's flat, while I continued on to the Times newspaper building.

I was most anxious to learn what Lucy might have discovered about Jean Luc Betard in her search of the newspaper archives.

# Nine

LUCY MET me downstairs at the attendant's desk when I arrived. She carried a notebook. She hooked her arm through mine as we left the building—out of hearing of those 'walls with ears.'

The Times archive was in the building adjacent and included not only copies of past editions of the Times dailies but also the newspaper archive that had been recorded on photographic film as I had some experience searching in one of our previous cases.

"Were you able to find anything?" I asked as we entered the adjacent building and went to the lift. The film archive was on the second floor.

"Quite a lot actually," she commented. "Most of it in the News about the City section of the papers for performances he's given in the past, and then more recently in the theater section. The first news article that I was able to find was from April of 1876 when he made his first appearance at the Tivoli. There was some information about his arrival in London. This was no easy task as Alan Ivers has taken upon himself to be most bothersome ever since we last met. That's the reason I chose to meet you downstairs."

The lift bumped to a stop, and she opened the gate.

"I've written down the dates of the issues I found," she said as she held aloft her notebook. "The ledger system is quite thorough." She smiled at the clerk at the counter and explained that I needed to see the archive for my next book.

He nodded and we entered the archive for the Times of London.

"The others frequently come here when they're following up a story that was written, instead of keeping files of copies of old newspapers," Lucy explained. She led the way to a long table with a half dozen of those viewing machines that were quite familiar from my forays into the London Library.

She then led the way past and down an aisle that was numbered and labeled with dates.

"Here." She pulled a metal canister from the shelf, dated April 1 to April 30, 1876, and carried it back to the table. She opened the canister, then threaded the photographic film from one spindle at the machine, across the viewing plate, then onto the other spindle.

She sat at the table, turned on the electric light inside the machine then began searching through photographs of issues of the Times as she scrolled the film across the plate.

It was one of those marvelous inventions that had come out of the Exhibition years earlier. That was before either Linnie or I were born, however my aunt had attended the exhibition several times and had told my sister and I of the marvelous inventions that were seen there.

*It really was quite exciting*, she had enthused. *Some of the inventions were quite ridiculous contraptions. There were photo machines where the inventors actually demonstrated how a photograph could be made on a roll of film. Then there was the invention of a horseless carriage powered by a steam engine of all things. The engine blew up and almost took down a section of the Crystal Palace.* She had given us both a wink then. *However, by far, the most entertaining invention was the machine that produced what was called the personal intimate balloon.*

She had been quite amused with that. *It was for making prophylactics from rubber. Most ingenious!*

This particular conversation about the Exhibition had preceded our first year at private school in Paris, when she emphasized that it was important as an enlightened young woman to be prepared for what we might encounter.

*Ah, yes, the French*, she had begun with a somewhat secretive expression that at the time made me curious what she wasn't telling us perhaps about her own time in private French schools.

*I digress*, she said then. *You must be prepared for enthusiastic young Frenchmen.* That, and the conversation about that wonderful invention at the Exhibition, then became the explanation of what occurred between a man and a woman which had thoroughly embarrassed Linnie. I had to admit that I wasn't embarrassed at all, merely quite curious about the machine.

Not that I didn't already have a fairly good idea of things. But this was something fascinating—the invention of a manufactured item that much resembled a balloon, as our aunt described it and prevented the woman from finding herself with child.

A detailed description followed for Linnie's benefit and to her horror. She could not understand the reason a well-married woman would want to prevent having a child. I was afterward forced to explain to her that it was possible not all women wanted children, or not immediately following the wedding.

It was said to be a vast improvement over sheep's intestine that was previously rumored to have been of some success when it didn't rupture. In addition, as our aunt pointed out at the time, the ones that were made by the modern machine could have different sizes.

*What do you mean different sizes?* Linnie had blurted out. Our aunt was the then forced to explain that men were not all the same size, just as their hands were different sizes. My sister's response at the time—she was twelve years old, was to simply say, *Oh*.

We laughed over that years later.

"Here it is," Lucy announced, jarring me from my thoughts.

She pointed to the viewing window with the photo archive from April 8, 1874 that featured, "Entertainers to appear at the Tivoli."

As I scanned the article, she disappeared into the archive once more, then emerged with the next roll of photographic film and threaded it through the machine next to me.

"There is this as well," she added.

And so we spent the next few hours, myself at one machine, Lucy at the other as I made my own notes about the articles she had found.

The earliest article made mention that he was quickly becoming known for his more complex illusions—no rabbit pulled from a hat, but with a flair for the dramatic and shocking.

There was then an announcement of his first tour. If nothing else, it appeared the man was quite a self-promoter. That first tour was to Germany and Italy, then returned to London, followed by his tour to the United States.

Lucy had found articles with questions regarding his techniques, and of course his secrets, which he refused to answer.

Several years earlier he had moved his tour to London, taking up residence at Hampton Manor, a rundown estate. In an accompanying article he explained that it provided him the perfect setting to create his latest illusions in privacy, along with easier travel options as his tours were more and more in demand, not only across Europe but return tours to New York and beyond. It was mentioned that he had taken his performance as far as San Francisco.

All of it was most interesting as demand for his performances grew far beyond the days of the early street performer. It presented the unusual demand and fame that he was achieving, as each season he presented more and more complex illusions. There were comparisons to the most famous illusionists at the time including John Maskelyne.

"I found this as well," Lucy indicated a mention she had pulled up on her machine. I peered over her shoulder.

"The family was quite poor. It seems that he was most curious about the art of illusion early on and performed on the streets. He spent countless hours as a child studying the illusions of Professor Liebholz, Jean-Eugene Robert-Houdin, and later performed with the Great Maxim—Maximilian Holt here in London.

"He lives in Aldgate according to this," she added. "I believe he also performs on the street from time to time, quite different from his early career. It also mentions early illusions, including one where he seemed to disappear in a cloud of smoke right before the audience."

Aldgate. One of the poorer areas of London. A sad end to a successful career. The same fate might befall Betard with Francoise's death.

Along with the early articles there were the usual artist renderings of his performances and a succession of assistants through the years. Of course, there were the latest editions of the daily promoting his performance at the Crystal Palace, with the promise of that entirely new illusion, 'to thrill and mesmerize the audience'. Written by none other than Alan Ivers, of course.

The editions of the last two days that had not yet been archived recounted the events of the performance including somewhat lurid details about the death of Betard's assistant during that performance.

It noted his fascination with the world of illusion and years of training. Then, mentioned that he had set out on his own, constantly experimenting with new and more fantastic illusions. According to one article, Jean Luc Betard had struggled and found fortune and fame, only to have that experiment at the Crystal Palace end in disaster.

And not an accident as Chief Inspector Abberline had hastily announced, but something far more sinister—murder.

Success, fame and fortune. And now a horrible tragedy.

There were other articles as well, including an interview with

John Maskelyn, and Albert Smyth who had performed at the Adelphi and was interviewed after one of his performances.

The person writing the article had asked for Mr. Smyth's response to the enormous success of other illusionists, particularly that of Jean Luc Betard. When asked about his disappearing illusion in a cloud of smoke. He had responded quite briskly according to the article—"As he should disappear!"

"A bit of envy, perhaps," Lucy suggested. "But it appears there was an accident that almost ended Betard's career. Here," she indicated.

It was a brief article about a fire during one of his illusions that exploded out of control. He was horribly burned, and it was thought he might never perform again. It appeared that he had recovered very well and achieved great success. Success that someone was willing to kill to destroy?

Templeton had experienced such a threat from a well-known actress who had accused her of stealing a role in one of the plays she performed in. And Mr. Alamy had spoken to the fact that illusionists carefully guarded the secrets of their illusions, even something as simple as pulling a rabbit out of a hat.

Was it possible that professional jealousy might have led to Francoise Dupre's death? Something dramatic played out before an audience with the potential to ruin Betard's career?

"I also asked Alex... Mr. Sinclair to make inquiries. It seems their people have connections in other countries. I thought it might be helpful to have him inquire about anything that appeared in the French newspapers," she explained. "They might have carried something early on before Betard became famous."

I thought I saw a bit of bright color at her cheeks at the mention of Mr. Sinclair.

"That could be useful. I will place a call to him," I told her. "Unless, of course, you would like to contact him," I suggested. She smiled as she leaned in close where we sat at the table.

"He has inquired if I would care to work for the Service," she explained. "It doesn't seem quite as exciting as the newspaper. I don't want to do the same thing I was doing before—running errands, providing tea or coffee, that sort of thing. However, I wouldn't have to put up with the likes of Alan Ivers. "

I didn't blame her. However, that was not for me to say.

"What do you think I should do?" she asked.

Good heavens! I was hardly the best person to be giving out advice on how to live one's life, or conduct one's relationships. I lived independently as a result of the royalties from the sale of my books and what was left of my portion of my mother's estate.

I lived quite well on my own without anyone to take care of me. However, I knew that Lucy needed to work, and that was different.

"Sir Avery has offered a fair compensation," she added.

I liked Lucy very much and, while I couldn't see her making a career of running errands at the Times, still she had managed to move beyond that and was now at least contributing to articles that appeared in the newspaper. And yet...

I knew better than most the difficulties women faced on their own from my experience in publishing. I was consistently pushed aside in favor of other authors—mostly men. Until I wasn't.

And then there were the things I had seen while working on cases with Brodie; the poverty of the East End where women, many on their own with children, worked demeaning jobs just to put food on the table, and often not enough of that.

I thought how best to answer her.

"It might be useful to request a list of duties you would be required to undertake," I suggested. "That might give you a better idea of what to expect."

She nodded, her mouth pulled into a frown. "What if it's similar to working here?"

"Then you negotiate."

Her eyes widened. "Negotiate?"

"As far as errands are concerned," I explained with thought of all the times I had filled Brodie's coffee cup as well as my own. "There might be some not unlike when I'm working with Mr.

Brodie and we're investigating a case." I hesitated. "You may need to assert yourself," I pointed out. "And it might be helpful to have them put in writing precisely what your responsibilities will be, much like a contract."

"That is quite brilliant," she excitedly replied, then looked up. "Oh, that irritating man!" she said with disgust.

By her reaction, it could be none other than Alan Ivers. Then I saw him as he entered the archive room.

He didn't bother to sign in but quite brazenly approached the table where we had been searching the microfilm archives. He glanced at the viewing glass and Lucy promptly shut off the electric at her machine.

"Imagine my surprise, finding you here," he commented, and I immediately thought of Templeton's pet iguana, Ziggy, slithering about and half expected to see that serpent-like tongue dart out and snatch a fly out of the air.

"Searching for ladies' fashions or the latest gossip?" he continued. "Or perhaps researching for your latest novel?"

This, of course, directed at me. I should have thought to bring Rupert with me. It would have been quite entertaining to simply let the hound have his way with the disgusting man. I had removed the film roll from my machine and returned it to the canister.

"Various methods for removing one's bollocks," I replied with a smile, then gathered up my notebook and joined Lucy as she returned from the storage shelves for those rolls of film.

"Have a good day."

"Marvelous," Lucy whispered as we left the building. "How do you do it?"

"Quite easily with annoying creatures," I replied. And I smiled to myself.

I left the Times building and Lucy to compose her list of questions for her potential pending employment with the Special Services. There was someone else I wanted to call on with my aunt's recommendation.

Juliette Delón was a French émigré who had come to London several years earlier from France—'Madame Juliette', as she was known to the ladies of London who followed the latest Paris fashions and paid handsomely for them.

That exclusive clientele included the queen, although her gowns were in black for mourning, and my great aunt as well, when she wasn't going about in the costume of the great hunter in Africa complete with field boots.

*A lady is known by the way she dresses*, she had told both my sister and I on more than one occasion. Quite ironic.

Linnie had followed that advice, that included the gown for her wedding that Madame Juliette had personally designed. My wardrobe had a tendency to be far more practical—my walking skirts and shirts, and of course the split skirts that had become the rage after the London tour of the Wild West Show with Miss Annie Oakley from the United States.

On the rare occasion that I could not avoid, such as accompanying my aunt to one of her holiday events, I had worn a fashionable gown after I had removed all the satin bows and flowers. I simply was not a 'bow and flower' person.

Madame Juliette had also provided elaborate gowns for Templeton's various incarnations on the stage, as well as creative costumes for my aunt's All Hallows Eve celebrations in the past. The goddess costume she designed for my aunt was still talked about. Juliette was indeed very talented.

"I have not given up on you, mademoiselle," she once told me. "One day, I will design a gown for you, and it will be most *spéciale*."

Her shop was on Bond Street, not far from the townhouse in Mayfair. It had a brick sidewalk and a recessed entrance framed by glass windows at both sides. An elegant vase of flowers was displayed on a Louis XV table in one window. The name of the shop was at the other, simply *'Juliette'*, with the royal warrant in the lower corner. No other signage was necessary.

Juliette had family in France and frequently traveled back to Paris. She attended the Paris theaters and knew many who were part of that circle. I hoped that she might be able to tell me something about Jean Luc Betard that had not been in those newspaper articles.

I entered the shop that was bustling with activity even late in the day, no doubt owing to several society functions that were approaching, including Royal Ascot. A young attendant greeted me, in French. I asked to speak with Madame and gave the young woman my card.

"Mademoiselle Forsythe." Juliette smiled in greeting as she swept from the back of the shop where there were dressing rooms for her clients.

She was dressed in a chartreuse gown that reminded me of someone else—

a woman barely clad I had once seen emerging from Brodie's office.

She was the only woman I knew who could wear such a color, with her dark hair and equally dark eyes, and an almost regal air about her.

"To what do I owe the pleasure? A new gown, perhaps?" she hopefully suggested.

"I need your assistance with something else," I replied. "However, I don't want to impose..."

She smiled. "As you can see, we are very busy. But come, let us talk. My assistants can handle everything for a little while." She inclined her head in the direction of her private salon where she met with her exclusive clientele, other than the queen. She met with her at Buckingham Palace.

She asked one of her assistants to bring wine. I would have preferred my aunt's very fine whisky, however when in France... Or very near that in the shop which resembled a French atelier.

Her assistant brought the wine and poured two glasses, then quietly left.

"Her ladyship is well?" Juliette inquired.

"Quite well," I replied. We exchanged the usual pleasantries over the wine.

"You spoke of needing my assistance," she said then, angling her head slightly. "Or perhaps not, but I am hopeful," she added with an amused smile.

"I was once told that you prefer wearing jockey silks at horse races." There was no criticism in her voice, only amusement. "That is something I would like very much to have seen," she added. "Perhaps next time."

I didn't bother to mention that the officials at Ascot had submitted an 'informal' reprimand, requesting that I not attend in the future. Not that it bothered me.

"I need information and I am hoping that you can help me."

"For your *Miss Emily Fortescue* novels, perhaps?" She poured more wine. "Such a delightful creature. I have read all the books. It helps with my English, you see. I seem to notice a resemblance, perhaps?"

That had been pointed out by my publisher as well.

She sat back in the Louis XV chair, watching me over her wineglass.

"Or perhaps you are here because of a new investigation?" she speculated.

Most perceptive.

"I'm hoping that you can tell me something about Jean Luc Betard."

"The man of a thousand illusions? I read about the death of his assistant. So very dreadful, tragic. The police are calling it an accident. But perhaps not?"

Once again, she was most perceptive.

I explained that I was at the Crystal Palace that evening, and that we had been called upon to make inquiries on our own as we were not convinced it was merely an accident.

"Ah, Monsieur Brodie," she replied. "A most interesting man."

I didn't mention the specifics of the note that Betard had received.

"And you are hoping that I might be able to tell you more about him from before, in Paris, *ai-je raison?*"

"Quite correct," I replied.

She nodded. "He has made himself into what he is and very successful, *certainement.* Something I understand very well." She smiled.

"He is from the lower classes like many, in the 13th Arrondissement as I remember," she reminisced. "There is much poverty. Very difficult and many leave in order to survive."

I had heard of it while attending school in Paris. There were stories of the cabarets, the prostitution gossiped about among ourselves, a place where no proper schoolgirl would go.

Betard, it appeared, had escaped as Juliette had. She'd learned her craft, working as an assistant to another woman, but with aspirations to make the finer creations she saw in lady's fashion books. It was a well-known story.

"And the 13th Arrondissement with its poverty is not the image he wishes to the world to see. Most particularly audiences that include kings and queens."

She rang a small hand bell and asked her assistant to bring pastry and more wine. Then she continued.

"It is said that he struggled for many years with performances on the streets and in the small theaters. But not long as he created more difficult and sensational illusions such as the one at the Crystal Palace.

"He became known as *'the man of a thousand illusions'* and performed in the capitals of Europe and the United States."

"I've been told that illusions are carefully guarded secrets," I commented.

"*Certainement,*" Juliette replied. "Can you imagine if the most successful secrets became widely known? One would become a pauper overnight, so the secrets must be closely protected. "

She was thoughtful. "I remember as a child, one of the street performers was found in Paris with his throat cut. The man had no enemies. And it could be most dangerous for one like Betard who has achieved such success. Then there are the dangers of the illusions themselves."

I was curious. "What sort of dangers?"

"There was supposedly a dreadful accident several years ago, an explosion and a horrible fire," she replied. "According to the newspapers it was from the chemicals he was using. It was most fortunate that he was not injured. It was about then that he left France and has only returned a few times. I believe that his mother still lives in Paris."

He'd been fortunate indeed. I thought back to what we now knew about his relationship with Francoise Dupres.

"What about other assistants, those he's worked with in the past?" I asked.

"It would be exciting for a young woman, of course," she admitted. "A handsome, charismatic man, the thrill of the stage, the attention of the audience, and travel to foreign countries. For Betard, he would be most careful with those he chose to work with him for they also share his secrets. *Oui*?"

I thought of Marie Genesse. A former assistant now relegated to cleaning and mending costumes for new assistants. Forced to watch as Betard carried on his affair with Francoise?

"Ah yes, she was once his lover," Juliette commented when I mentioned Marie. "She would know his secrets." She smiled. "I have not been very helpful," she said then.

I assured her that she had. Now, I knew far more about Betard than when I had arrived. However, the question still remained, what did it tell me?

I was more curious than ever about what Marie Genesse might know. She had been with Betard for some time and had once participated in his illusions. Then lovers, now set aside to mend the costumes of younger women who had replaced her.

There was a saying from a play I had once seen, *Hell hath no fury like a woman scorned.*

Marie Genesse had been reluctant to tell me anything about Betard, almost as if she were hiding something.

Even though it was already well into the evening, I was certain that I would find Marie at the hotel since Betard's people weren't to return to his private residence at the edge of the city until the morning.

The front desk clerk asked to assist me as I arrived. I told him that I was there to see Marie Genesse who was a member of the Betard party.

"I know the room number," I explained and continued to the lift.

Upon reaching the floor where Betard and his people were staying, I continued down the hall to the room where I had previously met with Marie. I hesitated as I reached her room. The door was ajar.

Perhaps she had stepped out. I looked both directions at the hallway, but saw no one. I pushed the door further open, and called out. I stepped inside.

The room was exactly as I remembered it except that it was now quite dark inside. I felt along the wall near the door and pressed the button for the electric. A single light came on beside the door, throwing shadows across the carpet and the furnishings. I called out again. There was still no answer.

I crossed the room to the small writing desk beside the windows where there was hotel stationary. I reached for the pen with the intention of leaving a note. There seemed to be something sticky on the pen.

I reached for the chain pull at the desk lamp and turned it on to see what it might be. Perhaps something Marie had spilled—or possibly one of the cosmetics used by Francoise and Sophie that had spilled as she was packing to leave in the morning.

I stared at the pen in my hand. It was covered with blood! And there was more blood smeared at the hotel stationary.

I stepped back. It was then I saw Marie Genesse. She lay sprawled at the floor just behind the settee, a dark stain soaking into the carpet beneath her, a stunned expression at her face. She was obviously quite dead.

I knelt beside her. From past experience, I have learned there is nothing that can prepare one for the sight of someone dead. It was most often startling, catching one by surprise, then filling one with horror. But there were also instances, as now, when it seemed that Marie might suddenly rise, look about herself with that frown at her face and demand in rapid French to know what had happened.

What indeed? I thought. Who had been there? Why was she killed?

It was then I saw the note clutched in her outstretched hand. Not precisely clutched as it seemed that it might have been put there after she was killed by the way it simply lay *over* her hand where it might be easily found.

There was writing on the outside of the envelope along with those blood stains. It was addressed simply—*Betard*.

I heard voices then at the hallway, distant at first, then much closer. The door of the hotel room was suddenly pushed open as the desk clerk and the hotel manager came into the room.

It was one of those moments when I could have sworn that I heard Brodie's voice calling me impulsive, stubborn, even reckless at times. I had heard all of it, more than once. It was my imagination.

"Good heavens!" the hotel manager exclaimed as Marie's body came into full view, then turned to me.

I had only a moment as the desk clerk let out a gasp. I seized the envelope and quickly thrust it into my skirt pocket.

Impulsive? Quite.

Stubborn? I saw no reason for them to have something that we might need very badly on behalf of our client.

Reckless? Well there was that, of course. But as I said, it had served me well in the past.

"Hoskins," the manager turned to the desk clerk, who stood at his elbow, gaping open-mouthed at the sight of Marie's body.

"Contact the Metropolitan Police immediately. Say nothing to any of the other staff," he added. "Use my private office. We have the reputation of the hotel to consider. And be quick about it."

I stood and smoothed my skirt. "As I said," I began again, thinking he had perhaps not heard me the first time. "I merely wanted to speak with Madame Genesse. The desk clerk is aware that I only just arrived."

"You may tell that to the Metropolitan Police."

I have a few rules that I have acquired in my travels and more recently in my association with Brodie.

One—don't get caught. This should be one's intention when going off with one's travel guide to a Greek Island; more specifically when taking off one's clothes to go swimming in the Aegean Sea.

Two—tell the truth, or as close to it as possible. I have discovered, however, that there are some people who simply refuse to believe the truth. In that instance, a small stretch of the truth had served me well in the past. That was before my association with Brodie.

Three—most particularly in my work with Brodie, try to avoid encounters with persons who are more concerned with their position than anything else. Most particularly, Chief Inspector Abberline of the Metropolitan Police with whom I'd had several previous encounters, and who had proven himself to be very concerned with his position and future promotions.

Two uniformed constables immediately arrived and informed me that I could explain everything to the chief inspector.

# *Ten*

I'VE NEVER HAD the experience of being *'nicked'* as they say
—arrested, or taken into police custody.

There was that one time at Ascot, but I don't consider that
the same. I had wandered into the stabling area and there just
happened to be one of my aunt's horses, saddled as others were
ridden to the starting stalls. I had managed to 'acquire' a set of
silks and proceeded to leg-up with the other jockeys.

I made it to the starting stalls without being discovered and
before Jimmy Balfour, my aunt's jockey, had alerted race staff.
And as they say, the rest was history. The race started and we
were off!

My aunt's horse was disqualified when it was discovered that
Jimmie was not aboard. And there had been several constables,
race officials, along with my aunt and Jimmie waiting when I
returned to the stabling area, covered in mud, grinning from ear
to ear—it was most exciting.

The race officials grumbled amongst themselves while Jimmie
tried to explain just how I had managed it, and my aunt fought
back laughter over the entire matter.

In the end I was banned from riding at Ascot—not that it was
any loss, as there were other adventures that beckoned; the police

were persuaded that there were no charges to be brought against me, and my aunt swore to all that I had her permission in the caper.

Now, I was at police headquarters in the room adjoining Chief Inspector Abberline's office. A uniformed constable stood guard in the event I tried to escape while I listened to the conversation that alternately rattled the door with Abberline's furious comments.

"Miss Forsythe was found at the scene of a crime!" he informed Brodie. "Standing over the body of the deceased! I have every right to have her arrested and charges brought!" Abberline thundered.

I then listened with curiosity for what Brodie's response might be as he had threatened to throw me to the police on more than once occasion. Granted, that was in a fit if temper that had soon passed. However, this was his opportunity as it were.

"She was acting in her in the course of investigating a case in the matter of the death at the Crystal Palace," he calmly replied.

"What bloody case?" Abberline demanded.

"In the matter of the case that Monsieur Betard has retained us to investigate," Brodie explained in a still-calm voice.

"A case," Abberline replied. I heard the disdain at his voice. "You're telling me that Miss Forsythe is an associate or partner in your investigations? That is the most absurd thing I have ever heard."

"Quite so, and invaluable in the resolution in the matter of at least three previous cases that I believe you are well aware of."

I smiled to myself, quite enjoying this in spite of the seriousness of the matter.

"And she just happened to be at the Metropole and stumbled across the dead woman!" Abberline replied.

"She was following up information she had in the matter," Brodie replied. "She had my authorization to do so."

A slight stretch of the truth, however I was touched by his words, defending me.

"What am I to make of this, Brodie?" Abberline then demanded.

"It would seem that two murders have now been committed," he replied. "Our client has the right to expect that the matter will be resolved," he added.

Direct, firm, yet in that same calm voice. I was quite impressed in consideration of the fact that there was a difficult history between Brodie and the chief Inspector.

"And what am I to make of the fact that I have had communication from no less than three persons demanding her release!"

Three? My aunt possibly, but two others? Most curious.

"Lady Antonia Montgomery..." he announced.

I would need to explain everything to my aunt.

"Sir Beaton, the Home Secretary, and Sir Avery Stanton!" Abberline added to the list with what sounded like a fist at the desktop.

I would have liked to have seen the expression at his face even as I was surprised at two of the names mentioned—the Home Secretary and Sir Avery? Good heavens.

"Sir Avery suggested that it might be in my best interest to set the matter aside, even though I could easily bring charges against her for interfering in police matters!" Abberline added. I did not have to strain to hear Brodie's response to that.

"As there was no active police investigation in the matter at the time, I suggest that ye release her."

I could well imagine Abberline's expression, flushed with anger, what remained of the hair at his head standing on end.

"You will tell me what information you have in this and not proceed on yer own!" Abberline replied after what I was certain were several deep breaths to control himself. "It is not the first time that you have chosen to avoid authority."

"I have a responsibility to our client," Brodie calmly informed him. "I have explained Miss Forsythe's reason for being at the hotel. Unless you wish to formally charge her with a crime, we will be on our way. You may, of course, wish to discuss further with Sir Avery."

I was quite impressed.

"You and I are not finished," Abberline finally replied in what could only be a threat.

"No, we are not," Brodie replied in his same measured tone. "Good evening, then."

I quickly sat back at the chair where I had been leaning to better hear their conversation as the door between the two offices suddenly opened and Brodie walked out.

"Miss Forsythe," he said with a look at the constable that might very well have been a warning not to interfere.

The young man nodded and resumed his stoic posture. Brodie slipped his hand beneath my arm, somewhat firmly, and escorted me from Abberline's office.

"Not a word," he whispered. "Or I swear that will leave ye here, and throw away the key."

We left police headquarters without interference, and in spite of the late hour Brodie was able to find a driver.

"Betard?" I asked.

"He knows and he's determined to leave the city in the morning."

I entered the cab. Brodie stepped in as well and we were off.

"Not a word," he'd repeated in a tight voice as he gave the driver the address of the office on the Strand.

When we were sufficiently on our way, I reached into the pocket of my skirt and retrieved the blood-stained envelope.

"What is this?" he demanded.

"This was in Marie Genesse's hand when I found her."

"Good God, woman!"

I handed him the envelope. "I do believe that I detect the scent of absinthe on that envelope."

· · ·

There have been times in our association when I thought Brodie might suffer an apoplectic fit or some other malady. This was certainly one of them as he paced across the office, the envelope in hand.

"Ye withheld evidence from the scene of a crime." He waved it at me.

"Not precisely."

His voice rose. "How not precisely?"

"It had not yet been established by the police that it was a crime," I pointed out. "As they had not yet arrived," I added, a bit of a stretch of the truth. "At the time, it might have been possible that Marie merely tripped and fell with it in her hand."

I crossed the office, stepped around an irate Scot—he really was quite handsome when he was in a temper— and went to the file cabinet.

I retrieved a bottle of my aunt's very fine whisky. "Will you be having a dram?" I asked.

I believe that was a snarl as he stalked over to the desk, seized his glass and held it out.

"Sir Avery was most interested in how you came to be arrested," he informed me.

"I will explain to him."

"He had a call, in the middle of the night from the Home Secretary, who had a call from her ladyship."

"I will send my apologies to the Home Secretary," I replied. "He's new to the office, I didn't realize that he and my aunt were acquainted."

He groaned, downed the whisky I had poured, then held out his glass for more. "Is there anyone who is not?" he demanded. "And then there is this!" He waved the envelope under my nose again.

We were back to that.

"Don't you think we should open it?" I suggested. "It was obviously left for whoever found Marie's body, someone with that unusual scent of absinthe. It's only that I happened to be the one who found her first."

"Just happened to be...?" There was a curse, he emptied the glass again, then slammed it down at the desk.

"Did it occur to ye that the murderer might still have been there, and might have...?"

"Might have what?" I asked, taking a healthy swallow from my own glass.

He shoved his hand back through that mass of thick dark hair that seemed to perpetually be in need of a trim. Although I quite liked it in waves, curling about his collar.

"That ye might have been in danger!" He was shouting now.

It wasn't the first time I had crossed paths with unsavory persons, and I did consider myself most capable of defending myself with that knife tucked into my boot, or other means if necessary.

He took hold of me then, the envelope temporarily forgotten, both hands at my upper arms as if he might shake me.

"I am quite capable," I reminded him as I managed to free one arm and attempted to pry his other hand away from my other arm.

"God knows, I'm aware what yer capable of!" he roared back, and it occurred to me that this might be something more than going off on my own.

"Why are you angry?" I asked.

He cursed again and suddenly let go of my other arm. He stalked away with another curse, his shoulders taut beneath the cloth of his shirt. Another curse and something else I couldn't make out.

"I may have found an important clue," I pointed out. "No one else has been hurt, except perhaps for Abberline's pride. We both know the man is incompetent."

He spun back around, and I took a step back or might have found my face buried at his chest, not that it was an unpleasant prospect.

I saw something in the expression at his face and those dark eyes that I had only glimpsed a time or two before.

"What is this about?" I again demanded.

"That ye might have been hurt or worse and I ..."

"What?"

Very definitely the possibility of apoplexy, I thought. Or possibly something in the office broken—the desk lamp or some other piece, as he was quite angry.

"... That I wasn't there to protect ye!" he finally blurted out, throwing both hands in the air.

Is that what this was about? Not the fact that I had taken the envelope, not that he had been forced to retrieve me from police headquarters.

I laid a hand at his arm.

"No one has ever said that to me before."

I thought my bones might break as he took my hand in his.

"I should have called before I went to the Metropole," I admitted. It truly was something I was trying to be better at in our work.

"Aye, ye should have," he whispered still holding onto my hand.

"However, I had no way of knowing what had happened until I was in the middle of it," I added. That dark gaze narrowed, and I quickly continued.

"I realize that I can sometimes be... headstrong and impatient..." I wasn't ignorant about my faults, and Brodie reminded me often enough.

"Aye, " he replied, his voice softening.

"And I probably shouldn't have made some of the comments that I made to Abberline. However, I attempted to explain the reason I was at the hotel. He refused to listen. The man is an ass." The expression at his face changed. One corner of his mouth lifted.

"Yer a rare one," he said then.

One minute I thought he might have a fit and fall in the

middle of it, then next he was kissing me. Not like others we'd shared. This was different, this was Brodie—fierce as his hands closed around my head, holding me so tight that I couldn't have escaped if I wanted to... I didn't.

"And I wouldna change a thing about ye, God help us both!" And then his mouth was on mine, his tongue thrusting between my lips, and I knew that in spite of the fact that I had been kissed before, I had never *really* been kissed.

To say that I was quite breathless when he finally let go, was an understatement.

"If ye ever do something like that again..." He paused and shook his head. We both knew that I probably would. However, I would call first.

"I do believe that I need another drink," I said then.

"Aye." He slowly let go of me.

"We need to see what is in that envelope."

As I had discovered, it smelled very much the same as the one sent to Betard—

with that faint scent of absinthe.

"Here." Brodie showed me the back of the envelope where the killer had tucked the flap inside and two smudged prints, very similar to the ones Mr. Brimley had retrieved from that glass box, the slightly smudged outline of one finger, those whorls and arches absent, and what appeared to be a stub of a much shorter finger. Brodie carefully opened the envelope, then removed the note inside.

*Then there were two.*

"Two?"

I looked up at him. "What does that mean— two more will die?"

I saw by his expression that our thoughts were the same.

Betard? Sophie? I told Brodie about my conversation with Lucy Penworth, and then Juliette Delon. There was something more, but I had no idea if it actually happened or if it meant anything.

"It's a feeling, nothing more."

"Tell me," he replied.

"Twice now, I've felt that someone might be following me. It could be nothing. The street was crowded."

"Perhaps, perhaps not," Brodie replied.

"Sophie needs to be told about Marie's death."

He nodded. "And Munro as well, to be safe. I'll go."

"I'm going with you."

"It's late, ye don't need too. The Mudger will be here if ye need anything, and there's the revolver in the desk."

I caught his meaning. I shook my head. "It might be easier if it comes from me. If she should have questions. After all I was there."

He touched my cheek. "Ye are a rare one, Mikaela Forsythe."

I called Templeton and briefly explained that something had happened, and we needed to see Sophie. Even though it was quite late, we would be arriving shortly.

My friend has been accused of being many things— vain, self-involved, even woefully untalented according to one scathing review. However I knew far better. She carefully chose her responses— Sophie was obviously in the parlor with her, then simply said, "Of course."

There were no questions that might have upset Sophie, no loud exclamations. Templeton was quite simply a friend helping someone. Of course there was Wills to consider. There was no mention of him.

Templeton's flat, very near the theater, was not far from the office on the Strand. We arrived and found Munro waiting outside her door.

"I have tea and coffee," Templeton said.

I would have preferred something stronger. However, this was not about me. It was about a young woman who had lost her sister to a brutal murder, and had now lost someone who had been very much like a mother to her.

There were tears, and then there were questions.

"Who is doing this?" she cried between bouts of tears. I exchanged a look with Brodie as I translated for them both.

"We will find the answers," he replied, gently holding her hand.

How many times had he done this when tragedy had befallen someone, and how many times had he been just as gentle with me?

"The danger is still there," he explained. "For that reason, ye must remain here for yer own safety."

I translated once more for her.

"Jean Luc?" she asked.

"Aye, he knows," Brodie replied. "It's his intention to leave in the morning ... after arrangements are made."

She nodded again as I translated once more. *"Alors je partirai avec lui. Ma place est avec, Jean Luc."*

"Then, she will leave with him," I told Brodie. "She feels that her place is with him."

"Try to make her understand how dangerous that could be," Brodie responded. "That it's much better if she remains here where we can protect her."

There was no persuading her. She was determined to return to the hotel. Munro agreed to escort her there, and he would remain at the hotel until their departure in the morning.

I returned to the office on the Strand with Brodie. I was both angry and sad. I felt helpless and terrified for her at the same time.

Brodie sat at the edge of the desk. He poured us both a drink of my aunt's very fine whisky.

He reached out and brushed the hair back from my cheek. "The decision was hers to make, lass."

"I know," I replied. "It's just that..."

"Ye want to protect her. I understand, not unlike yer sister."

It was sometimes frightening how well he understood me.

We had told Sophie about the second note and that message. There was no dissuading her.

"The best we can do now is to find who is doing this. That is the best way to protect her."

I nodded and took another sip of whisky. It warmed my stomach and helped ease that too familiar hollow feeling. He took the empty glass from me.

"Ye're tired and it's verra late. Stay here tonight. There's some of that soap that ye seemed to like and a brush in the drawer at the washstand."

Soap? And a hairbrush? Not, 'would I like to stay the night', or some argument that it was late, there were no cabs available at near one o'clock in the morning... just that simple the way things had changed between us. I nodded.

"And ye won't need to go down the hallway to use the accommodation," he added then, tossing back the last of the whisky at his own glass.

Most women received flowers or boxes of chocolates from a man. I received soap and a hairbrush. I wouldn't have traded either for flowers or chocolate. Well, perhaps chocolate.

"Will you be working late?" I asked.

He looked over at me. "Not so very late."

I nodded, then turned to the bedroom.

I found the soap—lavender of all things. Who would ever have guessed that Angus Brodie would be aware of something like that? I then found the hairbrush, still wrapped in paper from the shop where he'd purchased it.

I unpinned my hair. The bristles were soft, yet strong enough for my thick hair. Then I removed my skirt and shirtwaist and slipped under the bedcovers.

With everything that had happened, I was restless. I rearranged the covers, then the pillow, then the bedcovers again.

What sort of man purchased lavender soap and a woman's hairbrush?

But I knew.

It might have been the creak of the floorboards I heard, or the coffee pot as Brodie set it at the grate for the morning in his usual way. Then, the office was quiet once more, and he was there, faintly outlined at the doorway in the light from the streetlamp that spilled into the outer office.

"Are ye all right then, lass?"

Lass. I was far beyond that in years, but there was something in the sound of his voice, that faint Scot's accent, the gentle sound of it there in the shadows, and Brodie.

There were so many reasons... And none of them mattered. Then he turned, perhaps thinking that I was asleep after all.

"Don't go..."

I heard the whisper of clothes as he removed them, then the dip at the edge of the bed. He slipped an arm around me and pulled me against him.

No wound this time that needed care... perhaps only an old wound inside that would most probably never go away. But Brodie was there, his hands slow and gentle, my own less so, impatient as my fingers brushed his flat stomach and I felt that silk of dark hair there.

He brushed the hair back from my cheek. "Are ye certain?"

What man would ask? Only one man that I knew.

I slipped my hand behind his neck, my fingers curling in that thick dark hair as he slowly untied the ribbons at my chemise.

# Eleven

I'M certain there are guidelines for the 'morning after the night before', but I had no idea what those might be.

It was a new experience for me—not covered in any of my notebooks, or one of my novels. Well, perhaps one of them when my erstwhile heroine went adventuring on the Isle of Crete with *her* travel guide.

However, that was different. This was Brodie.

As I reached for my boots, I looked at my toes as I finished dressing. They appeared to be quite themselves this morning. However, last night...

I laced my boots and pinned up my hair.

Brodie, as I had previously learned was his habit, rose earlier. I heard him moving about in the outer office as I glanced back over my shoulder at the bed.

Damn the torpedoes, I once read, full speed ahead.

"Good mornin'," he said, looking over from the coal stove as I entered the office.

He handed me a cup of coffee, that dark gaze filled with questions which thankfully at the moment, he did not ask.

"Good morning," I replied, taking the cup and my first sip, and tasted that hint of my aunt's very fine whisky.

"Are ye all right, then?"

"Quite all right." I replied.

"Mikaela..."

There it was, the sound of my name, low, that look in those dark eyes...

"I've been thinking," I said before he could finish the thought and take the conversation in a direction I wasn't yet prepared to go.

"Have ye, now?"

I took another long swallow of coffee.

"We need to find out what Mr. Brimley may have been able to learn from the photographs he took of those prints with his box camera."

I averted my eyes as he watched me.

"There could be something important there," I added.

"Aye, something important."

I had the distinct impression we might not be talking about the same thing. As I said—*guidelines*. I seemed to be at a loss for those with Brodie, and not the first time. I held my breath as he set his cup at the desk, and I am not one to hold my breath.

"Munro sent a message round this morning." He gestured to a note at the desk.

"Sophie Dupres left with Betard first thing."

"Oh dear." I slowly let out my breath.

Whatever he had been about to say it had been pushed back for the time being—something no doubt about foolish mistakes, too much drink, although there wasn't, and things that needed to be said.

As I said, full speed ahead.

"Then, we need to meet with Mr. Brimley as soon as possible. Perhaps those prints will tell us something now." I went to the coat stand and retrieved my jacket.

"Right fine mornin'," Mr. Cavendish greeted us with a grin as we waited for a cab. "Wouldn't you say, miss?"

He seemed particularly jovial this morning. There was something definitely different about that grin.

"Yes, thank you, Mr. Cavendish," I replied, leaning down to give the hound a scratch behind the ears.

Mr. Cavendish handed me a copy of the morning paper. "I found this just down the way and thought of ye."

Down the way? Very likely lifted from someone's pocket.

"May I say that you look very fine this mornin', miss, with yer color up..." He paused with a look over at Brodie, then cleared his throat.

"Must be the weather after the long winter," he added as a driver arrived. I looked over at Brodie as we settled ourselves in the cab.

"I wonder what that was about," I commented.

"It might have been a late night at the pub," he suggested as we set off.

"Do come along," Mr. Brimley greeted us as we arrived at his shop in Holborn. Sara greeted us as well.

"I say, miss. You look real pretty this mornin'," she told me as we entered the shop.

I thanked her, taken back once again. I did hope that I wasn't coming down with some illness, although I have always enjoyed good health.

"Come along, Miss Forsythe," Brodie said with some amusement in those dark eyes as he escorted me through the shop to Mr. Brimley's work area.

"Most interesting," Mr. Brimley said as he led us back to that tiny, cramped room where he had a desk. He closed the door behind us, plunging the room into darkness. He then switched on the electric, a new addition to this part of the shop.

"This way if you please."

We followed him into the small adjoining storeroom where I had spent some time on that narrow cot as he had removed a bullet from my shoulder. I had recovered quite well with his care. And Brodie's, of course.

This room now had electric as well. The cot had been folded against one wall while several shallow basins sat at a table at the opposite wall.

"I set up my processing room here as there are no windows that might let in unnecessary light," Mr. Brimley explained. "I used a gelatin dry plate, then washed the film in silver nitrate. This is what we have." He showed us a series of photographic prints that he'd laid out at the counter.

The entire process really was quite remarkable. That simple little box camera, a roll of celluloid film, and now photographs. He handed me a magnifying glass and I bent closer to inspect the photos.

Unfortunately the prints revealed exactly the same thing we had seen for ourselves when we inspected that glass box where Francoise had been murdered.

The outline of three distinct prints were there in the photographs, however just as the actual fingerprints we had seen were void of any distinguishing marks, the photographs were exactly the same. I had hoped the photos would reveal something that might tell us something about who the prints belonged too.

"The images are most clear," Brodie commented. He exchange a look with Mr. Brimley. "What would you say might cause the usual marks to disappear?"

"It would seem that there might have been an injury, the one finger possibly maimed. There are chemicals that do that, or it might have been an injury from a fire."

Lucy Penworth had found an old article about an accident early in Betard's career. Was it possible that Betard was injured in an illusion that went horribly wrong?

He had worn gloves the night of the performance, and again when we first met. Was he hiding something? But even so, all that it meant was that his prints were on the glass box, as might be expected for the performance of the illusion.

Lucy Penworth was waiting for us when we arrived back at the office on the Strand. She was crouched down at the sidewalk, the hound at her feet like a docile puppy, of all things, as she scratched his head. He had flattened himself to the sidewalk with great soulful eyes and a grin. Fickle beast.

"Here you are," she said with that infectious smile and all those delightful freckles.

"I thought to come by rather than have you come to the Times office," she explained as she stood and greeted us both.

"Alan Ivers would be unlikely to know I came here straight away from my flat," she added conspiratorially.

She handed Brodie a note. "Mr. Sinclair asked me to have you ring him up this morning," she told him. "Something about a shipment. It's in the note."

A shipment? That was odd, yet it confirmed my suspicions that he might be working in some manner for Sir Avery with the Special Services.

"Oh, I say, Miss Forsythe. Catch a bit of the sun, did you? You look quite aglow this morning. I merely burn and then peel."

Glow? Another remark about my appearance. I caught something in Brodie's expression and chose to ignore it.

"I found something that might be helpful in your case with Betard," she continued and accompanied me as I headed for the stairs and the office where we might have more privacy, in the off chance that Alan Ivers might be lurking about.

I took a quick look at myself in the mirror beside the coat rack, and frowned. I didn't notice anything different. Glow, indeed. If one more person mentioned anything about my appearance...

I joined Lucy at the small table that had been added to the new furnishings at the office, as Brodie went to the desk to place his call to Alex Sinclair. Most interesting.

"I returned to the archive last evening and searched under the name of Maximillian Holt," Lucy was explaining as I brought my thoughts back to the situation at hand.

"I didn't find anything at first, so I then searched under his professional name, the Great Maxim." She took a note she'd made from her carpetbag. She handed it to me.

"He was quite famous at one time and toured extensively. It seems that he was the first to use disappearing smoke in his performances, quite unique at the time. There was an article that mentioned an assistant that he had taken on, an aspiring young man."

"Betard?" I asked.

"There was no name mentioned, but it did say that the young man was quite brilliant. That would have been about the time that Betard left France. I then found this." She pulled a copy of a daily from her bag.

"This is from less than two months ago, in the paper's 'News About the City'. Holt is still performing, most recently at the old Olympic Theater in Drury Lane."

Somewhat of a set-down from his earlier successes when he had performed at the Adelphi and other London theaters, as well as touring extensively. But there was something else about the article—a photograph, those incredible wonders of the modern world, taken at the time.

I recognized him! He was the man I had seen leaving the amphitheater at the Crystal Palace just as Betard's new illusion was about to begin!

"Wonderful!" I exclaimed.

"This is helpful to the case, then?"

"It could be," I gave her a squeeze about the shoulders. "I don't suppose we know what his performance schedule might be?"

She grinned. "As a matter of fact, he's performing each evening over the next month each evening as the leading act at the theater."

And yet, he'd managed to attend Betard's performance, or at least part of it, that night at the Crystal Palace. Interesting.

It might be useful to speak with the Great Maxim. The

Olympic Theater was in Westminster, I thought as Brodie concluded his telephone call with Alex Sinclair. There was a look in our direction.

That dark gaze met mine, then looked away. "I agree, best to proceed with caution," he replied to a question that was asked. Then the telephone call ended.

"I need to meet with Alex on a matter." That dark gaze fastened on me once more, as if there might have been something he wanted to say then thought better of it.

"I'll be attending the theater tonight," I told him. "Perhaps the Great Maxim can provide information about Betard that might be useful." And in the meantime, I wanted to speak with Mr. Alamy again about that disappearing smoke illusion.

Brodie eventually nodded. "I don't know how long I'll be gone."

"That's quite all right," I assured him, although I very much would have liked to have known what he was meeting Alex Sinclair about.

Since I hadn't yet eaten that morning, I asked Lucy to accompany me to the public house just down the way after he had gone.

Miss Effie greeted us with a huge smile. "I've meat pies today, miss. Fresh out of the oven, and a pint if you like."

I discovered that Lucy and I shared something else in addition to what Brodie would have called my backward thinking ways— namely my independence. Lucy Penworthy also had a healthy appetite.

"Alex says I have to go to work for the Service, otherwise he won't be able to afford to feed me," she commented, then caught herself. "That is on the occasions that I see him."

Of course, I thought with a smile to myself. It seemed that their 'acquaintance' had advanced somewhat.

She seemed quite pleased in spite of speaking out about it. Bright color appeared at her cheeks. It must be that sun she was speaking of earlier.

We returned to the Strand where I delivered an extra meat pie to the Mudger along with food left by customers from earlier in the morning that Miss Effie provided for the hound.

I inquired if Brodie might have returned. He had not. Just as well. I was not yet ready to discuss the night before.

"You are quite fickle," I told the hound as he launched into the food with a great deal of enthusiasm and quite noisily, I might add.

Lucy departed to return to the Times newspaper office, while I waited for a cab to take me to Mr. Alamy's Magicks Shoppe.

Having been there previously, I was prepared for the oddities to be found in the shop that included the proprietor who barely reached to the top of his counter. However, today he seemed to have gained a few inches as he concluded a transaction to a lanky young boy who tucked that 'magic' hat under his arm and turned with a grin.

Another budding magician in the making perhaps?

"Miss Forsythe!" he greeted me enthusiastically. "I thought you might return."

"I have some additional questions if you have the time."

He grinned as he took a jar that looked as if it might contain dead frogs and returned it to the shelf behind him. He and Mr. Brimley would get along famously I thought.

I stared, not my usual habit, as he then came from behind the counter, much the same height as the day before. I wondered what might have made the transformation as I leaned over the counter and saw the narrow platform that ran along the base of the counter at the floor.

Mr. Alamy grinned. "A bit of assistance, for when customers might argue over the cost of an item. Join me for a spot of tea, Miss Forsythe." He led the way to a table tucked amid the displays in the front of the shop.

"Your question?"

"How might someone disappear in full view of an audience?" I asked as he poured, and I kept a watchful eye for any of his occupants that might move about.

The tea, not usually my choice, was quite wonderful. I tasted vanilla and lavender of all things, and wondered if there might be a little something else as he smiled quite mysteriously at me.

Mr. Alamy sat back, fingers steepled before him as he seemed to contemplate both the question and myself.

"Illusionist, that many chose to call themselves instead of magician, comes from the word, 'illusion', what the mind sees or..."

I listened and waited. That smile as I caught a movement out the corner of my eyes. But when I looked, the falcon I had seen the time before, sat perfectly motionless at its perch.

"Or, what the mind believes that it sees."

"Please explain."

That smile again. "The most accomplished illusionists will make you think that you've seen something while something else has occurred."

"A diversion?"

"You may call it that. It's all part of the illusionist's skill. He holds your attention with one hand while executing the illusion with the other." He then demonstrated what he was talking about, as he began to tell a story.

He took a marble from his pocket. It was dark blue and made of glass.

"A boy was given the marble by his father. He was told that it was a magic marble," he continued. "He put it in his pocket so that it would be safe." With great dramatic flair he wrapped his fingers around the marble.

"But he lost the marble." He opened his hand, and the marble was gone.

"I suppose you're going to pluck it from behind my ear," I commented. He smiled.

"Not at all, Miss Forsythe. The truth of the matter is that the marble never disappeared at all."

He opened his fingers once more and displayed the marble.

"Sleight of hand?" I replied, a common magic trick. Now you

see it, now you don't. "The marble was hidden up the sleeve of your shirt."

"Was it? Once more, then." He went through the same rapid motions as before, showing his empty hand as he proceeded to tell me of other disappearing illusions. Then he extended his hand and opened it. It was empty.

He then reached across the table. This time he did appear to pluck the marble from behind my ear with his other hand and I would have sworn that I never saw him switch it from one hand to the other.

"You must be more careful, Miss Forsythe or you might lose the marble."

As it turned out he hadn't switched the one to his other hand at all as he then extended both hands, each with a marble, exactly alike.

"What other means are there that a person might disappear?" I asked.

"There are several ways. I would be giving away secrets," he grinned. "But since they are not my secrets..." He settled himself back in the chair.

"A trap door in the floor of a stage has been used behind a curtain or screen; possibly the use of mirrors as with the illusion at the Crystal Palace, compartments within compartments, a false door in a box, the way you escaped, my dear."

"What chemicals are used in the making of disappearing powder?" I was curious about that illusion that he had created on my earlier visit.

His eyes twinkled. "There are powders when mixed that have the ability to create a cloud of smoke allowing one to simply 'disappear'. They are found in any chemist's shop."

I thought of Mr. Brimley.

"Potassium nitrate, sodium carbonate, and sugar," he explained. "It is also possible to add a particular color of dye to the mixture in a glass tube. Then, when shattered the mixture will ignite in a cloud of colorful smoke and when the smoke clears..."

And when the smoke had cleared, Mr. Alamy had already taken himself off and disappeared for all intents and purposes, and then reappeared.

Smoke and screens. Deception.

"Of course there are some who use gunpowder with an accelerant," he continued. "It can be quite dangerous for the one performing the illusion and for those watching."

It was quite late of the afternoon when I left Mr. Alamy's shop. I knew more about how disappearing illusions might have been created than before. However, that still didn't tell me who had killed Francoise.

After leaving his shop I returned to my townhouse in Mayfair. I placed a call to Templeton and invited her to join me to see the Great Maxim's performance at the Olympic. She begged off and I wondered about that earlier comment about keeping company with another man.

I showered at the bathroom next to the bedroom in that wonderful new invention, then returned to the front parlor afterward to make my notes about what I had learned from Mr. Alamy.

My housekeeper, Alice, hovered near. "Your sister called this morning. She wants you to return her call. The mail is on the corner of your desk. I believe there is a piece from your publisher, and I have a roast chicken in the oven for your supper..."

There was that expectant silence that often followed her part of the conversation.

"How is Mr. Brodie?" she asked when I didn't immediately respond, her way of asking—but not asking—where I might have passed the night.

"Mr. Brodie and I worked late into the night," I replied. That was almost true as far as it went, and as much of a response as I was going to provide.

I dearly loved Alice, however there were things that weren't up for conversation. In fact, I hardly know what the conversation would have been—*Oh, and by the way Brodie and I...* As I said—not open to discussion.

"I see."

The way Alice said it, I suspected that she did in fact 'see' perfectly well.

"Supper will be ready in half an hour, then. Will Mr. Brodie be joining you?" she asked.

"No, he is meeting with people on another matter."

Supper was quite delicious. I complimented Alice and then dressed. I had the driver go by the office on the Strand.

Mr. Cavendish informed me that Brodie had still not returned. Whatever he was about with Alex Sinclair, appeared to be quite serious.

"Do you want to leave a message for him?"

"No. It's not necessary."

I caught a sound from the hound, the sort of sound that is usually a request for food.

"What are you looking at?" I asked. Not that I expected an answer.

"Mr. Brodie won't like you going off on your own," Mr. Cavendish reminded me.

"It's regarding our case, and Mr. Brodie isn't available." I softened my tone. "It's quite all right. I'm going to the theater."

Mr. Cavendish made a disapproving sound. "By yourself, miss?"

"By myself." I gave the driver the location of the Olympic Theater at Drury Lane and we set off.

I had sent a note round to the theater earlier, but I had no way of knowing if Mr. Holt had received it. Arriving at the theater, I paid my four pence and entered the Olympic.

I had asked the theater attendant to deliver a note to Maximillian Holt after his performance of the evening, then climbed the stairs to the gallery.

Over the years the Olympic had become the setting for comedy performances and burlesques. It appeared from the playbill at the sidewalk display outside the theater that the Great Maxim was an opening act for the evening's other performance.

I took my seat in the gallery just as the theater lights dimmed and the stage lights came up. The orchestra then played the opening overture as the curtain rose. The Great Maxim appeared in formal coat and tails, and the performance began.

He performed several magic tricks and illusions, first a white dove seemingly plucked from the air then sent off to fly over the audience. Next he sent crystal balls into the air above the stage, one by one, then and had them circle overhead to the accompaniment of the orchestra. A young woman joined him for his final presentation.

He had her lay at a platform that was wheeled onto the stage. He then removed the wheeled table out from under her, the young woman appearing to be suspended in mid-air. He indicated that there were not wires or ropes above or below supporting her.

The illusion concluded as he slowly turned her, then with a flourish he had her stand once more, and held out his hand to her, indicating that she was in fact real and not some theater prop or image recreated on the stage as she bowed to the audience.

Most of the audience remained as Holt and his assistant left the stage. I returned to the foyer. My message had been delivered to the Great Maxim.

With a little persuasion in the form of a half crown, he directed me to the dressing rooms at the back of the theater and behind the stage where larger props could be brought in through an alley at the back of the building.

The dressing rooms here were much the same as those at the Adelphi when I visited Templeton after a performance. A stage worker directed me to Holt's room where I found my note tacked to the door. I knocked.

There was no answer at first. I knocked again.

"*Do come in,*" a very pleasant voice came from inside the dressing room.

The dressing room was much the same as Templeton's at the

Adelphi. There was a dressing table with several small lights that encircled an enormous mirror. The dressing table itself contained jars of what appeared to be make-up—somewhat surprising for a man.

The rest of the room was dimly lit with a screen at one corner and a rack nearby with several costumes. It appeared that the Great Maxim might share the dressing room with someone, his assistant perhaps.

Most curious, a phonograph with a brass cylinder sat atop a wardrobe chest. My aunt had one, an enormous box invention, that played recordings made on the cylinder. A large speaker horn filled the house at Sussex Square with her favorite music—recorded at music halls, the raucous sound bouncing off the walls. That may have been what drove the monkey from the jungle.

My aunt's phonograph worked off electricity. This one, however, did not seem to be wired into the electric. Possibly batteries, I thought, much like the hand-held lamps the police used.

It appeared that Holt had not yet returned, when I caught a movement from the shadows opposite the door. A thin, lanky figure dressed in evening attire stirred. Startled, I took a step back as an overhead light came on and that figure seemed to emerge from the shadows.

"Good evening," that lanky figure greeted me, cocking his head so that the light fell across his features. The Great Maxim?

"So good of you to join me," he continued. "Please be seated." He gestured toward the table.

"It is so kind of you to visit me."

It was then I noticed that the cylinder at the phonograph was turning, the sound seeming to come from that enormous horn. It was playing a recording? Not music but what seemed to be a voice recording.

"Good evening," I greeted the figure before me with growing suspicion, approaching closer as he didn't make any attempt to step further into the room.

"A very interesting performance," I added as he stood motionless in front of me.

"A lovely evening," he then said.

"Lovely indeed for an illusion," I commented.

"You have discovered my secret," this came from the door behind me. I turned and greeted the man who stood there in full dress suit and tails that he had performed in earlier.

"Good evening," I greeted the real Maximillian Holt. I indicated the lanky figure who stood in those shadows, a perfect replica of the Great Maxim.

Holt chuckled. "He is most effective when I perform on the street. The children are quite fascinated, most particularly when he moves."

As my note had still been tacked to the door of his dressing room, I was quite surprised that he knew my name. He had obviously retrieved it when he returned.

"Please, do sit down, Miss Forsythe," he gestured to an upholstered chair. "Forgive me as I remove the stage make-up, but please tell me what has brought you to the Olympic Theater this evening."

He sat at that dressing table, opened a jar, and liberally applied a cream to his face, much as I had seen Templeton dozens of times.

"Jean Luc Betard's performance at the Crystal Palace," I replied and saw his hand hesitate as he grabbed for a towel. "You were there that evening."

"Ah, yes." He proceeded to wipe the cream and the layer of thick make-up from his face, his own features emerging—that pale blue gaze, the hawklike nose, and the lines at his face revealing a man much older than the audience saw that evening.

"A most unfortunate situation."

"You left before his final illusion."

"That poor young woman's death..." He glanced up at me, reflected at the mirror before him. "So very sad. I read about it in the daily paper. And I have read about you as well, Miss Forsythe, that dreadful business about your own sister, those children... Most dreadful. But what brings you here?"

"You have had a most successful career creating illusions," I replied. "Betard once performed with you."

That glance up again at me. He swung around on the stool before that dressing table.

"And you want to know what I can tell you about him. You are investigating the young woman's death?"

"Betard has asked us to learn what we can." I didn't bother to explain that there had been another death.

The phonograph clicked off and the replica of Holt in the corner stood motionless once more. A trick for children on the street as he explained? Or did he know I was there all along, and it was meant to frighten me? I did not frighten easily.

Holt smiled, the expression familiar from his performance earlier. Another performance?

"That was a very long time ago," he finally spoke.

"I know that he performed on the streets of Paris for some time, perfecting his act before immigrating to London."

He nodded. "That was over fifteen years ago. And, as you witnessed at that performance at the Crystal Palace, he has achieved great success."

"Success that might now be in jeopardy with the events of that evening," I pointed out. "There seems to have been an event that brought him to London."

"He spoke of the political unrest. He was a young man then and felt that he could not achieve success in a place with so much turmoil. He arranged to meet me here in London."

"Yet he returned to France from time to time," I replied with what Lucy had learned.

"I believe his mother was still there, though not well. And there were other reasons, he never spoke of."

"He found success here," I said the obvious. "Was there anyone in France whom he worked with as an apprentice perhaps?"

"Apprentice is such an... odd word," he replied. "Thief is perhaps a better description."

Thief? That was certainly revealing, along with definite animosity. Was he saying that Betard had stolen some of his illusions for his own?

"I understand that illusionists guard the secrets of their work," I said then, in an attempt to learn more.

I saw something change in Holt's demeanor, the lines deeper as he frowned, his voice suddenly cold.

"There is a great deal of competition. The one who brings a new illusion to the stage will reap the benefits," he explained. "But it has been known to be dangerous. Careers have been ruined. You might ask Betard about that," he snapped.

It appeared that Betard had indeed learned a great deal in his time with the Great Maxim, and had then surpassed him in recognition and reputation.

I caught the change in his voice at that last comment. Was he perhaps thinking of his own career and the assistant who had outshone the master?

"What about the final illusion that he presented that night?" I then asked. "A new illusion that he had created. Is it possible there was professional jealousy over that?"

"The girl in the glass box," he commented in an almost dreamlike voice. "Her death, most unfortunate." He spoke, almost as if he had gone away, then slowly returned.

"A brilliant illusion that ultimately failed," Holt replied. "Most unfortunate for him."

I didn't agree that the illusion had failed. Someone had obviously intervened so that it would fail. Unfortunate? Yes, for Francoise. Was he implying something more? Might he have had something to do with that failure?

Most assuredly professional jealousy might be a reason. But after all these years? And how would he have done it?

It was then the mannequin that resembled Holt came back to life as if by... Magic perhaps? He straightened and nodded in my direction—activated by some mechanism that Holt controlled?

"So good of you to come by," the mannequin commented, its voice almost identical to Holt's.

In full light now from the overhead electric Holt had turned on when he returned to the room, the resemblance between the two was quite uncanny and very unsettling.

That was obviously my cue to depart.

I thanked the Great Maxim for his time. In spite of whatever animosity he bore Betard, or possibly because of it, I had learned two things.

Holt considered his protégée to be quite talented. At the same time he resented his success that had very likely brought about the end of his own, reducing Holt to being the opening act to a vaudeville performance in a small theater at Drury Lane and street performances for pennies.

It seemed quite obvious that there might have been a less than amicable parting between them. Quite obvious in things that were said as well as that early departure from Betard's performance at the Crystal Palace.

The main act for the evening had not yet ended and those who had attended had not yet departed. The street was almost empty as cabs and hacks waiting for a fare had not yet arrived.

The evening had quite a chill and I had worn only the jacket. I walked toward the corner. The fact that it was May was deceptive. Mist wrapped around streetlamps as it rolled in from the river creating its own illusion, hiding those who walked past until they brushed against my shoulder.

I didn't see him at first, a man slightly bent against the cold of the night, dressed most unusual for this part of London, and I thought of Mr. Holt.

It wasn't him, of course, but someone else with that vague familiarity that moves across the senses not quite clear, and then suddenly it was.

Quite handsome, beneath the rim of his silk hat, features illuminated by the streetlamp, as a gloved hand reached for me and there was the oddest sensation, much the same as when the mannequin had bowed in the shadows of the dressing room, the man's face suddenly visible. And with that odd similarity came the scent of absinthe.

That gloved hand closed around my forearm with surprising strength. The startling combination of his appearance, the hollow eyes, and that scent caught me by surprise.

I struggled to retrieve the knife at my pocket.

"Mikaela?" the sound of my name, came not from my attacker but from the street behind me.

I was thrown against the side of a shop as my attacker thrust me away from him. And then, just as suddenly... he was gone.

"Mikaela!"

It was Brodie!

"Are ye all right?"

Surprisingly, I was, after something that could have ended badly. But there was something in my attacker's manner in those few moments, something in his hand at my arm and the look in those bleak eyes.

He could have hurt me, but chose not to. I looked down at the now empty sidewalk as I tried to make some sense of what had just happened.

"Are ye hurt?" Brodie demanded.

"No. What are you doing here?"

"The Mudger overheard the instructions ye gave the driver," Brodie explained.

When we reached the office, he poured both of us a dram of whisky. That dark gaze watched me as I emptied my glass and held it out for another.

"What happened?"

Not the usual scolding about going off on my own that I fully expected. I frowned as the whisky warmed its way into my stomach and told him what I had learned about Maximillian Holt, and then that strange encounter outside the theater.

"Betard returned frequently to Paris the first few years, then not at all in later years," I explained. "Holt thought it was because of family."

He listened. There was the usual frown, but he still said nothing, which was more aggravating than his usual comments. I went on to describe my impression of the man in formal dinner attire I had encountered, that sense of familiarity, the impression that it was like looking at a mask. Brodie splashed more whisky into both glasses.

"Absinthe," I commented.

"Are ye certain?"

"I'm certain."

He nodded as he leaned back at the edge of the desk, that frown encircled by that dark beard, arms crossed, glass in hand as I had seen a hundred times.

"It's no accident, or coincidence."

I knew that he was right.

"What do you want to do now?" he asked, a simple question filled with possibilities, not the least was a conversation about the night before. But not now.

There were too many questions about what happened the night Francoise was killed, about Betard, about what I had learned from Holt. I couldn't dismiss the fact that there had to be answers. I just had to find them. I had learned that from Brodie. However, they weren't here, at least not the ones that connected all of this.

And now, he asked what did I want to do?

"Paris," I replied, and expected the argument to come now. That dark gaze narrowed.

"Paris? Do ye realize what ye're saying? What do ye hope to find there?"

"Something that may tell us who is doing this... *'Now there are two?'*" I repeated the message in that last note.

"Francoise and Marie are both dead. The note said, *Now there are two.* It's very possible that note meant Sophie and Betard might be next. If I've learned one thing in speaking with Holt and with Mr. Alamy, the secret of illusions is guarded with one's life. What if it's someone Betard stole an illusion from?"

"Revenge?" Brodie replied.

I saw by the expression at his face that he believed I might be right.

"As you've told me, a killer will strike again," I reminded him.

The frown softened. "I've taught ye too well for yer own good."

"I've always been a good student."

He made a familiar sound then, a curse under his breath as he continued to watch me.

"And it wouldn't do any good to tell ye no," he said then. "I've learned a few things as well." He swirled the last of his whisky at his glass.

"There's no boat from Dover in the middle of the night," he commented.

"No, there's not." I knew well enough from my school years in France.

"Ye'll be wantin' to leave first thing then in the mornin'."

"If we take the first mail packet from Dover we can catch the train from Calais," I pointed out.

That dark gaze.

"It's late."

I didn't wait for him to suggest that I stay the night so that we could make that early departure as I set my empty glass at the desk.

"Yes, it is," I replied, then went into the bedroom. I left the door open.

There were other questions, but they would have to wait as I listened to the now familiar sounds as he set the lock at the office door, the switch at the desk lamp, then the click as he closed the bedroom door.

He slowly undressed me, loosening the buttons at my skirt, then just as slowly unbuttoned my shirtwaist, that dark look at his eyes in the light from the bedside lamp reaching inside me as he lightly brushed his fingers across the scar at my shoulder. Then, he slowly pulled the pins from my hair.

"Brodie..."

His mouth brushed mine, his beard soft beneath my fingers.

"Aye, lass," he whispered and that was all that mattered.

# Twelve

WE CAUGHT the early morning train from Charing Cross in time to make the first cross-channel ferry from Dover. With a smooth crossing, we arrived in Calais in less than two hours and boarded the next train to Paris.

It had changed since my last travel there. There were new buildings and others that had been rebuilt after fires set by the Paris Commune years before.

I had seen some of that construction, while attending private school, that included the Eiffel Tower, the Paris metro, and the completion of the new Paris Opera house. The exposition the year before had brought millions of people to the city as it transformed itself once more.

There were still signs of unrest at the rail station. The streets surrounding it were filled with groups of workers demonstrating against poor wages even that late in the day. Police surrounded them, while pickpockets took advantage of the unsuspecting person on the street.

I had read about the first May Day celebration organized by the socialist party. It was an unauthorized celebration and just weeks earlier had led to confrontations between the police and demonstrators. More change in this modern era.

As far as Brodie was concerned, it didn't seem to matter whether it was the streets of Edinburgh as a youth, London, or Paris. It was dangerous—the smoke from fires, the surge of crowds that had gathered, the air was charged with it, and that watchfulness that I had seen countless times was there as we secured a *fiacre,* the small horse drawn coach, to take us to the hotel.

It was just after seven o'clock of the evening as the driver made our way to *Relais Hotel du Vieux,* where I had stayed on my last travel to the continent, very near Notre Dame and the Sorbonne. The Eiffel Tower, with construction complete, was now lit up with electric lights in the distance.

I had directed our driver in French, however here at the hotel, more accustomed to foreign travelers after the Exhibition the year before, that was not needed. I signed the hotel registry and Brodie requested the use of the hotel accommodation to make a telephone call.

He had made two calls before our departure that morning, one a lengthy conversation with Sir Avery, the second, much shorter one, with Mr. Munro, asking him to continue his watch over Sophie and Betard now that they had returned to Betard's residence.

I continued to the room with those thick plaster walls and dark-beamed ceilings. There was little to unpack as I had only my carpetbag with my notebook. There was not time to return to the townhouse for more as this trip was most urgent.

As with many hotels who catered to tourist travel, wine and a platter of fruit and cheese was brought to the room. I had not eaten since early morning and fixed a plate and poured a glass of wine. I was on my second serving of fruit when Brodie finally arrived. I poured the second glass and handed it to him.

He quickly emptied the glass, and I poured him another. It wasn't my aunt's very fine whisky, however it would do. I waited as he took off his coat and emptied the glass.

"There's a man we need to see," he explained as he loosened

the tie at his neck. "Someone Sir Avery knows here. He spoke with him earlier."

Most interesting, I thought. It seemed that Sir Avery knew a great many people in other places. And Brodie as well? I wondered, thinking of that conversation I had overheard the day before about a shipment. A shipment of what remained to be seen as he had chosen not to discuss it with me, even on that long train trip from Calais.

"He may have some information for us by the morning. We're to meet him at the entrance to the museum..."

"The Louvre?"

He nodded. "Aye." He handed me the note he'd made with the name, Julian Lefevre.

I knew the museum well. During our school years, Linnie had spent hundreds of hours there and I was her somewhat reluctant companion. It was a magnificent place with paintings and sculptures from throughout Europe and beyond, and she had studied the works of Monet, da Vinci, and Degas.

As impressive as those works were, I chose to explore Paris itself, which was considered somewhat dangerous for a young English student. However, I had several friends who explored with me. That had undoubtedly planted the seeds for my further adventures.

"Ye best get some sleep," he added.

We had taken the only room available with tourist season well underway, the accommodation limited to a single bed.

"And you?" I asked. He'd had no more sleep than I had.

"I'll be along. I want to study the map of the city the clerk at the desk provided."

Brodie—cautious, thorough in a city he was not familiar with.

I undressed and slipped beneath the bedcover, and thought of the reason we were there.

What would we find? What might we be able to learn about Betard before his success? Before he arrived in London, and made those trips back here? Anything? Nothing? A fool's errand?

There was only the faint glow of light from the window as I wakened. Brodie slipped under the cover and found me.

"I could have managed quite well on my own," I whispered. I knew he didn't believe, as I did, that we might find anything that would help with our case. "You didn't have to accompany me."

He stroked my back as he pulled me to him. "Aye, I did."

We both spent a restless night—a strange place, a strange city that had never seemed strange to me before, his hand at my waist, my hand at his shoulder, and finding sleep once more.

I splashed water on my face, brushed my teeth, then dressed and it struck me that, in spite of the reason we were there, I felt at peace, as if everything... as if *I* was right where I was supposed to be.

Brodie had already dressed while I had admired those long legs, muscular shoulders, and the dark hair at his chest with the memory of them pressed against me.

We were to meet Monsieur Lefevre at ten o'clock which gave just enough time to catch breakfast at the café next to the hotel. I grabbed my jacket and carpetbag.

"Mikaela...?"

On occasion it was still *Miss Forsythe*, usually when he was determined to make a point, more recently it was *lass* which I liked the sound of. Only rarely was it my given name and a faint little warning went off in my head.

His hand was at my wrist, something far different at that dark gaze that I had only glimpsed once or twice in the past. I was fairly certain what it might be after the past three nights.

I wasn't ready for something complicated which, considering our partnership, seemed a bit of a contradiction. Not here, not now! I thought. But this was Brodie, and as I had learned only too well...

"We'll see this through." And in that way that he always seemed to know what I was thinking, "Then there are things that need to be said."

I nodded. "You're quite right." Then headed for the door.

Breakfast was croissants, more fruit, and strong black coffee. After that last conversation, I would have preferred something stronger. Afterward, we had the hotel concierge summon a driver.

Monsieur Lefevre was already at the Louvre by the time we arrived through morning street congestion.

He was slightly built, of medium height with graying hair beneath his cap, and watchful hazel eyes that, in spite of the contrasts between the two men, reminded me of Brodie.

"Mademoiselle Forsythe and Brodie," he greeted us, noticeably not Monsieur Brodie but the familiar, which raised the question of just what work he had been doing with Sir Avery of the Special Services.

"Sir Avery said that it was a most urgent matter. If you will come with me, I will show you what I have been able to find. We joined him at the outdoor café just outside the main entrance. There, people paused before continuing on into the museum which I knew from experience could not all be seen in a day, or even a week of days.

"You must understand," Monsieur Lefevre cautioned. "Many official records made before the Commune no longer exist, what with the bombings, and fires throughout the city. However," he continued, "In the arrondissements, many records were kept in churches and by the local magistrates. The name Betard is not unusual. But perhaps well known.

"Most particularly," he continued. "Jean Luc Betard and his success around the world, and particularly in your country these past many years." He turned to Brodie.

"You mentioned the 13th arrondissement and I made inquiries. Jean Luc Betard's family originally lived there. It was once a very poor part of Paris. Although there are efforts to restore the area, many working families now live there.

"I was able to locate the address where the family once lived in the older part of the district," he told us. "Very poor and no surprise that one who achieves the success of Jean Luc Betard would not return.

"Some of the streets were renamed after the Commune, but in this old area the names are mostly still the same—*Rue LaFouge*, number 8, from the information I was able to obtain from old records."

I showed him the information Lucy Penworth had been able to find in the newspaper archive, along with what the Great Maxim had told me about an early illusion where a young assistant had been badly injured. There was a possibility there might be something more about it in the French Newspapers.

"It is uncertain what might be found," Monsieur Lefevre replied. "You must remember that it has been almost twenty years since Betard left. In that time with many changes, the newspapers are mostly filled with articles about political unrest here and across Europe, but I know someone who might be able to tell us something. I will see what they can find about him."

"It's unknown what you will find at the address in the 13th arrondissement, if anything," he cautioned. "But I have someone who can take you there." A man he trusted.

"Even during the day," he continued, "the streets can be dangerous, especially in the old places where there is still much poverty and the police do not go. I urge caution, even though I know you have spent time in Paris before, mademoiselle."

He seemed to know a great deal about me. Most interesting.

I *was* grateful. It was more than I had hoped for in such a short time. It did seem as if Monsieur Lefevre had the ability to obtain information, even old information, that we might not have been able to.

"There was apparently a place near the theater district where those like Betard lived, created their illusions, and performed in theaters and on the street," I commented. "Where that might be?"

He nodded. "I have heard of these places, but of course with the political changes there was little opportunity for them. One place I know was near the *Théâtre Gaîté Montparnasse*. It survived the purge after Napoleon III was removed. It is still there, and there are places near there that might be what you speak of— ateliers of the artists and performers."

"Thank you, my friend," Brodie told him.

I thanked him as well. It was a start.

But where would it take us? What might we learn? Something? Anything? And with no time to waste considering the threat in that last note.

We left the café and walked to the street. Monsieur Lefevre whistled sharply and signaled with his hand. A driver swung his rig from across the boulevard and stopped at the curb.

"Armand will take you to the *Rue LaFouge* in the 13th arrondissement. I wish you well, Brodie and mademoiselle."

"As for you, my friend," he told Brodie. "I have information regarding the matter Sir Avery was most concerned about. I will have it sent to you at your hotel by one of my people. I do not trust the telephone... There are too many ears."

"You've been here before," I commented with more than a little surprise as I climbed into the French version of a hansom cab. Brodie climbed in after and settled into the seat beside me.

"A brief trip over on a matter for Sir Avery."

And that was the extent of his explanation. I was discovering there were many things about Angus Brodie that I didn't know.

With traffic in Paris it might have taken some time to arrive at the *Rue LaFouge*, however our driver knew several shorter routes through the city then into the 13th arrondissement.

There were no signs along the way, only street names and in some places, none at all. But the change was evident in the older houses and shops that had survived the Commune years before, but with little attention since. It reminded me much of the East End of London as Monsieur Lefevre mentioned the families of working-class citizens that now lived here.

Still, the streets were clean, women going about their daily shopping at the open-air markets, laundry hung at a line between apartments overhead, and an occasional stray dog that reminded me of the hound.

The *Rue LaFouge* was off the main boulevard, a quiet street with window boxes where an attempt had been made to entice flowers to bloom with marginal success.

Our driver pulled to a stop in front of Number 8, a three-story building with chipped plaster and broken tiles at the steps in the old Norman style. Our driver understood English. Brodie asked him to wait as I climbed the steps to the entrance of the building and stepped into what passed for a foyer.

There were a half dozen apartments on the main floor, each with a letter at the door. There was no answer at the first door on the left, or the second one. As I was about to knock on the third door to inquire if Madame Betard was there, the door at the end of the hall opened revealing a woman with graying hair pulled into a bun at the back of her head.

Having spent a great deal of time in Paris in the past, I was not surprised at the rude comment or the volley of French slang that accompanied it along with the suspicious glare.

There was surprise in the woman's expression along with the suspicion when I replied in French. Her eyes narrowed on me, then angled past to Brodie. Whether it was his somewhat intimidating presence or my language skills, she nodded and stepped out of her apartment.

"*What did we want?*" she asked, keeping a careful eye on Brodie as I translated.

I explained that we were looking for the apartment of Madame Betard. The suspicion was still there but there was a hint of recognition at the old woman's expression.

"*Anna Betard?*" she then asked, and I nodded in response.

She shook her head and turned back toward the door of her apartment. I told her that it was about Anna Betard's son, and that we were prepared to pay for information. She hesitated.

It was then that Brodie told her, "The information first, madame, then you will be paid for your trouble."

I translated once more, and she slowly turned back around. Yes, she knew Anna. They'd had lived in this same building through the troubles, for over twenty years, but the woman had moved into the building after Anna's son had gone.

She only knew about his success in the papers that were delivered to Anna's apartment at the second floor. Anna told her that Jean Luc paid for her apartment. Then, as her health declined, she moved, and Jean Luc paid for that as well.

I asked if she knew where she had gone. There was that guarded look once more. I handed her several francs that I had exchanged at the hotel. She took them and held her hand out for more. I indicated there would be no more coin unless she told us what she knew.

She had visited Anna once where she had gone to live, some distance away at the *Hotel Dieu* in the 4th arrondissement, in a private room, cared for by nuns. She was told that Jean Luc had paid for that as well, according to Anna Betard who boasted of her son's great success.

She had not returned to visit Anna as she could not afford the carriage fare for that distance. Perhaps now she could, if Anna was still alive.

"Do you know of it?" Brodie asked after I had paid her the additional francs that I had promised, and we returned to our carriage.

"Yes, it's across the river very near the Cathedral of Notre Dame."

The Hotel-Dieu, or God Shelter was a hospital on the Ile de la Cité, over near the cathedral. I had learned about it in my school years in Paris. The original hospital was supposedly founded by Saint Landry in the seventh century, although there were no records of it. The first official records of were from the ninth century.

"It was burned several times over the centuries, and rebuilt several years ago. I remember my aunt speaking of it. It's still run by Augustinian Nuns."

"A hospital run by nuns," Brodie commented as our driver set off. There was a hint of disapproval.

"Are you afraid for your soul, Angus Brodie?"

"That is for those who believe in God!" he replied.

Another insight. Most interesting.

Having been raised by my aunt, my religious education had been somewhat lacking, although she had seen to it that both Linnie and I were baptized—just to be on the safe side as she once explained it.

Still, I was widely read and traveled, and while I didn't necessarily believe in the usually accepted concepts of God and creation, I very much left that door open as they say. Just to be in the safe side. As for Brodie, it seemed that he did not.

The spires of the cathedral appeared within view long before we reached the hospital. I had visited Notre Dame during my school years, the last time after abandoning my classes for the day and accompanying three other young ladies from school. Linnie had been certain we would be caught and severely reprimanded and so chose to remain behind.

We were caught and reprimanded, but the punishment had been well worth the risk.

Our aunt was made aware of it in the weeks that followed and had replied that she would see the matter dealt with upon our return to London. In a separate letter, she admitted that she had once done the very same thing, several times. Her advice was not to be caught the next time. I wasn't!

Now as we arrived at the Hotel-Dieu, Brodie grimaced as two nuns came down the steps and made their way to the cathedral for midday prayers. Very definitely something there, I thought.

We entered through the colonnaded entrance at the street, with its gargoyles and the name of the hospital carved into stone overhead.

The newer hospital, built only a few decades earlier across the river from the old site and in the shadows of Notre Dame, was inhabited by nuns much the same as the older hospital. But here its buildings were arranged around a central garden courtyard connected by colonnaded walkways that led to other parts of the hospital—offices, the surgeries, patient wards and private rooms, along with research facilities.

We were met at a desk by a nun in the usual attire of black tunic and scapular with a black mantle and veil, and a long white apron over.

"Good afternoon," she greeted us in French. "May I help you?"

Also in French, I explained that we were there to see one of the residents, Anna Betard. She asked us to follow her down a hallway lined with a long wood bench, that intersected another hallway. We passed several rooms, a ward, and then were escorted to a windowless room that turned out to be an office. There we were greeted by another nun, Sister Mary Louise, Administratrix, according to the name plate at the desk.

We were asked to be seated and I explained the reason for our visit. Sister Mary Louise then asked our relationship with Anna Betard. I explained that we had been sent there on behalf of her son, Jean Luc.

She paused, and I was afraid she might refuse to let us see her, or worse, that she might not still be alive. Then she smiled.

"You are the author of the books by Emma Fortescue, are you not?"

To say that I was surprised was an understatement. Her English was flawless! However, the revelation that a sister of the order of Notre Dame in Paris would know about my books caught me quite by surprise.

"I was born in London," the nun said. "My sister lives there with her family. I chose a different path, and it brought me here. Still, I think of other places that I might have visited, and you have taken me there. Although, I must say that Mademoiselle Fortescue is not exactly... saintly."

There was a sudden cough from Brodie at the chair beside me. Well and good, I thought. Whatever his past experience might have been with the church, it appeared that Sister Mary Louise might have tempered that somewhat with her comment. He was most definitely struggling to keep a straight face.

It turned out that she could help us. She pulled a ledger from the shelf and found her name.

"She has been a resident for almost eight years. She came to us when her health declined."

I asked if Betard had returned to visit her.

"He has made certain that her care is paid for, very generously," she replied. Which answered the question without specifically answering it. It seemed that he had not returned, but made certain that Anna was cared for.

"She is in our residential wing," Sister Mary Louise then told us. "She does not have many visitors. I am certain she will be happy to see you." She picked up a bell and rang it. A young novice appeared, and Sister Mary Louise gave her the room number and asked her to escort us there.

She rose from behind the desk as I thanked her and turned to leave.

"You will have another book soon?" she inquired.

I was trying to hide my surprise that a nun had read my books.

"Yes, it's with my publisher now." I hesitated. "However it's more about a murder case that Emily Fortescue becomes involved with." I exchanged a look with Brodie.

Sister Mary Louse smiled. "How very exciting. I will ask my sister to look for it. Murder?" She cocked her head. "Very interesting."

How very interesting indeed, I thought. She then took Brodie's hand between hers in parting.

"You have a good heart, Mr. Brodie. Follow it."

Where had that come from? I wondered as we left her office. They hadn't exchanged more than two words after the introductions were made. I looked back at the door to the office as we followed the young woman who was taking us to Anna Betard's room.

Through the windows at the hallway I glimpsed the dome at

Notre Dame Cathedral. It suddenly gleamed in the afternoon sunlight. I glanced over at Brodie and wondered if there might have been some presence in that office. Templeton would have been certain of it.

There were several private rooms in the wing where the young novitiate escorted us. Anna Betard's room was at the end of the hallway and faced out onto the courtyard below. The young novice knocked lightly then escorted us inside.

Whatever I expected, I was pleasantly surprised. The room was brightly lit by the windows at one end of the room. There were two chairs that sat about a small table. Anna Betard sat at that table, looking out at the garden. She turned as the young novice told her that she had visitors.

She was small and frail with snow white hair and was dressed in a floral gown. Faded blue eyes lit up at first, then clouded with confusion as she stared at us. The young novitiate introduced us, then smiled and left.

As I crossed the room and took the chair beside her, I knew by that first reaction that she had hoped it might be her son come to visit her. Eight years, I thought, and only strangers were here now.

She must have been near ninety years old, and I could not help but think of my aunt, and where the next years might take her—safari, perhaps China, and then. My aunt had sworn she was going out in a Viking longship in the North Sea. But I digress.

I took Anna's hand and again introduced myself and told her that we had been sent by her son, Jean Luc. There was confusion at first, then a soft smile, and in that way that time perhaps slows down and the memories returned, she told us of her son, how hard he had worked, the tours that took him around the world.

The pride was there along with the sadness from not seeing him, her memory clouded as she told us that it had been some time.

She spoke in French, and I translated, as Brodie listened and slowly moved about that small room. I learned of her youth, the young man she had married and the family they had. Then he was gone, he had deserted the family and she spoke no more of it. But she was not alone.

I told her that we were working for her son, that we had seen him only days before in London. She wanted to know more, and I was careful not to mention the circumstances.

In that way that the mind then wanders, she spoke of his career, how hard he had worked to support all of them before he left Paris.

Apparently there were other children and the struggle to hold her family together was constant in those difficult years of the Republic and political upheaval, with little work and often no food. There had been other losses along the way, a young daughter, age four. But always her sons found a way to provide for them.

"Mikaela," Brodie caught my attention where he stood beside the small table at her bedside. He pointed to photographs of children, two older boys standing and a younger girl and boy sitting stiffly, staring back at the camera. This was Anna Betard's family.

She had spoken of the little girl who had died and of Jean Luc, but nothing of the other two boys. The smaller one, seated, looked as I had seen in other old photographs, when parents desired to have one last picture of a child in death.

He was propped up at a chair, held in place by one of the older boys who stood behind him, the expression in his eyes vacant. It was so very sad. Anna Betard had obviously lost two children. But what of the two older boys in those grainy photographs?

Photography had come a long way since they were made, but even with the obvious age of the photographs, creased and faded in gray and black tones, those two faces stared back at the camera.

I handed the photographs to her. She stared at them, tracing those images with her fingers.

"Tell me about them," I asked her in French.

She didn't seem to hear me as she continued to stare at the

photographs. When I would have asked again, I felt Brodie's hand at my shoulder. He shook his head.

"Leave it be, lass."

The lap blanket across her legs had fallen to the floor. He picked it up and gently tucked it about her once more.

We left her dozing, the photographs clasped in her hands.

# Thirteen

**THERE WAS** a note from Monsieur Lefevre waiting for us when we returned to the hotel. He had information for us, and we were to meet with him at his apartment on the Rue Rivoli.

Brodie gave him the address and our driver nodded.

Lefevre's apartment was in one of the Haussmann buildings that had been built along Paris boulevards over the past decades.

"Ye know of them?" Brodie asked.

"The apartments are quite well known throughout Paris."

The family of a student my sister and I attended school with had lived in one of the apartment buildings and we had been frequent guests, far from our own home in London.

The Hausmann buildings all much the same, supposedly following strict guidelines by Baron Haussmann who provided the original design. It was said that the facades of all the apartment buildings were to have cream colored stone, mansard roofs, and that no building would exceed six stories.

Lefevre's driver delivered us to number twenty-six on the Rue Rivoli. His apartment was on the ground floor.

He nodded to Brodie, then at me. "I have information one of my people was able to find that might be helpful, mademoiselle."

His apartment was one of the smaller ones that I had seen,

with an adjoining bedroom, a small fireplace and a desk where he obviously worked. However the question remained, what sort of work that might be that involved Brodie and Sir Avery.

He poured cognac as we sat before a table in his small salon, a man after my own heart and something I had acquired a taste for while in Paris.

"The man I know was able to find several articles from some time ago about Monsieur Betard after he became well known and returned for performances here in Paris." The notes from 'the man he knew' were written in French.

"There is mention of a place where he performed in the streets while perfecting his illusions."

As I translated the scrawled handwriting, he drew Brodie aside and handed him an envelope.

"You will provide this to Sir Avery."

Brodie nodded and tucked the envelope into his coat pocket.

I returned to the notes Lefevre had obtained regarding Betard. Almost twenty years ago, Betard struggled to perfect his illusions on the streets of the theater district at Montemarte.

He had lived and worked at perfecting his illusions at an atelier that was apparently an old communal warehouse in the district. The information was much the same that the Great Maxim had provided about the time just before Betard arrived in London. The warehouse was in the Montmarte district, at Rue Lamarck.

I looked up from the notes Lefevre had provided. "We need to go there."

I didn't ask Brodie about the envelope Lefevre had given him as we climbed into the carriage for the ride to the theater district at Montmarte where Betard had once lived and worked.

I had learned that he would share information when he chose, if he chose to. And I was not one to poke and prod. Whatever it was that he was doing for Sir Avery obviously included Monsieur Lefevre. But I would have to wait.

I had attended theater in the Montmarte, most notably plays

performed by the great Sarah Bernhardt when she was in Paris and not on her next tour. I remembered the district as quite colorful with billboards and sidewalk board walkers announcing everything from the entertainment in the cabarets to the Opera Garnier.

It was all most exciting for two young girls and that first taste of freedom. Linnie preferred the opera while I had managed to take in more than one performance at the cabaret with its risqué performances.

Little had changed in the years since, the overhead signs advertised scantily clad young women who performed daily in the smaller cabarets and clubs.

"Ye attended school here?" Brodie commented.

"Not exactly here," I replied. "Our school is very old and in another part of the city. "The Montmarte was for the days when we were allowed personal time."

"Personal time," he replied with a glance up at one of those advertisement boards. "I can well imagine."

The Rue Lamarck was off the main boulevard, a mixture of old buildings and warehouses, some covered with signage advertising rooms to rent, others that had fallen into disrepair. Our driver pulled up and inquired about any buildings where artists lived or gathered. We were directed to an old building at the end of the street.

Our driver waited as we approached the building that was very much like some of the building at the East End off the Strand. There were sounds from inside the building just beyond a large sliding door that stood open.

Inside the building there were signs and easels, and other equipment of artists, while overhead were other parts of the building that appeared to have been converted to small nooks for residents to sleep.

A young man stood before one of the easels, head cocked to one side as he seemed to consider the painting before him—perhaps a budding Renoir or Rubens, although by the slashes of color that went in all directions very likely not, but some new artistic style.

My sister would undoubtedly have recognized it while I... my influence had been the cabarets.

I approached him as he turned and selected another brush, and inquired if there was someone who might be able to tell us about the building from several years before and someone who had once live there.

That look, bold and quite familiar among the French, slid over me. The old man who keeps the building, Lescoule, who was about somewhere, I was told. He might be able to tell me something. There was that look again.

"French!" Brodie commented under his breath in a tone that was hardly complimentary.

"We need to speak with a man by the name of Lescoule," I replied amused. "He's about somewhere."

A question for a young woman who it appeared might have been 'working all night', directed us to a short, stout man with a wild mane of white hair as he swept the back of the building.

"Eh?" he replied when I asked if he could answer some questions for us. "Betard?"

I was almost certain he would shake his head that he knew nothing. Then he nodded.

"Come with me," he said in broken English.

We accompanied him to a small room at the back of the building where there were chairs and a small table, and we listened to stories of the district—the various actors and artists who had lived and worked there.

"Atelier they called it, bah," he exclaimed with a sweep of the building. "What was left after the fire. I was here." He then nodded. "I know about Betard."

Jean Luc had lived there for two years, performing on the street as he struggled to create illusions far beyond what magicians performed on corners.

There was one trick, the man called it, with an assistant—poor girl. It required her to disappear in a cloud of smoke.

It had all gone wrong, made worse by the wind from the storm that swept the street. *La bombe*, he called it, had exploded, fire everywhere, including the girl. Betard tried to save her. He shook his head.

*It was of no use.* What of Betard, I then asked.

He was badly burned and might have died if he hadn't been taken to hospital. The other one came then, and collected all of his things. So tragic.

The other one? I exchanged a look with Brodie. A friend perhaps? Or possibly someone from his family? A brother, from that photograph we had seen?

"*Quel hôpital*?" I then asked. Did he remember which one?

The hospital where those who were injured in the bombings about Paris that year were taken. I thanked him and paid him for his time.

Our driver, Paul, was able to tell us more. Betard was most likely taken to the Hôtel des Invalides. His father was once there. It would have been the nearest hospital for such a horrible injury.

"It's been a long while," Brodie reminded me as we set off. "And with all the troubles here the past several years..."

I knew that he was preparing me that we might not learn anything, but we had far more information than we started with, and I needed to follow it through as far as we could. For both Betard and Sophie.

The Hôtel des Invalides was a sprawling complex of structures and courtyards originally built in the seventeenth century for the care of wounded soldiers. And according to our driver it was also here that the wounded from the bombings had been taken.

Our driver entered the courtyard off *Place Vauban*. We were directed to the office of the administrator of the hospital where records were kept.

It was late afternoon, and I was well aware that most offices and facilities closed that time of day. I hoped there might be someone who could provide us information.

The clerk at the administrator's office was hesitant to help us. We were told that hospital records were private matters.

Paul had accompanied us. A discussion in rapid French followed, that included Monsieur Lefevre's name. It seemed that our host carried some authority in unexpected places. The conversation abruptly ended.

Paul turned to me. "If you will provide the name and when the person might have been here, he will be most happy to search their records."

Most happy, indeed!

I provided Betard's name and the time period he might have been there, and we waited.

I made notes in my notebook while we waited. After all these years, I was prepared for the clerk's search to take quite a bit of time, and perhaps result in nothing with all the turmoil Paris had gone through.

I was grateful for Paul's assistance. When not arguing with reluctant hospital clerks, he was most congenial but with that same watchful expression as Lefevre and someone else I knew.

The clerk returned far sooner than I would have expected and explained to Paul that we would have to see the administrator for the information we were after.

"The administrator will see you," Paul explained. "I will wait for your return."

I frowned. What was it that the clerk couldn't have told us? Confirmation that Betard had been brought there? How long he stayed? The extent of his injuries?

The administrator greeted us with a cool demeanor. And once again, it was explained that it was not usually the policy of the hospital to provide information regarding its patients.

However, he was made aware of the special request. He read from a large ledger filled with entries.

Jean Luc Betard, age seventeen years, was admitted to the hospital on 4 April 1881 with severe injuries from a fire.

The list of injuries as entered by the surgeon at that time was staggering, that included extensive burns to his hands and other parts of his body. I caught the look Brodie gave me.

What did that mean now with what we knew from the illusion that night at the Crystal Palace and the prints found on the glass box?

Betard was hospitalized for several months and then transferred to another part of the hospital for what they referred to as rehabilitation.

I then asked when he was released. Had someone in his family, perhaps that same person who retrieved his belongings from Montmarte, then come for him? Where had he gone then? How long had it taken for him to recover and then go to London to resume his training?

"You do not understand, mademoiselle," the administrator replied. "His injuries were... most severe. To the brain as well as the body."

"What are you saying?" I asked.

"Monsieur Betard was here until recently, in the psychiatric ward."

"What do ye mean recently?" Brodie then asked.

"He was discovered to have left, nine days ago. We attempted to contact his family, but there was no longer an address."

Nine days...


I was still trying to understand what we had learned at the hospital.

According to their records, Jean Luc Betard had arrived at the hospital nineteen years earlier barely alive after a horrible accident. Only through the efforts of the surgeon and over a great deal of time, had his life been saved although he was left an invalid. The irony of the name of the hospital—*Invalides*, was not lost on me.

Years of care and rehabilitation followed, but were minimally successful in restoring him to what he had once been. The trauma of the explosion and the death of his assistant, with whom it appeared he had been in love, had shattered him. The patient the hospital knew as Jean Luc Betard was only a shell of the young man he once was, barely able to speak, given to violent outbursts.

Then, nine days ago, he had slipped out of the hospital and disappeared.

We had what we had come for. We had answers, but what did they mean? How was it possible that Jean Luc Betard had arrived in London only nine days ago?

It was well into the evening when Paul delivered us back at the hotel. Monsieur Lefevre had arrived some time later and met with Brodie. I heard little of what the discussed. Then he stood to leave.

"Be careful, my friend," he said. He had exchanged a look with Brodie, then bid me farewell in that typical way of the French with a kiss at my hand.

I thanked him for his assistance. Without it we might have spent days trying to find information that he and Paul had provided in a day. But what had we learned?

I was tired, frustrated and angry, and we only had more questions.

"How is it possible?" I asked about what we had learned about Betard at the hospital.

"It's not possible," Brodie replied.

I wanted to argue with him, to go back over everything that we and the entire world knew about Jean Luc Betard. There had to be something we were missing.

He poured us both another cognac. We had eaten late supper, having not eaten since the breakfast of pastry and fruit. Now, the cognac warmed into my stomach.

"If it's not possible, then what is it? If the man that the hospital knew as Jean Luc Betard left nine days ago, where did he go...?" I asked and held my glass out for more.

It was there of course, just at the edge of my thoughts as a memory returned of the night I had met with Maximilian Holt. He had even spoken of it—that Betard had come back to Paris briefly, a family matter, then returned to London where he was mentored by the Great Maxim.

Afterward, as I left the Olympic Theater, a man came at me through the fog. He had been dressed for the theater in formal coat and tails with a cape, but his face was hidden by the rim of his hat, shadows, and poor light from the street. It had looked like... a mask.

"That is enough," Brodie was saying as he took the now empty glass from my hand. "Ye need some sleep. We'll leave in the morning."

I nodded then stood, admittedly a bit off center from the long day or possibly all that cognac.

"Can ye walk?"

"Of course I can walk," I replied.

At last I was fairly certain I could. I was not intoxicated. It took far more than two drinks— or was it three? —for me to even begin to feel the effects. But of course that was usually my aunt's very fine whisky. However at the moment my feet did not seem to be moving.

He made that sound that I was so familiar with, something that resembled a curse and picked me up. No mean feat considering that I was not small, something that I was oft reminded of as whoever happened to be meeting or speaking with was forced to look up at me. It intimidated most men. Not Brodie.

"What are you doing?"

"Making certain ye get to bed without damaging yerself."

I smiled as I rested my cheek against his shoulder. I could not remember the last time a man had put me to bed. To be quite honest, it had never happened.

But this was Brodie and somewhere in my slightly muddled thoughts I remembered the night before... and the night before that. And then he set me at the edge of the bed.

"Can ye undress yerself?" he asked.

That handsome face with that dark beard and those dark eyes.

"Of course," I replied as I fumbled with the buttons of my shirtwaist. There was that curse again as he brushed my hands aside, and proceeded to unbutton me.

"What do you think it all means?" I asked. I wanted very much to know.

He had finished with my shirt waist, then unbuttoned my skirt.

"What is that?"

"That the man at the hospital was supposedly Jean Luc Betard?"

He took my hand and pulled me to my feet. He pushed my skirt from my waist then the shirtwaist from my shoulders.

"Could it be a coincidence?" I knew that he didn't believe in them. It was that part of him from those years living on the streets, then with the Metropolitan Police. He made another sound, that thoughtful sound.

"Perhaps."

I knew better, and that earlier thought teased at my brain. "An impostor then."

He folded my clothes and laid them at the nearby chair. He looked at me then.

"If not an impostor, then who is the man in London?" I continued, standing there in my chemise. It didn't occur to me to be embarrassed. We were beyond that now.

"Who was the young man the Great Maxim mentored all those years before? Why were Francoise and Marie murdered?"

"Be quiet, woman."

Be quiet? I wanted to know who was doing this. I wanted to protect Sophie.

"Brodie..."

He cursed again. "Ye are the only woman I know who would be asking such questions in the middle of the night when ye should be asleep. I don't know why I put up with ye."

"Yes, you do," I replied, a bit more brazenly than I might have if not for the cognac. Or at least more than *I* would usually have put up with.

"Because you care what happens to Sophie as much as I do, and there is another other reason."

"I suppose you're going to tell me what that is."

"You like that I think for myself, and you like me." That was definitely the cognac. I would never have made a statement like that to a man nor cared to. But this was Brodie.

"Aye," his voice softened. "I like that ye think for yerself..." Then he added, "Most of the time, but not when ye take it upon yerself to go off alone."

He didn't say the rest of it. It was enough for now.

"You need sleep as well," I told him, bold as brass my aunt would have said. That pot calling the kettle black. I crawled under the covers.

That dark gaze met mine. "In a while. I have a message I want to write up for Lefevre before we leave in the morning.

He paused and looked back at me. "Ye are a bold lass, Mikaela Forsythe. Now go to sleep."

I smiled as I drifted off.


I had once experienced a different sort of *'morning after'*, quite young and after one of my aunt's holiday parties where I had managed to lift two bottles of champagne when her butler wasn't looking.

I had made off with it back to Linnie's bedroom. I was fourteen years old at the time, and she was twelve. We had emptied both bottles, dancing around in her room to the music that drifted up from below at the salon at Sussex Square. We both ended up quite foxed.

The morning after, I vowed never to touch champagne again.

There was, of course, my aunt's very fine whisky that I developed a taste for over the years, and that one encounter with ouzo while on one of my travels. And cognac when we were previously in France.

Cognac couldn't hold a candle to the whisky.

I slowly sat up, my head still attached quite nicely, and glanced to the other side of the bed. It seemed that Brodie had been up much later through the night and possibly slept at the settee. Not wanting to disturb me?

In spite of the early hour, he was fully clothed. I couldn't deny that I was disappointed... Then I caught the smell of food.

"Breakfast?" I said as I finished dressing and headed for the small table. I was starving.

There was definitely something to be said for a man who ordered up breakfast along with a silver pot of steaming coffee.

He had obviously already eaten, evidenced by the pastry crumbs at the plate. I scooped up the sliced croissant that was left with a thin sliver of ham and cheese between.

"Have you sent your message to Monsieur Lefevre?" I asked as I caught sight of a different sort of message at the desk. It was a telegram.

"Aye, first thing. He'll send round his driver. We have just enough time to make the first train back to Calais."

Just enough time translated to quickly gathering up my hair as I took bites of the pastry and fortified myself with coffee. I then made use of the wash basin, used a cloth to clean my teeth instead of my brush that was at the washstand at the office on the Strand, and was ready to leave most efficiently.

He retrieved the telegram and tucked it inside his coat. Whatever message it contained would have to wait.

We had arrived only with what we were wearing and my carpetbag, and that was all we carried as we left the room. Paul, our driver from the day before, had arrived and was waiting for us at the porte cochere. He handed Brodie an envelope. Another message from Lefevre?

I looked at Brodie with some surprise as I was informed that the account for our room had already been settled.

"Monsieur Lefevre," was the only explanation Brodie provided. Which again raised the question of his previous acquaintance with the man. I saved that for later, along with whatever might be in that telegram, as we entered the carriage and made the trip to the Paris central rail station.


The French did appreciate their coffee; dark, strong, as if a spoon might stand up in it as my friend Templeton had once described after her tour of the United States. And I had an appreciation of good strong coffee.

With at least seven hours ahead of us before we arrived at the port of Calais, I decided to learn what was in that telegram.

"Was it in English, or perhaps French?" I asked as the attendant moved away from our table. That dark gaze met mine, and so that there was no confusion. "The telegram you received at the hotel."

Brodie took a long swallow of coffee, that dark gaze narrowing.

"There are times, Miss Forsythe, that ye are too clever for yer own good. Aye, it was in French."

"You might have had the desk clerk translate it for you," I pointed out.

"I might have."

But he hadn't. He reached inside his coat and pulled out the telegram. He handed it to me.

The telegram was from London, received during the night and delivered to the hotel. It was from Alex Sinclair.

There had been another murder!

Maximillian Holt, the Great Maxim, was found dead inside his dressing room at the Olympic Theater the night before. Right after I had met with him.

Then there were two...

# Fourteen

I HAD READ of efforts to build a cross-channel train tunnel that would cut travel time between England and France. It had been postponed due to concerns with political upheavals across Europe that might prove dangerous for England.

How I wished for that now however as our train arrived in Calais in the late afternoon and there was still a two-hour crossing as well as the return to London from Dover.

"The man I encountered outside the Olympic theater that night? If I'd only known..."

"Ye canna blame yerself, lass," Brodie told me as we boarded the late afternoon ferry for Dover. "There is no way to know it was the same person as the one that killed the magician."

But what if it was? And that second message that was found with Marie— *Now there were two.*

I had assumed that the note meant Sophie and Jean Luc. Did it mean something else?

The late ferry service provided no amenities except what the passengers brought with them. It didn't matter. I had no appetite. What I wanted was to know who was doing this.

It would have to wait until we reached London.

At Dover we had to wait for the next train. Brodie sent a

telegram to London as telephone service was only sporadic, and as he said telephones had ears.

It was very near eight o'clock of the evening when we returned to Charing Cross Station in London. We caught a cab, not to the office on the Strand, but to the office of Special Services where lights burned well into the night at those discreet offices. Alex Sinclair greeted us.

"I got your telegram," he told Brodie. "Do come along. There's something in the matter of the case that you need to know."

The 'something more' was another note, found on the body of the Great Maxim.

*Now there is one...*

I had assumed that the message I found with Marie Genesse's body was a threat against two—Sophie and Jean Luc. If we were to believe that there was to be one more, then it was possible that Sophie was safe. But was anyone safe?

The records at the *Hospital Invalides* made reference to violent spells the patient known as Jean Luc Betard had suffered, followed by long silences.

He had been treated and received what they referred to as rehabilitation. And then he escaped from the locked wing where he had lived for the past nineteen years. Now three people were dead—three people whose lives were connected to Jean Luc Betard. But who was he? And who was the man who had escaped the hospital in Paris?

We ate for the first time since breakfast, food provided by the office of Special Services. Quite ironically, I had little appetite. Instead, I went back through the notes in my notebook. The answer had to be there, somewhere.

"What about Mr. Munro and Mr. Conner?" I asked as Brodie returned from meeting with Sir Avery.

He nodded. "A man was sent to let them know what's happened, and that we've returned. He'll let us know when he's made contact with them."

"What about any clues other than the note that was found?" I then asked. "Something that might tell us who this person is and where he went... afterward."

I thought of that feeling I had twice, that I might have been followed and couldn't help my feelings of guilt.

If the man I had encountered was the man who escaped in Paris and had followed me, I might very well have led him to Maximillian Holt.

"Ye need to let go of it," Brodie said gently. "Ye had no part in the man's death."

"If the killer followed me..."

"It wouldn't have mattered," he continued. "If he was after Holt, it would have been easy enough to find him, just as ye did. The man's name was on the board, and he was well known about the district. It would have ended the same, and ye might have been hurt as well. Or worse."

I knew what he was trying to do, but it didn't make me feel any better. And the worst of it was, we didn't know who was doing this. An impostor? Someone who had admired Jean Luc Betard and his success, and then taken his name? Or was it something else?

*Now there is one.* It was obvious what the killer intended next.

"We need to speak with Jean Luc," I said then. "He needs to be told what we learned so that he can protect himself and Sophie."

Alex had joined us and nodded. "Sir Avery had additional people sent to his residence."

Brodie nodded. "I'll go to meet with him, first thing in the morning."

"I'm going with you," I announced. It didn't hurt that Alex was there. In the very least, it prevented an argument.

Then, there was later as he accompanied me back to my townhouse in Mayfair.

"That is the most damned fool thing I ever heard," he bluntly informed me as he accompanied me into the townhouse. He then proceeded to check all the rooms, the alleyway where deliveries were made, Alice staring and listening with great curiosity.

"Her ladyship called today," she informed me. "She wanted to speak with you, something about a monkey that the municipal authorities are saying she cannot keep at Sussex Square. And Miss Templeton as well."

"Has there been anyone calling at the house?" I inquired, not that I believed that I as in any sort of danger.

"Just the delivery boy for the grocer and the gas man, miss," Alice replied as she watched Brodie with great curiosity. "The mail is on your desk. Two days' worth," she added pointedly, a frown at her face as Brodie returned from his search about the house and garden.

"What is Mr. Brodie looking for, miss?"

How best to answer when I suspected that I knew exactly what he was looking for? I said the first thing that popped into my head.

"Broken windows."

"Broken windows, miss?"

It was better than telling her there was a killer loose and about. I nodded.

"There's been a rash of them about the city."

She sniffed. "That's something I would expect in the East End," she said, again rather pointedly. "Not in Mayfair."

I left it at that. I knew when to pick my battles, and this was not one of them. The truth was, the less Alice knew, the better.

"I suppose it could be malcontents," she commented. "We might think of getting a dog. They set up a bit of a ruckus at a disturbance."

I thought of Rupert. He was no doubt a most effective guard dog few would dare to cross. However, I wasn't certain that was what Alice had in mind when she made the suggestion.

Brodie returned from the back of the house, apparently satisfied that no one was lurking about as I went to my desk and sorted through the mail. There was a letter from my publisher, what was most likely a bill from the gas company, other assorted envelopes including one with my sister's handwriting—undoubtedly the invitation to the garden party she had planned now that she was in her new home. Another envelope bore what had now become a familiar scrawl. I looked over at Brodie.

"What is it?"

"It appears to be from the person who left the other notes," I replied, glancing at my name at the front of the envelope.

I said nothing more as I didn't want Alice to overhear, walls with ears and all that. And there was no point in alarming her with an explanation.

I held the envelope up, then looked at Brodie. "Absinthe."

The scent was there, telling me who it was from in the off chance I hadn't recognized that scrawled handwriting.

"Open it," he replied.

I slipped the letter opener into the envelope just at the corner, then pulled out the note. I handed it to Brodie.

*Death will come when it will come!*

It was quite ironic and a threat, but against whom? The man we knew as Jean Luc Betard? Sophie?

"It's from Shakespeare," I explained. "It seems the person who wrote this is well read."

From the weeks, months, and years in that hospital in Paris, I thought. As to the meaning...

"Aye," Brodie replied. "With what we know it could also be a threat against ye. Ye'll not stay here alone."

It was a warning, and I knew that he was right, as far as it went. More importantly, I couldn't put Alice in danger. The person who had written that note knew where I lived, had perhaps even been watching the townhouse as part of some maddened scheme. But if Alice wasn't there...

She was in a fit of a mood as I gave the driver instructions to take her to Sussex Square. As my aunt would have said, 'her Irish was up'.

"It's not proper for a young lady to entertain a man without a chaperone," she reminded me as she packed. "What will her ladyship say?"

I had almost laughed at that. And as for being a lady, I was beyond that by society standards. I assured her that I would be quite safe.

"Safe?" she exclaimed. "I've seen the way the man looks at you," she said in an aside as she stepped up into the cab when it arrived. "As if you are a sweetmeat and he'd like to take a taste."

She wasn't finished. The driver was certainly getting an earful.

"There are precautions you should take."

Good heavens! A lecture about intimate relations. Brodie and I were somewhat beyond that.

"Our relationship is strictly professional," I assured her, and that was as much as I was prepared to say in the matter.

"In a pig's eye!" she snorted as she settled herself in the cab and the driver set off.

"What was that about?" Brodie asked.

"Something about a pig's eyes," I replied. "It seems that Alice believes that we are *avoir une liaison,* as they say. "

His eyes narrowed. "And what might that mean?"

"That we are involved in an affair," I translated. "I assured her our relationship was strictly professional."

There seemed to be no reason to go to the office on the Strand that time of the night, and since Brodie was convinced that I needed protecting, I headed for the kitchen.

"I thought ye said that ye don't cook," Brodie commented after setting the lock at the front door.

"I don't, but Alice always has food about. It must be an affliction of the Irish."

"It's a wonder ye have survived this long."

I opened the cold box, blessed invention that it was. Inside I found eggs, a ham that had obviously been purchased without knowing that I was going to be gone for two days, fresh baked bread, and some of her Irish sweet cakes.

I pulled everything out and set it at the counter, then went in search of a carving knife for the ham.

"Good heavens, woman! Be careful with that thing before you hurt someone," he told me as I pulled a knife from a drawer.

"You seem to forget that I am quite skilled with a blade."

"Aye, but I have no wish to be cut up like a ham."

I handed him the knife and he set about carving off two slices. I contemplated the eggs, then would have put them back in the cold box.

He looked over at me with that carving knife in one hand. "Ye don't know how to prepare eggs?"

"I know that it involves a pan and the gas at the stove."

He made a sound. "It's a wonder that ye have survived this long."

"I make certain there is food whenever I am out and about, or on one of my travels."

"Aye, resourceful, like the Mudger. Hand me the eggs."

I handed him the bowl Alice kept them in. It really was quite fascinating to watch a man prepare food.

After we ate at the small kitchen table, I removed the plates to the kitchen sink. I would simply have left them for later, but Brodie would have none of it.

One of the wonders of modern inventions was the hot water he filled the sink with. He found the can of dish flakes, sprinkled several in the basin, then let the water run until it covered the dishes.

"You're quite good at this," I complimented. He gave me a dark look.

"Ye learn a few things along the way."

A common reply with no explanation.

"Ye might want to dry the dishes with that towel," he suggested as he placed a second plate at the drain board.

I dried both plates and the silverware we had used. I would like to think that Alice would be pleased. However, astonished was more accurate.

While I didn't expect anyone to wait on me, I was in the habit of eating something far more simple that the meal Brodie had prepared. Something on the order of bread with jam. Quite simply, I didn't see the point in preparing a meal for one person.

I finished and hung the towel at the rack.

We returned to the small parlor where I had my desk and talked about what we had learned in Paris, then that note that had been sent to me as we sat over a drink of my aunt's very fine whisky.

"We need to meet with Betard," I commented.

"Aye, it's obvious he hasn't been forthcoming in the matter. The murderer, whatever he chooses to call himself, is still out there and both Betard and Sophie are in danger."

Before we left the office of the Special Services earlier, Brodie had asked Alex Sinclair to send someone to Betard's residence with a message for Munro to call first thing in the morning. We agreed that we needed to meet with Betard as soon as possible.

"What was it Mrs. Ryan said before she left?" he asked over a second drink.

"She believes that we are having an affair. She was most concerned about precautions we should take."

"Precautions."

"I believe that she meant…"

"I know what it means, lass." That gaze fastened on me. "What was yer response to that?"

The conversation had definitely gone in a different direction.

"I assured her that I was quite safe."

"Safe? Ye have a guarantee of that?" he asked.

I stood and set my empty glass at the table. "There is no possibility of the 'situation' occurring." I went to the door and checked the lock, then climbed the stairs. I was not used to sharing personal details.

"What is it, lass?"

He caught up with me just outside the door of my bedroom, his hand at my arm.

"You needn't worry," I assured him.

"Is that what ye thought?"

"Isn't it?" I asked, quite calm now. "Isn't that what most concerns a man?"

"I would be a liar, if I said I hadn't thought about it."

"As I said," I repeated, and I could have sworn my voice caught. "There isn't a possibility of an accident."

"Is that what ye think of it?" His voice changed. "An accident? Something to be gotten rid of with one of Mr. Brimley's medicines?"

I heard the anger at his voice. There was something more here, but I wasn't of a mind to examine it. I pulled my arm away.

"Do you think so little of me that you would believe that? Do you believe that I could do such a thing?"

We were both tired. The last several hours had revealed some difficult things about the case, two people's lives were in danger, and it was possible that two drinks of my aunt's very fine whisky made me less cautious than I should have been.

"The truth is," I heard the emotion at my own voice. I took a deep breath. "The truth is... I cannot have children. So you see, neither of us has anything to worry about."

I would have gone into my room and left him to find his way into the second bedroom for the night. But this was Brodie. He had followed me and slowly turned me back around. He brushed his fingers across my cheek.

"I never thought that of ye, lass. Ye are good and strong, sometimes in spite of yerself. Ye would simply spit in someone's eye and the devil take them. But the truth is, I thought that if something happened then we would find our way through it together."

"In spite of myself?" I repeated.

"Aye," he said softly. "Ye can be most stubborn. And whatever the reason..."

How could he possibly know what it meant for me to hear him say this.

"It was a long time ago," I explained. "A fever that I caught, and the physician told my aunt that I would never be able to have children."

"Ye didn't need to explain it. I apologize to ye." He turned to leave.

"What are you apologizing for?"

"For hurtin' ye that way."

"You didn't hurt me. It's something that is... part of me. "

"Makes ye who ye are? Makes want to protect others? Makes ye take the risks ye take?"

He understood. In spite of the arguments, his stubbornness, the risks he took; he understood.

I nodded. "I leave it to my sister. She is quite enamored of babies. I cannot understand the fascination. My aunt and I are of the same opinion. They are helpless and mostly wet, and quite obnoxious once they start to speak."

He smiled and touched my cheek once more, then turned to leave the room. "Good night, lass."

"Stay," I said, never before more certain of something that I wanted, with no idea what it meant or where it would take us.

I went to him then, and slipped my hand behind his neck, my fingers curling in his overlong hair just at his collar.

"I want you to stay."


Nothing was said the next morning. Nothing needed to be said as I took a shower then dressed and came downstairs. There was simply that look in those dark eyes, different now, that met mine.

"I called Alex Sinclair first thing," he said, sitting at the desk.

I said nothing. It seemed quite natural.

"He heard from Munro first thing," he continued. "And explained that we need to meet with Betard and Sophie this morning."

It was time that Betard told us everything.



Hampton Manor was at the edge of the city in Richmond, an overgrown estate had been empty for some time before Betard took it as his London residence when he wasn't on tour.

It was private, behind a high wall with a gatehouse that we rode past for our meeting with Betard and Sophie.

Eventually the main house came into view among the forest of trees that surrounded it. My aunt had described it as a grand manor in the Elizabethan style, built somewhere in the sixteenth century. It was rumored that Henry VIII was known to use it as a hunting lodge I explained to Brodie. "Undoubtedly to seduce his next wife," I added somewhat sarcastically.

Now the brick two story manor was a shadow of its former glory or notoriety, having sat empty for almost twenty years since the eighty-nine-year-old Lord Northridge was found dead, quite naked amid rumors of his scampering about after one of the maids.

According to my aunt, who knew a great many things about a great many people in high places, that sort of thing happened when one lived so long. The condition Northridge was found in made it doubtful that he could have consummated anything had he caught the poor girl.

"It appeared," my aunt had shared at the time. "That there was little left of the thing. Shrinkage, I'm told. The better reason to find a young man."

The conversation had taken place just after Mr. Munro became part of her household. Although, I had my doubts about the success of her plan in that regard.

Our driver pulled to a stop before the main entrance to the manor. We were met by Mr. Conner and Betard's manager, Monsieur Fouquet.

Brodie had spoken with Alex Sinclair after our return from Paris. But I had no idea how much he had told Munro or Mr. Conner about what we had learned. Given the Special Services' penchant for secrecy, I suspected little might have been mentioned other than our need to meet with Betard as soon as possible. And along with that, inform him of the death of the Great Maxim, his mentor.

Needless to say, it was a somber atmosphere in the very least that we found upon being escorted into what was once a very grand salon at Hampton House. There, Betard eventually joined us, sleeves rolled back at his shirt, wiping his hands on a cloth. His expression was what I would have called annoyed, as if we had disturbed him at something of great importance.

Without his formal attire and cape that he had worn the night of the performance at the Crystal Palace, he was still a very handsome man, lean with that sort of restlessness that commanded attention.

"Monsieur Fouquet has been able to postpone the tour for a few weeks," he explained. "But there is little time for the changes to be made. I have been working in the shop, you see," he indicated by his smudged hands. "When not being spied upon by the people you sent here. So, tell me what you have learned about this unfortunate situation."

Spied upon? Munro and Mr. Conner? Both of whom I was certain had little interest in his illusions, and had been sent to protect him. But the show must go on, according to my friend, Templeton.

I exchanged a look with Brodie. In that way we had discovered over the past several months and our past cases, this was the part where he explained where we had been and what we had discovered. And it was quite obvious as he began that Betard was not aware that we had been to Paris.

Sophie had joined as well, and sat at a chair apart, hands clasped before her. Her gaze constantly returned to Jean Luc, her expression quite pale and solemn. I wondered how much she was aware of or had guessed, as to what we had learned.

"We went to the old neighborhood, and were able to find yer mother as well," Brodie told him. He then looked over at me.

"She had several photographs, one of four children," I explained.

If I had been waiting for a reaction. It came now.

"You have no right to do this... to disturb her! She is very old!" Betard exclaimed as he came out of his chair and confronted Brodie.

"There were two smaller children in the photograph," I continued. "And two older boys."

I saw by Sophie's reaction that it was quite obvious she was not aware that he had family still alive in Paris.

"We then went to the *Hospital Invalides*," I then explained. Betard's expression changed, a vein standing out at his forehead, as control slipped.

"If you would prefer to hear the rest in private?" Brodie suggested to him.

"No!" Sophie spoke for the first time since our arrival, quite shaken but most forceful. "All of it," she managed to say in her limited English. She looked at me with a pleading expression.

"Mademoiselle Forsythe?"

I understood what she was asking and felt a deep sadness at what she would learn about the man she had obviously fallen in love with, in spite of the fact that her love wasn't returned. Or was it?

We had learned at the beginning that Betard and Francoise were lovers. Her tragic death had sent us all on this case. Was it possible that he had some small affection for Sophie at the tragic loss? Her feelings had been obvious from the beginning, and then again when she chose to return here with him, even with the murderer still out there.

I told her that I would translate anything that she didn't understand, she had only to let me know.

It was obvious that Betard was deeply shaken by the news that we had been to the hospital, though he said nothing.

"There was a patient who called himself Jean Luc Betard," Brodie then revealed. I translated for Sophie. Her shocked gaze immediately fastened on the man she knew as Jean Luc Betard.

Still, Betard said nothing.

"He had been there for several years after some sort of an accident," Brodie continued. "He was badly burned and given to violent outbursts..." He looked over at me as I translated for Sophie once again.

"He escaped the hospital ten days ago."

"Ten days?" Betard repeated in a shocked whisper.

As I translated this last part of what Brodie told him, Sophie came out of her chair and went to Betard.

His head slumped to his chest. He slowly shook his head.

"It was all a very long time ago," he replied. "Impossible."

"There's more," Brodie then explained. "It's almost certain it was the same man Miss Forsythe encountered outside the Olympic Theater three days ago. And ye should know that Maximillian Holt was found dead at the theater the night before last."

I watched both Sophie and Betard at this last bit of news. It was obvious neither had been told.

As I finished translating for Sophie, she crumbled beside Betard, her arms around him as she wept at his shoulder. As for Betard's reaction, it was as if all the strength, every last breath left him as he slumped at the chair.

"I am sorry," Brodie said then.

It was several moments before Betard was able to collect himself. He gently patted Sophie's hand as she stared at him with a stricken expression. He whispered something to her in French.

I didn't bother to translate, by his tone of voice it was meant to comfort her. Then he looked up at Brodie.

"I understand." Betard stood then. "I am grateful for your diligence in the matter. I will, of course, see that you are compensated."

I looked over at Brodie. It seemed that our services had just been terminated.

"Ye don't understand, monsieur," Brodie replied. "Three people are dead. This man, whoever he might be..." he waited, but there was no explanation offered. "Whoever he might be, is here in London after escaping from the hospital in Paris. Ye have received the notes."

"I am grateful..." Betard started to say.

"He is not finished!" Brodie told him, his meaning unmistakable.

"I have people," Betard explained.

"And they have not been able to protect ye and those who are now dead."

The words were blunt even brutal. I saw Sophie's reaction at the stunned expression at her face. I knew Brodie. The words were brutal, but they were meant to be honest, clear about the danger in order to make Betard understand the gravity of the situation.

"I can leave. The tour..." he said then.

"Perhaps," Brodie acknowledged. "But I've seen it before. He will wait, until ye return and ye think it's over. It won't be over until he's found and stopped," he then added.

"Are ye willing to risk her life as well as yer own?" Brodie glanced over at Sophie, then back to Betard.

Betard shook his head. "No, I will not," he said with a gentle smile at her. "There have already been too many lost."

There was something more at his voice. Sadness to be certain, but something I had seen in people who grieve deeply.

"You said that it won't be over until he's found."

Brodie nodded.

"Then there is only one way to put an end to this. He must be stopped."

That sense of sadness deepened, but along with it there was a resolve. I had seen that once in my brother-in-law's expression in the case he had asked us to investigate. Then he was dead.

"But how?" Sophie asked.

Betard took her hand once more and gently stroked it.

"A performance on the stage. He will come then."

There was still a question that hadn't been answered.

"Do you know who the man is?" I asked him.

Betard slowly nodded. "You saw the photograph. He is my brother."

# Fifteen

"HIS BROTHER!" I exclaimed as we left several hours later and returned to the office on the Strand.

"Aye," I suspected it.

"It makes no sense..." But it did make sense. One brother's success, the surviving brother left to watch it, an accident that hadn't been explained. One that had obviously taken from him any opportunity he might have had in the upheaval and chaos of Paris, torn apart by politics as it struggled to emerge from a series of wars of decades past that had left only poverty.

"And a performance?" I exclaimed, never one to hold back when I disagreed. "The man is insane!"

"Perhaps," Brodie replied. "Perhaps not." He looked at me across the inside of the cab. "You don't agree."

As much as I appreciated the fact that he asked, the truth was that I had enormous misgivings.

"It's too dangerous. Three people are now dead. You cannot possibly mean that you will go along with this," I argued. "There has to be another way... more guards to protect him, bring in the police on this." But even as I said it, I knew perfectly well how ridiculous that was.

In the first place, it required Abberline to see that there

was a connection between the deaths that we had discovered in Paris, and therefore risk to Betard and Sophie. He would have to admit he was wrong when he had declared Francoise's death an unfortunate accident and then to be willing to cooperate in the matter. And that came back to the difficulties between him and Brodie. I knew perfectly well that it would never happen.

Abberline deeply resented Brodie over that situation in the past that had separated Brodie from the Metropolitan Police. I didn't know the details, only that it was something that still existed to this day and Abberline's resentment of Brodie was quite obvious as we had been forced to proceed on our own in our past cases.

"And Miss Sophie?" Brodie then asked.

It was so like him to point out that part of it. Until the murderer was caught, neither Betard nor Sophie would be safe. Betard might be able to protect himself, but Sophie?

"How will it be arranged?" I then asked of the one-night performance Betard had suggested and was determined to carry through, a prime opportunity that it was hoped would draw the murderer out.

He and Brodie had spoken of it at great length while I had done my best to console Sophie and convince her that everything would be all right with Brodie, Mr. Munro, Mr. Conner, and others from his days with the MP, to provide protection. But it did little good.

"He has suggested the Olympic Theater, temporarily closed after the death of Holt. His manager will make contact with the owner and make the proposal for a one-night performance by Betard."

"What of the audience?" I replied. There could possibly be hundreds who would attend a free performance.

"It will be put out that the performance will be a private performance," he replied.

Francoise's murder at the Crystal Palace had created a sensation, already reported in the dailies. When as it was made known that Holt had been murdered—

someone who was connected to Betard, it would only add to the sensationalism. Brodie knew that as well as I did.

"You could ask Sir Avery to see that Holt's death isn't made known yet."

"I could."

Which meant that he would not.

"Two murders already carried in the dailies, with Holt's to appear in the next issue, would surely draw curiosity seekers," I had pointed out.

"There's only one that matters. And once he's caught, it will end."

I wished that I was as confident as he was.

The man who claimed to be Jean Luc Betard might be insane, but he had already proven himself most capable in accomplishing what he had set out to do.

"He will come. He won't be able to stay away," he said, as if he had read my thoughts. "He will be caught."

We received a call that afternoon that Fouquet had managed to persuade the owner of the Olympic to provide the theater for that one-night performance, for an exorbitant fee that Betard was willing to pay.

'Persuade' might have been a bit of an exaggeration as he was most enthusiastic and saw it as a great opportunity to promote the theater afterward and draw even larger audiences. The date was set for two days away, just enough time to put the information out in the dailies and for Betard to put together the illusions he would be performing.

I had then put in a call to Lucy Penworth and shared the date of the new performance with her. She promised that she would have the announcement in the next edition.

Brodie had made contact with Mr. Dooley of the MP, who

had once served under him and continued to provide 'expertise' from time to time in our cases, outside the purview of Chief Inspector Abberline.

He had then placed a telephone call to Sir Avery and informed him what was to take place. An opportunity, he had called it, and Sir Avery had assured him several additional men would be made available for the night of the performance.

I saw it as something other than an opportunity. It was dangerous even foolish on Betard's part. It was putting himself and Sophie center stage, no pun intended, for the killer. However, I also knew that everything Brodie had told him was true.

There would be no safe place for either him or Sophie, until the killer was stopped.

What had happened that set one against the other, willing to commit murder?

What Jean Luc did tell us was that there had been a fire, a horrible accident, and his brother had been badly burned and very nearly died. More than that he wouldn't say.

And now he had escaped from the hospital in Paris and committed three murders?

Revenge? For what?

I thought of the seven deadly sins from my somewhat abbreviated religious knowledge that ended when I was twelve when I had asked my aunt what sodomy was.

There had been a hazy explanation that ended just as quickly as my religious education. I had eventually learned the meaning on a tour of the Louvre years ago.

"Pride, greed, envy, lust, gluttony, sloth, and wrath," I quoted what I remembered as I sat across from Brodie at the desk and wished that the blackboard might have survived the fire. I needed to see everything that we had learned set out before me, to try and understand what had happened, and the reason one brother had turned against the other."

"Which is it?" I asked.

With the fame and success Jean Luc Betard had achieved, I

would have chosen envy, possibly greed. Although it appeared that the man at the *Hospital Invalides* had been well provided for after that devastating accident.

Lust? That seemed unlikely as both Francoise and Sophie were quite young and had only become part of Betard's performances less than two years before. Although that did not rule out an earlier affair that might have driven the brothers apart.

"There are different kinds of lust," Brodie commented.

That seemed a curious comment to make. I looked up from my notes.

"Such as?"

"The lust of a man for a woman."

I had to admit that I had thought of that, and found that dark gaze on me in a way that had changed over the past few days.

"Or a woman for a man?" I suggested.

"There is the lust to survive, deep inside, no matter what it takes, that drives a man—or woman," he explained, "to do the things they do. It could be said that lust drives envy, greed, and most certainly wrath."

Had I apparently just seen another side of Brodie? Something out of the past that he knew only too well, or perhaps had experienced from another?

I knew almost nothing about his past beyond where he had spent his youth, the struggle to survive, then his arrival in London with Munro all those years before.

Or possibly it came from what he had experienced in his years with the MP.

"Which one is it?" I asked.

"Perhaps all of it."

And enough to set brother against brother, and commit murder? But for what?

"For some, it is never enough," he continued. "Two who are the same, yet different. Envy. And there is only one way it can end."

We had two days to put everything in place for the performance Jean Luc was to give at the Olympic.

"I'm going to meet with Lucy Penworth at the Times to make certain the editor will be running the announcement of the performance tomorrow," I commented. "She wants to meet away from the newspaper building because of Alan Ivers," I added. It was one of the things on our list of things to be taken care of in order to make this work.

"Where will ye be meeting her?" Brodie asked looking up from the diagram he had obtained of the Olympic Theater.

"At the coffee shop at the Emporium at six o'clock after she leaves the Times. She's already spoken with the editor about the announcement for the performance. She wants to go over what it should include. I have Betard's note about the illusion he will be performing."

I saw the frown at his face.

"The Emporium is a bit far from here," he replied.

"She chose it because it's quite far from the Times and less likely that Alan Ivers would go nosing about, and it's very near her flat. I can take a cab there." I didn't bother to explain that it seemed that Alex Sinclair had recently moved into her flat and that would undoubtedly deter Alan Ivers as well.

"With everything that's come down, I don't like ye going out about on yer own, particularly after yer one encounter with Betard's brother."

I gave him that look, one he was quite familiar with by now. Or at least, should have been.

"I'm to meet Munro to go over the layout of the theater or I would go with ye," he explained. "It's the best time to meet him before that announcement comes out in the paper, then he's back to Betard's residence with some other people Sir Avery has made available."

"I don't expect you to change your plans and I cannot change mine if we want the announcement to come out in the morning edition," I replied. "I will have the revolver with me, and I'll take

Rupert," I added. "He's proven himself to be quite effective warding off unsavory sorts."

Brodie made a sound at his throat, definitely not a compliment. "That bloody hound," he said then.

"You must admit there are few who would choose to tangle with him. I'll have Mr. Cavendish obtain some biscuits and sausage for him before I leave."

"Mikaela..."

Conversations that began with my given name usually included some comment from Brodie that I might not like. Whatever he might have been about to say, he seemed to change his mind.

"Take enough coin to pay the extra fare. It's a bit of long ways to the Emporium then back here." He hesitated again.

"I want ye to stay here," he added. It seemed to hang in the air between us.

"Until this is over," he added. "If ye need more of yer things, I could see you to the townhouse at Mayfair."

If there was more that he would have said, it would have to wait as the bell sounded at the landing.

He frowned. "That would be Mr. Cavendish with the workmen." He got up and went to the door, then out onto the landing.

Workmen? I thought.

He returned, two workmen behind him, one on each end of an enormous chalkboard that they had maneuvered up the stairs and now into the office.

It was magnificent, framed in oak, with a chalk rail along the bottom edge. I was immediately out of my chair at the other side of the desk.

"Oh, do be careful," I told them as they angled it through the doorway.

A question was directed at Brodie about where he wanted it mounted. He looked over at me.

"The lady can tell ye where she would prefer to have it."

The original chalkboard that I had used previously had gone up in flames with the rest of the office furnishings. It had been scuffed and cracked, undoubtedly confiscated from some abandoned building. Never let it be said that Angus Brodie wasted his coin.

The old board had been mounted at the wall behind the desk in the darkest part of the office with only a single overhead electric light. That had been improved upon with the repairs that had been made after the fire with an additional lighting including the one in the adjoining bedroom that had once been no more than a storeroom.

I surveyed the office, then made the logical decision for the best location at the wall beside the door where it might catch the light from the window at the opposite wall during the day, and from the additional light that had been added at night since our investigations did seem to run into long hours. It also allowed whoever was sitting at the desk to see it without having to turn constantly turn about.

When the workmen hesitated, Brodie told them, "Ye'll not want to argue with her. She has a bit of a temper."

They maneuvered, shifted, then maneuvered the cumbersome chalkboard until I was satisfied with the location then set the board against the wall, pulled their tools, and set to work. In no time at all the new board was installed. It was like Christmas... it was marvelous.

After they had gone, Brodie shook his head. "Most women want a new gown or some expensive perfume. You get excited over a chalkboard."

"I am not most women, Mr. Brodie."

"Aye, I've noticed."

I stood back and admired it, running my fingers along the chalk rail.

"You will need this as well," he said, removing a package wrapped in brown paper from the bottom drawer of the desk. He handed it to me.

It contained a box of chalk sticks and a wool felt eraser. The chalk was colored!

"For adding yer thoughts and suggestions to your list of notes. I was told the colored chalk makes it easier to find a specific note," he explained.

Lavender soap, a fine hairbrush, and a brand-new chalkboard —no small expense. And colored chalk!

"Does this mean that perhaps you like me just a little?" I suggested. There was that rare smile, his eyes softening.

"Aye, perhaps a wee bit."

I'd had things said to me by men in the past, with the obvious suggestion or a smirk, but I had never had a man tell me before that he *liked* me.

"Ye'll go straight to meet with Lucy Penworth, then return straightaway," he told me when it was time for me to leave for my meeting with her. Then he handed me the revolver.

I tucked it into the pocket of my skirt. There was a worried expression at his face.

"With all these new inventions ye would think someone would make a sort of phone where ye could make a call any time of the day or night, perhaps call boxes here and there. I would know when ye left after meetin' with her."

That was definitely something that could be useful, I thought. Perhaps for the next Great Exhibition along with motorized wagons I'd heard so much about, some sort of flying machine that was the next step beyond the hot air balloon, or the cross-channel rail tunnel that had been proposed some time before.

I assured him that I would be fine.

Mr. Cavendish waved down a cab as I reached the street below the office.

"Thank you kindly, miss for the steamed pie for me supper," he commented with a grin. "And the hound is grateful as well."

Rupert's grin matched his, along with the wagging of his tail.

"I cleaned him up a bit fer his ride with you, tho' he's not one to take kindly to a bath."

That was most certainly an understatement, however it was also part of the hound's disguise as well. No one on the street gave him a second thought. Unless, of course, they made him angry, or attempted to take a bone away from him.

"We will get along just fine, Mr. Cavendish, and return promptly after my meeting."

"Right yer are, miss," he acknowledged, then admonished the hound, "Behave yerself ye flea-ridden mass of bones or I'll drop ye off at the docks."

It was a frequent threat that went unnoticed or at least appeared to. It was ignored once more as Brodie opened the gate of the cab and the hound leapt inside. I followed and joined him at the narrow seat.

"Ye'll come back straight away," he reminded me as he closed the gate.

"Of course," I assured him.

I could only imagine the image we presented as we set off for my meeting with Lucy Penworth, me in my walking skirt and boots, with my hat, jacket, and carpetbag, the hound sitting up, looking about at those we passed by like a distinguished gentleman.

I sat across from Lucy at the coffee shop, the hound sprawled at my feet under the table. Lucy pulled out the evening edition of the paper and opened it.

"I was able to get this into this evening's edition. Tomorrow there will be a full spread about the performance—the date, time, and the fact that it's a closed engagement."

It would run in the next day's edition as well.

I caught the frown at her face. "I know that it's supposed to be a closed performance, rehearsal as it were for his next tour." She hesitated, then continued.

"I would like an exclusive on it," she then explained.

I had previously assured her that any story about the outcome of the murder would be hers to write, even if she was considering leaving the Times for work with Alex Sinclair.

"Of course," I told her.

"The only way I can do that," she continued, "is if I'm there that night, in order to get the details right."

I suppose it could be said that I saw a bit of myself in Lucy Penworth—

intelligent and unafraid to assert herself in a particularly male dominated profession. Brodie, of course, would have disagreed with me. The very reason for a closed performance—rehearsal as it were—was to limit the risk to anyone at the same time we hoped to draw Betard's brother out.

It was, of course, a risk for Betard. But he had been determined in the matter and Brodie had eventually agreed that it might be the only way to apprehend a man who had already killed three people.

In the end, I agreed with her.

"I'll make Mr. Brodie aware of it."

"He'll object," she replied.

Smart girl. "He objects to a great many things, but I'll persuade him."

We finished our coffee and prepared to leave.

"Is he still alive?" Lucy asked with a look down at the hound who had rolled onto his back, all four paws in the air and making quite a scene in the coffee shop.

"Just taking a bit of a nap," I replied, having seen that same pose before, one eye one closed, the other eye half open, and that faint grin. Guard dog on duty.

We stepped over him as we made our way to the door.

"You'll take *that* with you," the proprietor of the coffee shop called after me with a gesture to Rupert who still lay mostly under the table, undisturbed.

"I won't have 'im scaring off me customers."

I might have explained that the hound mostly did exactly as he pleased, and with his size there was hardly anyone who would argue a point with him.

However, the man had been good enough to allow Rupert to join us when I purchased a half dozen small cakes that he had immediately devoured. Never let it be said that the hound couldn't be persuaded.

It wasn't necessary to call to him as Lucy opened the door, the bell overhead ringing. As if the *'dead'* had suddenly come back to life, my protector leaped to his feet, shook himself off and joined us.

Lucy and I had spent the last two hours going over the plans for Betard's closed performance as well as the information that would appear in the article of the Times daily the next morning.

We parted at the sidewalk just outside the Emporium where she found a cab to return to the Times office where she would write the article that was to appear in the newspaper the next day.

There wasn't another cab in sight.

"It appears there isn't another cab about," I told the hound, ignoring the odd looks I received from a couple who passed by at the sidewalk. I Ignored them.

"We will undoubtedly be able to find one at the high street." I set off. However, the hound seemed to be of a different mind.

He stood at the sidewalk as if he would have followed, however his attention was drawn in the opposite direction. I had seen that same posture before.

"What is it?"

Ears perked up, or as near to that as possible with one torn from some past encounter, his entire demeanor changed, and there was a rumble that I had also heard before.

I looked past him, into the shadows at the edge of the street where the light from one streetlamp ended in darkness then met and slipped into the next pool of light. Someone *was* there, waiting in the shadows.

I do not frighten easily. I have seen and experienced far too much, particularly in my association with Brodie, to give in to that foolish emotion that numbs one's thoughts and ability to protect oneself. And I did have the revolver in the pocket of my skirt.

Before I could call out and demand that whoever was hiding there show himself, the hound decided to take matters into his own hands... or paws at it were. He launched himself down the sidewalk at a full run with much snarling and snapping.

I might have called him back, but I have also learned from past experiences that when the hound was on the chase, it was impossible to reason with him. Much like Brodie.

I then heard loud barking from farther down the street, followed by a sudden silence, then a horrible scream. Brodie's warnings cast aside, I ran the direction the hound had disappeared.

"I never seen nothin' like it!" I heard someone say, followed by, "Like the hound from hell, come through the night!" And then, "Sent chills right up me spine. Got what he deserved, though!"

A crowd had gathered, or at least as much of a crowd as a half dozen people might make. I pushed my way through, expecting the worst.

The *'worst'* was the hound sitting at the sidewalk, a grin at his face, or as much of a grin as he could manage with the mouthful of cloth in his teeth. The cloth had a distinctive herringbone pattern, along with another piece of fabric along with it.

It appeared that *someone* had lost a good piece of his coat along with a portion of his pants.

I pocketed the revolver and patted the hound on the head. "Good boy!"

"Everythin' all right, miss?" Mr. Cavendish asked when we finally arrived back at the Strand.

"Perfectly all right, " I replied, giving the hound a scratch behind the ears.

Rupert was still grinning as I climbed the stairs to the office.

# Sixteen

"ABSOLUTELY NOT!" Brodie replied when I told him of my agreement for Lucy to have an exclusive story for the newspaper— with the small detail that she would need to attend the Olympic theater the night of Betard's performance.

"The fewer the people who are there the less likely someone else might be injured, or worse. We are dealing with someone who has already killed three people," he pointed out.

"I am aware of that."

"And yer not to be there either."

That, of course, was going too far.

"I beg your pardon?"

"That's my final say in the matter. I'll not have Miss Penworth putting herself in danger for a story for the newspaper."

Where was this coming from? I thought. This was our case. I had put in as much effort and time as he had. I had as much say in this as he did. And it had been the information Lucy had found for us that had sent us to Paris and brought us to this point. I was not about the let her be set aside in this.

"As I remember, Alex Sinclair is to be there," I pointed out.

"Aye, and several of Sir Avery's people."

"I'm certain that he is capable of seeing that she is safe."

That dark gaze narrowed on me. "What are ye talkin' about?"

I had noticed in the past that whenever Brodie's temper was up, that Scot's accent thickened.

"They are together."

"What is that supposed to mean?"

Men could be so obtuse, refusing to see what was right in front of them.

"It means Alex has moved into her flat. They are together," I repeated. "I believe it would be described as in the biblical sense."

There was that dawning moment and a curse.

"I'll have a word with Alex in the matter," He finally announced. "That will be the end of it. And where the devil are ye going?"

"To bed," I informed him. "I'm tired and there are a great many things to be done tomorrow."

"Such as," he demanded.

"Such as determining the best location for Alex's people, along with Mr. Conner and Mr. Munro at the theater. I do believe you said that it's important for everyone to be in their place for Betard's performance." I turned and went into the bedroom.

"What I told ye was that everyone needed to know their responsibility— the reason I will be meeting with Alex and Sir Avery tomorrow."

There was a brief pause. I waited.

"And ye'll not be going as well!"

There it was, I thought, the male of the species exerting his authority over one and all. Especially true, I had discovered, of the Scottish species. I let him have his moment with that, then asked, "Are you coming to bed?"

There was, of course, another curse, also a requisite for a disgruntled Scot who should know by now that he had just lost this argument. Again. However that did not mean that he was going to surrender the point just now.

"Mikaela..."

He had followed me into the room. I turned.

"Yes?"

"I will have my say in this."

I moved closer and began to unbutton his shirt, my fingers brushing warm skin.

"Cease, woman!" he snarled.

I brushed my lips against that warm skin and made a faint sound at the taste of cinnamon and Brodie.

Then, his hands were in my hair, and his mouth found mine. There was another soft curse and something in Gaelic as several of the buttons at my shirtwaist scattered to the floor. He swore again.

"Ye'll be the death of me." His beard was soft at my bare shoulder.

"Not just yet," I whispered as I brought his mouth back to mine.


I had encountered Brodie's different moods in our association, and thought that I knew them all. It wasn't the first time he had refused to let me participate in an aspect of an investigation, and it certainly wasn't the first time I had refused to do as he said. It was, however, the first time that he simply refused to discuss anything with me.

As my aunt would have said, it seemed that he was having a fit and falling in the middle of it. Of course, in that Scottish way with much grumbling and grousing about, impatient, along with several complaints when Sir Avery postponed their meeting for the planning of the next evening.

There was no improvement as he grabbed his coat, with the theater layout in hand, and was about to set off for that meeting.

"I told ye…"

"Yes, I know, however I will go as well. As you have told me in the past, I am intelligent and might be able to offer some insight into the planning." I stepped past him at the door and proceeded to the stairs.

"A fine day, miss," Mr. Cavendish greeted me with a glance past to Brodie as he followed.

"And to ye sir, as well," he added, which simply brought a snapped reply.

"A cab, if ye please," Brodie replied.

Mr. Cavendish, far more familiar with Brodie's temper, looked at me with a narrowed glance. "Supper disagree with you?" He suggested as he maneuvered to the curb and waived down a driver.

"Or did you not sleep well?"

I smothered back the smile at that one.

"You might want to check for bed bugs, sir," Mr. Cavendish suggested then. "The little buggers can be most irritating."

I was forced to laugh behind my hand at that one. Bed bugs indeed, I thought.

Brodie glared at both of us. There was one last comment for my benefit.

"Ye are not coming along on this."

"Of course," I replied and stepped past him and into the cab.

"Would ye have me acquire ye another cab?" he asked Brodie while exchanging a glance with me.

"I can see that the two of ye are in this together," Brodie replied. "I never thought that ye could be persuaded by a woman!"

Mr. Cavendish merely grinned. "And ye as well, sir," he replied as our driver set off.

We arrived at the offices of the Special Services at the Tower for our meeting with Alex and Sir Avery. Betard and Sophie arrived shortly after, escorted by Mr. Conner.

Sophie's presence was required as she was to be part of the performance that Betard gave the following evening—not merely pulling a rabbit out of the hat as it were or anything as simple as that.

The performance—his final rehearsal before leaving on tour as it had been announced in the paper— was to be a series of the illusions he had planned for the tour that also included Sophie. It was assumed that the original illusion would be eliminated as it required two small, slender women who resembled each other. In the case of the original illusion, he had used the twins—Francoise and Sophie.

Sir Avery was thoughtful as the diagram of the layout of the theater was spread before him at his desk.

He looked over at Brodie. "It has been my experience that someone who has planned such an elaborate scheme is often very intelligent, even brilliant. Your murderer has eluded capture so far. There is always the chance that he will be wary of such a performance and choose not to appear.

"In that case, " he continued, "all of your efforts will be wasted, and he will still be out there to strike again. Murder is after all, an act of arrogance."

I exchanged a look with Brodie. He didn't disagree.

"What if Jean Luc was to create the exact same illusion again?"

To say that everyone's attention fastened on me, would have been a slight understatement. Everyone, that is except Brodie, who suddenly rose from that chair across from Sir Avery. He took hold of me by the arm.

"Ye will excuse us for a moment," he announced and pulled me out into the hallway outside Sir Avery's office.

"I know exactly what ye are thinkin'. Have ye lost what sense I thought ye had?"

I was prepared for his reaction, and quietly waited as a clerk passed by and Brodie continued to make his objections known.

Another man passed by, made brief eye contact with me and, with a sympathetic smile, continued past.

"I will not have it. Do ye understand?"

"It's perfectly all right then for you to go to the theater and encounter whatever may happen?" I asked. I will admit my voice had raised a small bit.

"It's my job," he replied. Two curses at this point, his not mine, then, "It's what I do."

"And it's what I do," I told him and discovered that the more calm I remained, the more irate Brodie became. Most interesting.

"I say where I go, and what I will do. I have my entire adult life." Aside for those few years in there before I became an adult, with a few exceptions.

"It could work, and I know my way around a concealing cabinet."

He had gone from shouting, cursing, to silently shoving his hand back through that dark hair. From experience, I knew that did not necessarily mean victory.

"Ye canna do it," he said then, suspiciously calm. "Yer too tall, ye would never fit into that glass box."

I started to protest, to inform him that he was simply making excuses and knew that I was right about being perfect for it. Except... that I knew that he was right.

I was very near five feet ten inches tall, in my stockings. Sophie, and of course Francoise, were barely more than five feet tall, a critical difference when it came to the confines of the box.

"You know that I'm right, lass. It wouldn't work."

*Lass*, was it? Much calmer when he believed that he had made a case for his argument.

I was not what is often referred to as a 'sore loser'. I didn't consider that I had lost the argument at all.

I could concede that point about my height preventing me from being part of the illusion, but not the proposal that was in fact quite ingenious and would all but guarantee that Betard's brother would be there. I had only one thing to say.

"Templeton."

If his reaction to my suggestion that I might perform the illusion with Sophie had been irate, it might have been outdone by the suggestion that my friend would be willing to play the part.

"The woman is...!"

I didn't give him the opportunity to finish. I had heard it all before.

"She is almost the same height as Sophie and with the proper make-up and identical costumes, she would be perfect," I interjected. And with that I walked right back into Sir Avery's office to the curious glances of those inside his office, and presented my idea.

And I discovered that there was at least one person present whom Brodie would not argue the matter—Sir Avery.

Plans were finalized. Everyone was acquainted with their role, the positions they would take up in the theater, and the fact that I would immediately contact Templeton. I had no doubt the answer she would give.

To say that it was a long, silent ride back to the office on the Strand was another understatement in a day that had been full of them.

"This is so exciting!" Templeton exclaimed.

"*So exciting*," her feathered friend repeated.

"Of course, I'll do it."

I had finally connected with her after she returned from a séance she had attended.

"It was most exciting," she rattled on. "I thought that Wills would pop through of course, but no. He's been in a bit of a temper lately. I criticized a character in one of his plays—a woman. I attempted to explain that her reaction simply was not consistent with women that I know and that he had it quite wrong. He was not pleased and has taken himself off."

Oh, dear.

What little I knew of her supposed interactions with the bard, the spirit of William Shakespeare that is, had been limited to his opinion of an oversized, and over embellished statue in the foyer of a theater where she had performed. In short, he didn't like it at all and had made that clear to Templeton. Supposedly.

However, I was not one to argue with one's habits or talents.

"I'm sorry," I commented.

She waved a hand through the air, dismissing the situation.

"He will be back. No one else puts up with his tantrums. Now, tell me, what do you need me to do?" And we were off to the races, as they say.

To say that she sparkled was yet one more understatement. Or that she was absolutely beside herself with excitement.

"What am I to wear?"

I explained that Sophie would be able to provide once of Francoise's costumes that was identical to her own for the illusion.

We would also need the assistance of Mrs. Finch, who assisted her in her different roles with make-up, and possibly a wig to make her look more like Sophie. I would arrange for her to meet with Sophie before tomorrow night's performance.

Brodie was still not speaking to me when I returned to the office on the Strand late in the afternoon. And it was most commonly said that women were difficult to get along with!

I ignored him as I went about adding more notes to the new chalkboard while he studied the theater layout and a list of his own with each role that everyone was to play.

When it had grown very near the supper hour and I was quite hungry, I left the office and went down the stairs and asked Mr. Cavendish if he would like to accompany me to the public house just down the way. To say that he was surprised was one more understatement for the day.

"I don't think you would like to be seen with the likes of me, miss," he replied, briefly doffing his cap in that way of his. I caught the way his kind gaze glanced past me at the same time I heard steps at the stairs just above.

"Not at all, Mr. Cavendish. Your company is far preferable to others I might name."

Never one to refuse a free meal or the opportunity to twist Brodie's tail, he replaced his cap and swung his platform about at the sidewalk.

"I heard from one of the lads that Miss Effie had put up some 'spotted dick' earlier," he said, his way of accepting my invitation.

I glanced back at Brodie as we set off.

"Spotted dick it is then," I said. So, Mr. Cavendish had a taste for steamed pudding with currants. I would have to let Mrs. Ryan know.

I could only imagine the sight we presented to those on the street—myself, Mr. Cavendish with his cap set quite jauntily at his head, paddling his way along beside me, and the hound.

When we returned, I seriously contemplated having the driver take me to the townhouse in Mayfair.

"I've never seen Mr. Brodie so taken with a woman," Mr. Cavendish commented as he lit a cigarette. "Most of 'em want just one thing—coin for the night or a while longer, and not with the sense God gave a goose."

"Are you suggesting that I'm a goose?" I asked with some amusement at his philosophical musings.

"I'm sayin' that an intelligent woman with spirit who would just as soon be by herself is an unexpected thing for a man like Mr. Brodie. It takes some getting used to. But to my way of thinkin' it's something like a taste of fine whisky," he added, with a look at me.

"Once you've had the good stuff, nothin' else will do."

Whisky, indeed.

"Of course, an intelligent, independent woman would need to make allowances for a man like that," he continued.

I wondered how much he might have heard about my argument with Brodie.

"Just sayin', you might keep that in mind." He spun about on his platform. "I'm off to the Old Bell for a bit of a nightcap. The whisky there is not worth the time, but the ale is good."

The Old Bell was a place he frequented. The hound waited expectantly for him. They were an interesting pair.

Brodie stood before the chalkboard as I entered the office. I will admit that I thought he might have considered having it removed after our last conversation.

I removed my jacket and hat, then turned to the desk. It was then I noticed the two tumblers there, the light from the electric light gleaming at the amber liquid in each one—my aunt's very fine whisky, of course. Both glasses were full.

He had waited for me to return. I cannot say why that small thing meant so much. His way of apologizing perhaps? Or acknowledging that perhaps, just perhaps, my idea regarding Templeton had merit.

"She will arrive in the afternoon for us to go to the theater," I told him. "There will be plenty of time for Sophie and Betard to go through everything with her."

He turned, that dark gaze angled away from me. "She knows the risk?"

"Yes. After all, she was there the night of his performance at the Crystal Palace. I assured her that she will be well protected."

He picked up one of the tumblers and handed it to me, then took the other. "It was a good idea. It's just that..."

"I know," I replied.

What had it taken for him to say that? We both took a sip.

"She is quite taken with the idea," I added. "She insists that Wills will most certainly see that she's safe, once he returns. However, I know that you will see that she's safe as well."

"Once he returns?" He took another long swallow.

"It seems that he's taken himself off over a disagreement with her," I explained. Whatever I might have expected at that, I was not prepared for what he said.

"Aye, well, I can understand how that might happen. The woman can be very difficult."

I ignored that specific reference. His acknowledgement about Wills was a great deal more than I would have given him credit for, not being one to believe in such things.

"As ye are as well," he said then, perhaps needing to get in the last word.

"And stubborn?" I added.

"Aye!" he acknowledged, a little more forcefully than I thought necessary, but I let it go.

"Unpredictable?" To quote an unpredictable and equally stubborn Scot.

"To try a man's soul. As I said, ye are unique. And will probably be the death of me, Mikaela Forsythe."

"That might be a bit of a problem for solving crime," I replied. "And I'm certain that heaven might not want you, arguing with everyone, going about like a bear with a wounded paw, and you should consider the possibility that God may be a woman."

I laughed at his expression at the last part.

"A woman? Then, God help us both," he replied. "And considerin' the things I've done..." He didn't explain that, and I didn't ask.

He poured us both another dram.

"Ye will need to add those new notes to the board," he suggested.

We now had more answers, I thought as I added my latest note about Templeton to the board. At least we knew who had written those notes and who had killed both Francoise and Marie. But I couldn't help but think that there was more that we didn't know.

"What about the residue we found on the glass box?" I asked standing back to survey the board that had filled up quite nicely now. "From your experience," I added.

"Severe injuries that Monsieur Betard spoke of," he replied. "All those years in that hospital, the man's mind gone. Most likely the morphine was provided for the pain. And then it's not enough. I've seen it before."

"His own brother," I commented. "And now three people are dead." I shook my head, still trying to understand.

"What would drive him to do this?" I thought of our earlier conversation about the reasons someone committed murder. The man who called himself Jean Luc Betard had been committed to that hospital in Paris—deranged, prone to violent outbursts.

Was that all it was, a crippled body and the ravings of a lunatic mind? Or was there more? I wanted to know.

"He was able to escape, to come here, for what reason?"

Brodie had spoken of the things he had seen and done. He tossed back the rest of the whisky at his glass.

"Revenge."

"For what?" Jean Luc had said nothing more after that one revelation that the man who had escaped from the hospital and had come here was his brother.

"It's between the brothers."

Revenge. I added the word to my notes at the board.

"Let it be, for now," Brodie told me. "We'll have the answers soon enough." I heard the unspoken at his voice. A question that waited between us.

"Let it be."

And it was that simple.

I turned and he was there, that question in that dark gaze after the angry words between us, and I knew what he was asking.

I stepped into his arms and closed my eyes at the strength of him, the gentleness, the way he reached past his own dark secrets and held me. Not a truce as they say, but... acceptance.

He was who he was, and I was who I was. There was no changing it, but we both accepted it.

And I let it be.

# Seventeen

I LOOKED DOWN at Rupert the hound who slept at the floor of the office. He had been assigned to official guard duty as Brodie left for his meeting with the man we knew as Jean Luc Betard. They were to finalize the plans for the rehearsal performance that evening that included that illusion in the glass box, while I waited for Templeton and Elvira Finch to arrive. A copy of the morning edition of the Times lay at the desk.

Lucy Penworth had been quite successful in persuading her editor about the article she wrote. It was meant to draw Jean Luc's brother to the theater, and appeared on the front page that now included the announcement that Betard would be rehearsing the glass box illusion in preparation for his world tour.

It was a rarity for a theater performance to appear on the front page. That was usually reserved for news of the latest political upheaval or war.

When Templeton arrived, I was to escort her and Elvira Finch to the theater, arriving some distance away and then proceeding afoot in the off chance that Betard's brother might be watching the theater.

The others who were part of the plan, among Sir Avery's people and those Brodie had brought into the scheme, were to appear as theater attendants, delivery persons, and workmen going about their usual tasks at the theater.

Mr. Munro and Mr. Conner were to enter the theater from the adjacent building and a shared entrance at the back alley. Brodie would arrive later with Betard and Sophie in the disguise of one of Betard's entourage assisting with the delivery of those glass boxes.

"Good heavens!" Elvira Finch said and backed away to the door at the sight of Rupert. "What is that?"

*That*, namely the hound, lifted his head and growled.

"It's quite all right," I patted him on the head. "He is my unofficial escort," I explained as Templeton dropped to her knees at the floor and stroked his head.

"I had an iguana," she started to explain, as if the hound understood. "He was quite a handsome fellow, but not as handsome as you."

Apparently he did understand, as his tail thumped at the floor, and he grinned. Another friend in the making.

"Will he be coming with us?" she asked. "We will need a coach."

And that settled the matter of whether he was coming with us or not.

For Elvira's benefit, I explained what was needed for the performance that night. She had brought her kit with the usual assortment of make-up and wigs that might be needed for one of Templeton's performances.

I thought, somewhat fondly, of the fake wart she had provided me on a previous occasion for a disguise I had worn. It had not been a favorite of Brodie's, something about reminding him of his grandmother.

I had, however, not told Elvira any details about the reasons for the performance, thinking that might be better.

"I mentioned that it was about the murder at the Crystal Palace," Templeton added, and there went my intention to not mention the more serious aspects of the performance for that night.

Elvira Finch reminded me of a mouse—gray hair, gray eyebrows, small, with hands clutched before her like one of those creatures who had just found a piece of bread or cake, nose twitching. But she quite surprised me.

"Sounds exciting," she declared. "When do we begin?"

I wondered if that might be Wills' influence—William Shakespeare that is. He had written extensively about the subject in his plays.

The telephone rang, irritating sound. I was inclined to agree with my great aunt in that regard. It was Brodie, the sound of his voice crackling over the line.

With Sophie's agreement, he and Sir Avery were able to convince Jean Luc as to the merit of performing the glass box illusion.

"I explained that Templeton would provide the role that usually went to Sophie in the second box," he said over the telephone from Alex's office at the Special Services.

"She knows the part her sister played in the illusion."

From my closeness with my own sister, I could only imagine how difficult this must be for Sophie.

He then informed me that Templeton needed to be at the theater no later than one o'clock in the afternoon to learn her part in this.

The call ended and I looked over at the two women. "You will need a disguise in case he might be watching the theater," I told Templeton. Elvira Finch nodded.

"I may have just what is needed," she announced as she looked over at Templeton.

"The part you played in Macbeth."

I knew the play well enough. That did seem a bit extreme.

"Did you bring the wig?" Templeton asked.

"I have it here," Mrs. Finch replied. "I'll fix it up a bit and with the right make-up, I'll have you looking like a charwoman." She turned to me. "We'll need a bucket and a broom as well."

I wondered if the make-up might include a wart. It did seem that Mrs. Finch was most enthusiastic at the prospect of transforming Templeton, a very attractive woman who was rumored to have attracted the attentions of Bertie, the Prince of Wales.

Although she had never actually admitted to that, at least not in the Biblical sense.

I set off, Rupert lumbering along behind me. There were undoubtedly the basic tools of a cleaning woman somewhere in the building.

We arrived at the alleyway entrance to the theater just after one o'clock, remarkable for Templeton as she never arrived anywhere on time. She had once explained it as raising the enthusiasm of the audience and admirers. I wondered if that included Mr. Munro as he opened the door at the back entrance.

An estrangement, between them, she had described it. It seemed that it might be a bit more than that. Usually quite stoic, preferring a look when a comment would have sufficed, and being quite tall, he simply looked past her to me.

"Miss Forsythe, Mrs. Finch." And nothing for Templeton.

Oh dear, I did hope that did not bode ill for our plans.

I greeted him in return.

"Mr. Brodie is with the owner at present, explainin' what is to take place, and attempting to persuade him that he shouldna be here tonight."

I suspected there might be some resistance to that suggestion.

"The glass boxes?" I inquired.

"They arrived some time ago and we have set them up at the stage. Damned contraptions."

I glanced past him from the back entrance into the back of the stage area.

"Dressing rooms for performers?"

"If ye'll come with me, I'll show the way." He looked past our small party at the hound who had accompanied us from the office on the Strand. A dark brow lifted, much the same way I had seen at times with Brodie.

"He's a guard dog," Templeton announced in a certain tone so that there would be no misunderstanding.

"What is the beast guardin' against?" he demanded.

It did seem as if we might all be in the middle of a confrontation. Estrangement indeed.

"Against dangerous persons and other miscreants," Templeton replied as if delivering a speech. I wondered which play that might be from. She seemed to have it down quite well.

"Come along. The dressing rooms?" I hinted and was ignored.

"I can find my way," Mrs. Finch announced. "Seen the inside of one theater, you've seen them all."

I was inclined to agree, and we set off to find the dressing rooms. Rupert, however, seemed most fascinated with the somewhat heated conversation that was now in progress.

"*I did no such thing,*" I heard Templeton reply to some comment.

"What about the marks at yer breasts?"

"You might ask! In any event, what business is it of yours?"

"I am askin'!"

Oh dear, these walls did seem to echo a bit. And that part of the conversation did seem quite familiar, from a similar encounter I had written about in my last novel—in particular that comment about, 'what business'. Apparently, Templeton had been reading my books.

We left them to their bickering, much like some old married couple, and much like...? Well, Munro was a Scot after all, and that sort did seem prone to difficult temperaments.

With her vast theater experience, we easily found the dressing rooms back of the stage where Mrs. Finch would transform Templeton into a lookalike of Sophie. Or as near as possible with

CARLA SIMPSON

make-up, a wig, and the costume that already hung over the screen.

Templeton arrived some time later, quite flushed. Or was that a whisker burn at her neck. It seemed that it might take all of Mrs. Finch's considerable skill to transform her into a shy, demure duplicate of Sophie.

We were eventually introduced to Mr. Strempole, the owner of the Olympic, who refused to leave the premises for his own safety. Or rather, I should say that he introduced himself, euphoric—that was the only way to describe it— that the *incomparable, magnificent* Theodora Templeton, was actually going to be part of the performance that night.

Those were exactly his words. Munro would undoubtedly have agreed after that little encounter at the back of the theater considering Templeton's high color which was still there some hours later.

I had persuaded Brodie that Lucy Penworth would be arriving as well. After all, she was to have the exclusive story for the newspaper, and she couldn't very well write about something if she wasn't there.

"Is there anyone else that ye've invited?"

I caught the obvious sarcasm, and it was simply too tempting.

"I thought of inviting my aunt. She is quite a fan of Templeton's."

"Ye have a wicked sense of humor, Miss Forsythe."

"It must be the company I've been keeping of late."

The humor was gone now from that dark gaze that fastened on me.

"If the man takes the bait and shows up tonight, this could be a very dangerous undertaking."

"Do you believe that he will?"

"It's the opportunity he has no doubt been waiting for. And he has nothing to lose. That makes him particularly dangerous." He brushed his fingers across my cheek. "Ye have to promise to do as I say. If anything were to happen to ye…"

"What could possible happen?" I replied, taken by the gravity at his voice and far more than he had ever said in the past.

"I'm concerned for Sophie and Templeton," I continued. "You're certain they'll be safe?"

"As safe as can be considerin' yer friend's habit for stepping in the middle of a mess."

I knew he was thinking of her own recent situation with the French Ambassador.

"It wasn't at all her fault," I defended her. "It had to do with things far more serious than entertaining the ambassador." That was, of course, putting a fine polish to the whole thing that might very well have ended in an international incident as those in high places like to refer to them.

"Still, I would prefer that ye keep to the dressing room and out of sight."

"Of course," I replied.

His eyes narrowed. "What is that supposed to mean?"

"It means that I understand."

He wasn't satisfied. "Yer word on it," he insisted.

"You have my word." And I would do my best to keep it.

"Aye," he slowly replied.

"You cannot expect me to stay in Templeton's dressing room until the performance. And I would like to see them rehearse."

There was that narrow-eyed look again.

"For rehearsal and then ye're to come back here."

I nodded, and hoped that I would be able to keep my word on that.

It was amazing how easily Sir Avery's and Brodie's people blended in behind the scenes as they say, posing as workmen, cleaning people. All of them seemed part of the staff for the upcoming private performance where Betard would once again perform the illusion that had ended so tragically. His assistant, Sophie in the first box where her sister had been found with Templeton in the second box. Each woman in those compartments inside, hidden by mirrors set at specific angles. One would appear to disappear from one box and then reappear in the second box.

Sophie was quiet and somber while Templeton was quite excited. With Mrs. Finch's expertise she had transformed my friend into a startling resemblance to Sophie. With only the footlights at the edge of the stage it was possible that the three of them, including Jean Luc, might pull this off. Quite possibly the most important illusion of all.

As the hours slipped toward the time that had been published in the newspaper for rehearsal to begin, it seemed there were fewer conversations. Even over the meal that Mr. Strempole had brought in for everyone, where there were usually boisterous conversations, it was oddly quiet, the air heavy, much like before a storm.

Afterward, everyone went about their assigned tasks, and Templeton returned to her dressing room to slip into the costume identical to Sophie's. That startling resemblance that Mrs. Finch had created was almost eerie as both women stood together in the dressing room. Except for Sophie's somber expression, they might have convinced me that they were twins.

I took Sophie's hands in mine. Under other circumstances I might have sent them off with the saying, 'break a leg', but that seemed morbidly inappropriate even though as Templeton had once explained that it was a wish for success according to Wills.

"Everything will be all right." I said a little prayer that it would be, and I was not usually one to resort to prayer.

"This is so exciting!" Templeton repeated for what had to be the hundredth time. She did have a somewhat distorted perception of things. However, this was someone who spoke to spirits in the afterworld. Or possibly the present world?

"Be careful," I told her.

"As you said, everything will be fine. After all, Wills has joined us before rehearsal is to begin."

Of course. What could possibly go wrong? I thought as I accompanied them to the back of the stage for the 'practice' rehearsal, before the actual rehearsal. That had been publicized to begin at eight o'clock, still an hour away.

I must say that once Templeton set her mind to something, or a script, or the plan as it were, she really was most impressive in her role.

However, it must have been excruciating for Sophie to go through the motions of the illusion as she had that night at the Crystal Palace, now playing the part of her sister.

With what I now knew about how the illusion was created, I watched from the curtain area at the left of the stage as Betard entered from the right with Templeton, and went through the steps and motions of the illusion, describing how he would create it. He explained for the imaginary audience that his 'assistant 'would appear in the first box, and then magically transform into the second box right before everyone's eyes.'

I glanced about the stage area, opposite where Betard had emerged, then down across the orchestra pit and into the main part of the theater that was brightly lit. I wondered where Brodie might be. Then I saw him at the back of the theater with Mr. Conner and another man nearby who diligently swept the floors that had already been swept several times.

There were others, I knew. Brodie had assured me that there were more than thirty men there, all in disguise.

Was that enough to protect Sophie and stop Betard's brother? Would he even appear?

I looked back at the stage as Betard held his hand out, and Sophie crossed the stage and joined him. Templeton had already entered the second box after learning how to hide herself in that narrow compartment with mirrors all around.

Step-by-step, the illusion was recreated. It was flawless in the hands of a master illusionist, as it should have been the night at the Crystal Palace as Sophie stepped inside the first box, lay at the floor, and then smiled out at an audience that wasn't there.

Only those few of us saw the way her hand shook and the sad expression that no amount of makeup could hide. The cover was lowered into place over the first box, then at the second box as Betard spoke and made those sweeping gestures as if creating the magic spell that would 'transport' Sophie from one to the other.

Then, in those slowly measured steps and in a voice that seemed to be magic itself, he returned to the first box and ordered the cover to be lifted. It revealed what appeared to be an empty box. He then stepped to the second box and ordered the cover to be removed.

Inside the box, it appeared that Sophie had indeed magically left one box and then appeared in the second one. Betard held her hand and they both bowed to the audience. The curtain came down and he went to the second box where Sophie had hidden herself. He said something and she smiled, staring up at him with such love.

Templeton in that way of hers all but flew across the stage. "That was quite marvelous."

And out on the street, somewhere, someone waited and approached. Would the murderer be convinced?

"Once more," Betard announced. "We must practice it once more. It must be perfect."

"The man is a perfectionist," Brodie commented beside me. He frowned as he watched it all begin again.

"Ye will remember yer promise to me. As soon as this next one is over, ye will go to the dressing room and stay there."

Rupert looked up from me to Brodie then back again, his head cocked. I felt much the same way.

"It's possible that Betard's brother won't appear," I replied.

"He'll come," he replied with certainty. But there was something that still bothered him.

"What is it?"

That dark gaze met mine, briefly, then angled back to the stage.

"The man has managed to stay well-hidden until now, and he's also moved everyone around as he chooses. Much like the parts in a play."

"Or an illusion?" I added.

"Aye, and that's what bothers me. I don't want you caught in the middle of it."

"With Templeton and Sophie on stage, I would say that I am not in the middle of it," I pointed out.

"Ye know very well what I mean."

The problem was that I did know very well. It was one of those things we had yet to maneuver our way through if this, whatever it was, was going to work—my independence that included an incurable penchant for *'finding my way in the middle of things'*, and his need to protect me.

"Yes, I do know," I replied quite simply because this was not the time to have that conversation, and because it was far easier than trying to figure out how we might maneuver that glaring difference.

He left then and I turned my attention back to the stage. I could have sworn the hound frowned at me. At the very least he lay down, head at his paws with a soulful expression at those dark eyes.

"Not you as well," I commented, then told him, "Do not start with me, if you want me to continue to bring you Alice's cakes."

He grumbled at me in answer.

As the hour gave way to minutes and Betard, Sophie, and Templeton went through the motions of the illusion one more time, it seemed that the air in the theater prickled with tension. And a warning?

I was standing at the edge of the stage, contrary to Brodie's instructions to keep to the dressing room. I glanced at the pendant watch I wore. Eight o'clock had come and gone, and nothing. No sign of the man who called himself Jean Luc Betard.

I exchanged a look with Alex Sinclair then Mr. Conner. Their responses were the same, a shake of the head that indicated they had seen nothing. Alex then went to see to the men Sir Avery had sent as the theater owner appeared at the orchestra pit below the stage and applauded loudly.

"Wonderful, absolutely wonderful. I will be able to fill the theater after tonight when word spreads that Jean Luc Betard has performed once again!" he announced enthusiastically.

I saw the shadowy figure that moved overhead where two of Betard's attendants had earlier lowered those covers into place. Then entire stage exploded in fire and smoke.

Sophie had just emerged from that first box and screamed and over it was terrifying laughter overhead as I fought my way through the smoke to reach her and Templeton.

The smoke choked at my throat and stung at my eyes as I reached Sophie.

"Get her out of here!" Jean Luc shouted at me as he turned toward those boxes and that shadowy figure swept down from the rafters on one of those ropes, his cape swirling around him like some creature from the depths of hell, and lunged at Jean Luc. Then like a deadly illusion at the wave of a hand they disappeared into that wall of fire and smoke.

"Rene!" Sophie screamed, clawed at my hand, and tried to pull free.

Rene? There was no time for questions as I pulled her with me.

I glanced back. Even if I could have seen across the stage for all the smoke, there was no sign of Templeton. Shouts went up throughout the theater and that blinding smoke thickened as fire ran up the stage curtains.

As we reached the other side of the stage, I glanced back, and caught a brief glimpse of Jean Luc as he struggled with his attacker. Then they were gone in that cloud of thick smoke...

# Eighteen

**THERE WERE MORE SHOUTS.** Somewhere in all that chaos and smoke, I heard Rupert barking, and the sound of my name. Brodie?

The smoke briefly thinned like some monster as if it took a breath, and I caught a glimpse of Mr. Munro and Mr. Conner running toward the stage. Then, they too disappeared amid more shouts and the sound of shattering glass, and the sound of the fire as it found new fuel and roared toward us.

Stage curtains at this side of the stage whipped past us as the fire seemed to create its own wind, and swept our way.

Terrified, sobbing, Sophie stumbled, fell, and I pulled her back to her feet. I continued to follow what I remembered of the layout of the theater I had fixed in my head as it was impossible to see more than two feet in front of us.

Following that diagram, I turned to my left, pulling her with me as I heard the frantic sound of a horn followed by the clanging of bells as the fire brigade arrived.

Another turn, then another, the smoke lighter as the hallway opened onto the area at the back of the stage where props and equipment were delivered and stored.

There was the sound of someone running, a muffled curse,

and a loud crash. Sophie screamed, her hand suddenly pulled from mine. I spun around. He was there, that figure dressed all in black—the formal suit with tails and that black cape that swirled around him as he dragged Sophie back with him.

Where was Jean Luc? Was he still alive? Was Templeton alive?

Smoke slipped through and swirled from the back of the stage as I faced that stooped and twisted figure who had managed to get inside the theater without anyone knowing. Somehow he had climbed to the rafters where the ropes were secured for the covers of the glass box, and had then dropped down onto the stage like some avenging angel.

Or an angel of death? And had then attacked Jean Luc.

Revenge. Brodie had spoken of it.

I thought of what we knew, what we had seen—those photographs in Anna Betard's room, the notes that had been left behind when Francoise was killed, and then Marie.

'Now there are two.'

A threat? Or a promise, in the message left for the one person who would know what it meant—the man we knew as Jean Luc Betard, world famous illusionist who performed before kings and queens. A man who concealed his own dark secret.

None of it made sense at the time.

Connections, pieces of information and evidence that were like an enormous puzzle waiting to be solved.

Brodie spoke of that too, and I had certainly seen it in the cases we had pursued. It was there now, right in front of me as I stared at the face of Sophie's attacker.

He'd lost the mask I had seen in that encounter at the street, wild eyes staring at me now, the skin at one side of his face marled with hideous scars. The hand at Sophie's throat as he pinned her against the hallway wall twisted with more scars, and only the stub left at one finger.

"You killed Francoise."

That last piece of the puzzle slipped into place, the finger-prints that Mr. Brimley found at the back of that glass box, void of the marks that would usually be found there. Burned away by the fire of some accident. Or an illusion that had somehow gone very wrong?

That wrinkled and faded photograph of two boys of the same height with similar features. Not merely similar, but identical?

"It is almost done now," he replied. "I have destroyed him. The fire will finish what it should have finished years ago and there is only one left," he shouted back, a distorted, horrifying figure.

He meant to kill Sophie, I was certain of it, in some bizarre, twisted plan for revenge.

The name in those hospital records was Jean Luc Betard. Yet, Sophie had called out a name as I pulled her from the stage —Rene?

What did it mean? Was I now facing the real Jean Luc Betard?

It didn't matter. I didn't care what his name was. I didn't care about what had happened in the past and drove him to kill three people, possibly four now. And Sophie?

Revenge was a powerful emotion. I knew that well. But not here, not now, not an innocent young woman fighting to draw a breath as he pinned her by the neck, a knife at her throat. The same knife that had killed her sister.

"Let her go," I told him. "She has nothing to do with this."

That head with hair burned away at the scalp and those distorted features swung toward me, and the thought sliced through everything else, that the man I was staring at wasn't human. Not any longer, and with nothing to lose.

"She is part of it, the two of them, the perfect illusion...! My creation all those years ago! It was mine! He took it from me! Now, I will take it back!"

Take it back, by destroying it? By killing everyone who was part of it at the Crystal Palace? Revenge that had waited for years?

There was no way to stop a madman, to reason with one. Hadn't Brodie told me that once before?

But I had to try.

"She is innocent," I told him. "Would you condemn yourself for her murder?"

He laughed, that chilling, mad laugh I had first heard as he set off that explosion on the stage, the fire and smoke used to conceal himself. Another illusion?

"I am already condemned!" he screamed at me. "Condemned to this body and the loss of everything... and everyone! Nothing matters any longer!"

Everyone? Someone he had cared for? Was it possible the accident that he had survived might have killed someone else? Someone he cared for?

It was no illusion now as I saw his expression change—the madness that had been deep inside for years and had driven him to this. It burned through him, the way his eyes gleamed. He would kill Sophie. Nothing I could say would stop him.

I had left the revolver Brodie gave me in the dressing room. But I had the knife that Mr. Munro had given me when I set off on my first adventure years before, down the side of my boot.

Could I convince him of something long enough to free Sophie? An illusion of my own, real enough to make him believe it for just a few seconds?

I had practiced the move with the knife often enough to Mr. Munro's satisfaction, his voice in my head: 'Ye must be quick, sure of yerself, there are no second chances. Strike first, and remember fear is just as good a weapon.'

I had been forced to use it once before on the streets of Shanghai when a boy at the street had attempted to steal from me. But that had been a boy, far smaller and easily frightened. I could have squashed him like a bug.

I had to admit that I was afraid. Not for myself but for Sophie. What if I simply provoked this madman to carry out his threat to kill her?

He pressed the knife against her throat and all I could think of was the sight of her sister lying in the bottom of that glass box in a pool of blood.

I was no match for a man. I had been taught that. My only advantage lie with surprise and then possibly another move.

I heard a sound from down the hallway, someone running toward us. He heard it as well, momentarily distracted.

Only a few feet away, I attacked, throwing him off balance as I swept his feet from under him. It threw him against the wall, his hold on Sophie suddenly broken.

"Run!" I told her, as he recovered then launched himself toward me. He was amazingly strong in spite of those old injuries and a blow at my wrist sent the knife through the air and skidding across the floor as Sophie ran past me and toward the exit door at the back of the theater.

Insane, and now enraged, the man who had escaped that hospital in Paris, grabbed my arm and wrenched it behind me, pulling me back as clouds of smoke swirled around us and that figure that ran toward us.

Brodie halted as he finally saw us. I had seen him several times 'on the hunt', as Mr. Conner who once served with him on the MP, had called it. That place where a man goes in his head, when confronted with a dangerous situation, the way a coldness takes over, closing off everything else.

I saw that now at Brodie's face as Betard dragged me back, an arm about my shoulders, the tip of his knife pressed against my throat, and I smelled the strong scent of absinthe.

Whatever happened next, at least I had bought enough time for Sophie to escape.

"Yer all right then, lass," Brodie commented absurdly calm, his gaze never leaving me.

Not a question, but a simple statement and not so much what he said, but the way he said it, low, almost tender, the last thing I expected but needed, and in it a silent promise that I would be all right.

I saw the revolver he had brought with him.

"One chance," he told Betard. "I'll give ye just one chance to throw down the knife and let her go. One chance only."

I felt the rumble of laughter begin, from Betard's chest pressed against my back, then heard it at my ear. That crazed laughter I'd first heard at the stage as everything erupted in fire and smoke.

I watched Brodie, that dark gaze fastened on mine. I should have been afraid. But I wasn't afraid. This was Brodie.

"Do it," I told him and meant it, and at that moment I put my life in his hands.

I saw the moment he understood, the way his gaze softened in a silent message only for me, then the way it hardened once more, dark, cold, as he brought his hand up, took aim, and fired.

The bullet exploded past my cheek. I felt Betard stagger behind me as he was struck. He almost pulled me down with him, but I managed to twist free.

Without a word, Brodie stepped past me and fired a second shot, the smoke from the revolver mingling with the smoke from the stage that spilled into the hallway.

Then he was there, his hands rough, urgent as they swept over me as he checked to make certain that I wasn't hurt. He pulled me against him, a hand in my hair, his fingers pressing into my scalp, that dark gaze fastened on mine.

Anything I might have imagined—a curse, my name, something about not following his instructions, for the first time didn't come. He simply stared at me. He shook his head as if in disbelief.

"Do it?" he repeated what I had told him only moments before. Then he swore.

"I could have missed!"

"But you didn't."

# Epilogue

## TWO WEEKS LATER...

THE FIRE at the Olympic had eventually been put out, much to the owner's regret. Firemen had swarmed through the building, soaking everything with water, creating what appeared to be an even greater mess of ruined stage curtains, charred wood, and theater seats that were covered in soot and reeked of smoke.

"If it had been a total loss," Mr. Strempole lamented when he finally emerged from the rubble of the theater looking much like an owl with soot at his face. "I could have filed the insurance and had it rebuilt."

It was the first time I had seen Templeton with her make-up smeared and her costume askew, quite a different stage performance for her.

Munro had pulled her from the box where she had hidden in that secret compartment during the illusion, and was then unable to get out. That was the sound of breaking glass I had heard. Munro had a few cuts at his hands.

"No worse than other things," he had brushed it off, with no explanation what those 'other things' might mean.

He and Templeton did seem to have reached some sort of accord in their relationship, although the writer in me was convinced that this was only the latest chapter.

Now, I continued to add to my notes about the case, completing the sad tale that Lucy Penworth could not write for the newspaper—the facts only according to her editor, sensational to be sure. All in the interest of selling more newspapers. But I had learned the story firsthand, and felt a need to put it all down on paper.

Perhaps a book was waiting to be written, the identities changed to protect the innocent.

The man we first knew as Jean Luc Betard, who had performed at the Crystal Palace the night Francoise was murdered, was in fact Rene Betard, the name Sophie had called out as we fled the burning stage at the Olympic.

It seemed that Sophie had learned at least that much as she and her sister had worked the past two years as assistants as 'the great Jean Luc Betard' worked to perfect the glass box illusion and others.

Rene Betard—his real name—would recover from the attack by his brother the night of the fire, but it would take time.

In a cruel twist of fate, he had been badly injured in the fire as he fought with his brother. His hands were burned as well as his back. But Sophie was there. She vowed to care for him and assist with his new illusions when he was able to return to the stage.

I couldn't have written a more twisted tale than that between the twin brothers.

They had begun together as lads desperate to leave the poverty they'd grown up with in that part of Paris and sharing a growing fascination with the art of illusion.

They had watched, studied, and attended street shows and theater presentations, that fascination growing into a desire to join those who created illusions behind a curtain or in a cloud of smoke.

They learned the disappearing tricks that some used—a trap door in a stage, almost invisible wires that created the illusion of someone being suspended in air, and the disappearing trick of a cloud of smoke.

And another illusion that used mirrors set at those angles with a secret compartment to show to an audience that the first glass box appeared to be empty, only for the participant to 'magically' appear in the second box.

The idea for that illusion had come from Jean Luc Betard, and it was first performed in Paris when the brothers were still very young. But as young men will do, both grew, their height making it impossible to fit their lanky bodies into those secret compartments and the illusion was set aside.

Then one evening as they performed, they had tried an experimental device for creating smoke. It had not yet been proven safe, but they'd ignored the dangers. The device exploded and Jean Luc had been engulfed in flames. Only the quick actions of Rene had saved his brother's life.

The aftermath was heart-wrenching. Jean Luc needed constant care. There were weeks afterward in a hospital for the poor man, then months more at that apartment in the 13$^{th}$ arrondissement. And then there was their mother, with no means of support except what her sons had been able to earn before the accident.

Rene might have gone to work in one of the factories or at the riverfront. But the illusion of fame beckoned. He knew what had gone wrong the night of the explosion and fire, and was determined to return to the work that had drawn both young men from the beginning.

By day he worked at the market, hauling fruits and vegetables, or barrels of wine. By night, he worked on those early illusions, as well as the one that had crippled Jean Luc.

The glass box illusion had been Jean Luc's creation. His genius first envisioned illusion, and his determination had taken them from lowly street-performers to an engagement at a legitimate theater in Paris before the accident. Jean Luc had a contract that promised to provide not only the opportunity for a theater performance for the first time, but the coin it would bring.

It was then that Rene became Jean Luc Betard.

He worked hard and other engagements followed. They were small, in local cabarets at first, and he realized that he needed to know more. The decision was made to come to London with its thriving theater district and world-famous performers who commanded large audiences. And it was in London that he was eventually mentored by the Great Maxim who saw his raw talent.

As he became more creative and skilled, he eventually left the Great Maxim and created his own show. There was a tour back to France as his reputation grew, Europe beyond, then a tour to the United States. He was able to afford care for his mother, an act of love and devotion, and protect his brother after the horror of the accident.

The real Jean Luc, confined to that hospital, descended into delusion and madness fed by his brother's fame. It didn't matter that Rene was able to send him to the finest hospital for rehabilitation that might allow him to leave one day, his pain managed by medications that included increasing amounts of morphine.

The explosion and fire had crippled the brother he once knew, the one who had been so brilliant, and the drugs had pushed him into madness. They had loved each other once but Rene's presence only seemed to intensify Jean Luc's violent outbursts and his visits to the hospital became fewer over the years.

I truly believed that Rene never meant to hurt his brother, only to help him as best he could.

The glass box illusion they were forced to give up had always tantalized. That lost spark of genius was just out of reach, until Rene realized that it could be done with the right participants— twins, small enough to fit into those secret compartments.

He began the search for two young women who might work with the illusion—identical twins— and eventually found Francoise and Sophie Dupre, two struggling young actresses.

The pieces of it all fell into place—Rene's affair with Francoise even as Sophie fell in love with him from afar. Jean Luc's escape from that hospital in Paris and my encounter with him on the street with that mask hiding his scars. Rene's determination to protect his brother even as Jean Luc descended into insanity.

As for his motive for murder. It was clear that he wanted to destroy anyone who knew the secret of how his creation, the glass box illusion was done, and that would have included his brother if he had succeeded.

Rene was grieving not the monster his brother had become, but the brother who had been lost.

"Perhaps he is at peace now," he had told me.

I could only imagine the pain he felt, having almost lost my sister in a previous case.

I folded the daily edition of the Times with that last article Lucy Penworth had written that I had read earlier. She had turned in her letter of resignation to the editor just after delivering the article, persuaded by Alex Sinclair to join the Special Services.

Alan Ivers, contemptible worm that he was, had attempted to claim credit for the article, insisting that the story should have been his to write. He was still limping about, the after-effects of his encounter with the hound.

Such a pity, I thought as I reached down and scratched the hound behind the ears as he lay sleeping and obviously dreaming, his legs moving back and forth as though he was chasing something. Rupert huffed and snarfed, then settled once more. He had much recovered from his latest duties as my guard dog after the fire at the theater.

According to Brodie, he ran through the fire to get to me and Sophie. He was a bit singed in a few places, but nothing serious. According to Mr. Cavendish it added character. Nobody would mess with a beast that looked like he'd been to hell and back. There was some truth to that.

We all seemed to look as if we might have been to hell and back, emerging from the fire into the street that night.

Brodie and I were in a different place in our partnership, although I still didn't know quite what that was. It didn't matter.

The chalkboard had been erased and I was now working on

my next novel about Emma Fortescue's latest adventure. Meanwhile, Brodie pursued his somewhat vague work with Sir Avery of the Special Services, that he chose not to discuss in that way of his.

However, I was confident that I would eventually find out exactly what that was. I knew exactly how to get around that gruff, secretive demeanor.

There were footsteps at the landing outside the office and the hound perked up his head. He had become a regular fixture in the office, much to Brodie's grumbling and grousing over the matter. Something about the way the hound smelled and bad habits that often included a dead carcass of some kind. They were mostly quite small and easily disposed of.

Brodie came through the door, faint lines at his forehead, that dark gaze lost in thought. He took off his coat.

It would have hit the floor in that slightly distracted way of his if I hadn't been there. I took it from him and hung it at the coat rack. Brodie looked at me and frowned if returning from wherever his thoughts had taken him, seeing me for the first time. Then he saw the hound, sprawled at the floor.

"What the devil is that beast doin' here?" he grumbled, but not quite a snarl.

I handed him a glass of my aunt's very fine whisky that I had poured earlier.

"I'm protecting him," I replied, which brought the familiar sound at the back of Brodie's throat.

"From what for heaven's sake?"

"Mr. Cavendish. He's decided that he needs a bath." Admittedly a bit like the pot calling the kettle black, I thought.

"I doubt one bath would do."

"That's the reason I'm protecting him."

He took a long swallow of whisky as he went to the desk, surveyed the contents at the desktop—the daily newspaper, my notebook and pen.

"Have ye been working on yer next novel?"

"I have. I'll transcribe my notes later when I return to the townhouse."

That was another part of our relationship that had yet to be defined. Brodie was most often found here at the office on the Strand, while my work—when not working together on a new case, was best accomplished at my townhouse in Mayfair where I had my typing machine.

Brodie had recently pointed out however that I could have my typing machine brought to the office. I wondered precisely what that might mean.

"What is it ye have there?" He gestured with glass in hand into the adjacent bedroom.

"Miss Effie sent over supper," I replied matter-of-factly, as if it were something that happened every day, which it was not.

"I believe there is roast chicken, potatoes, and some vegetables along with one of her pies," I added.

"A pie?" he said as I poured him another dram.

"Blackberry." I casually replied as I poured myself another dram was well. That dark gaze narrowed.

"In the bedroom?" He was beginning to repeat himself. Then something changed in that dark gaze. "That's not usually the place..."

"That is if you're not too tired," I suggested.

He downed that second dram. "Supper and then...?"

"Dessert, of course," I replied as I set my own empty glass at the desk and started toward the bedroom. I looked back over my shoulder at him as I removed the first pin from my hair.

"Ye're a bold, lass, Mikaela Forsythe."

Lass. No one before had ever called me that. Only Brodie.

He watched as I continued into the adjacent room, then set his own glass on the desktop.

"Supper, ye say? And dessert?"

# Author's Note

Some of this, and a little bit of that...

Brodie and Mikaela's cross-channel excursion to learn more about secrets in Paris—the channel crossing in 1890 might have begun from Folkstone, London, or Dover, by steam ferry. The Dover crossing to Calais was said to be much quicker, under two hours with the current, while the others would take longer. From Calais the trip to Paris by rail was a trip of seven to eight hours. It was a frequent trip made by tourists, and those investigating a murder.

The cross-channel tunnel is a modern invention—20th century, that had its beginnings much earlier. The idea for a cross-channel tunnel was set in motion in 1880 with excavations between Dover and Folkstone with the plan for a pilot tunnel to be enlarged that connected with the South Eastern Railway. It was abandoned however, over concerns about invasion from Europe should there be a war in those unsettled times. Those first excavations were back-filled, however the tailings from the hand digging can still be seen.

Construction on the Eiffel Tower was completed, with the original intention that it was to be a transmission tower for communication. Lights were installed with electric service, then a lift that took people to the top. A communication cable across the channel for telegrams already existed.

Mikaela's experience with exposure to morphine is quite possible according to sources I consulted. It would take a considerable amount and would immediately be absorbed into the blood stream with the potential for the symptoms that I described.

My research into certain means of... ahem, birth control, i.e.: prophylactics, revealed that latex prophylactics were available at the time, a definite improvement over animal intestines. They could be obtained at a pharmacy or men's barber shop. And they did come in different sizes.

Moving pictures were first shown at the Roundhay Gardens in England, 1888, quite an innovation at the time that later became the motion pictures of the twentieth century and our streaming videos.

Flying machines were very much on the minds of inventors. First, the hot air balloon, but actually a bit farther back as shown in illustrations envisioned by Leonardo da Vinci centuries earlier, and the first 'motor wagen' as it was called, was built in Germany in 1866.

Mikaela's colored chalk, a 'gift' from Brodie, first appeared in 1814.

Lavender soap, a fine hairbrush, a new chalkboard, that colored chalk. And of course—Brodie. What more could a woman ask for?

*And next...*

A DEADLY VOW

**Angus Brodie and Mikaela Forsythe Murder Mystery**
**Book 5**

*A thirty-year-old murder...*
*A boy found standing in his mother's blood...*
*A vow made, a promise to be kept...*

# About the Author

"I want to write a book... " she said.

"Then do it," he said.

And she did, and received two offers for that first book proposal.

A dozen historical romances later, and a prophecy from a gifted psychic and the Legacy Series was created, expanding to seven additional titles.

Along the way, two film options, and numerous book awards.

*But wait*, there's more a voice whispered, after a trip to Scotland and a visit to the standing stones in the far north, and as old as Stonehenge, sign posts the voice told her, and the Clan Fraser books that have followed that told the beginnings of the clan and the family she was part of...

And now... murder and mystery set against the backdrop of Victorian London in the new Angus Brodie and Mikaela Forsythe series, with an assortment of conspirators and murderers in the brave new world after the Industrial Revolution where terrorists threaten and the world spins closer to war.

When she is not exploring the Darkness of the fantasy world, or pursuing ancestors in ancient Scotland, she lives in the mountains near Yosemite National Park with bears and mountain lions, and plots murder and revenge.

And did I mention fierce, beautiful women and dangerous, handsome men?

They're there, waiting...

Join Carla's Newsletter